DEADLY PARCEL

DEADLY PARCEL

"WHO'S THERE?!" BOOK 1

BARBARA HINSKE

Casa Del Northern Publishing
Phoenix, Arizona

Copyright © 2020 Barbara Hinske.
Cover by Elizabeth Mackey, Copyright © 2020.
All rights reserved.

ISBN-13: 978-0-9962747-8-4
Library of Congress Control Number: 2020906864

Casa del Northern Publishing
Phoenix, Arizona

DEDICATION

To my father, Edward R. Hinske, who started my lifetime
love affair with reading and writing mysteries.

CHAPTER 1

The knife blade, honed to a professional sharpness, traced the orbital bone and along the ridge of the nose, slicing open a neat fissure. The dead man was beyond caring. It circled the lips, bluish-purple in the early stages of lividity. The tip of the knife sank easily into the ridge between lip and chin. One swift motion and the lower lip swung free.

The knife moved upward and hovered over the body, laid prone on the floor. A slim shaft of moonlight glinted on the blade.

The tip moved down and found the knot on the lace of the right shoe. It sliced the knot open and worked its way along the loops, breaking the laces. The shoe came off.

The blade probed the ankle, poking and pressing until it found the indentation between the ankle bone and the fibula. The blade pressed until it encountered the tendon, rigid and tough. A small trickle of blood, aided by gravity rather than the pumping of the now-still heart, trickled onto the floor.

The knife carved through the tendon and sliced through the tissues until it separated the tibia from the calcaneus. The foot dropped into the blood below.

The tip plunged into the fleshy underside of the foot, skewering it and lifting it up and into the Ziploc bag that was its intended destination.

The blade wiped across the corpse's shirt as it made its way to the dead man's right hand. Once more, the tip poked the bruised flesh until the wrist joint was penetrated. The tendons proved less dense than those of the foot. A series of precise cuts yielded the desired result. The severed hand was removed to another Ziploc bag.

The corpse's face was the next target. The handle pressed into the left cheek. Rigor mortis had set in. Considerable force was needed to turn the face to the side, exposing the left ear.

The blade meticulously outlined the soft fleshy junction between the skull and the ear. This final prize was the easiest yet. The ear came off with one expert cut and plopped into its own Ziploc bag. An oozing hole gaped in its wake.

The three bags—with their heinous contents—were now ready.

CHAPTER 2

Earlier that day…

He had been surprised how easily he'd been able to find out which funeral home had taken custody of the body. He hadn't even had to bribe anyone. Yet. He'd have to bribe someone at the funeral home now if he were to accomplish his goal. Surely one of the employees would welcome some extra cash. Where was the harm in what he wanted to do? The victim was already dead.

He stood outside the back entrance to the funeral home and ran through his plan in his mind. It was perfect. What did they say about revenge? That it was sweet? He had to agree—what he had in mind would be sweet.

He walked into the funeral home. The pungent aroma of stargazer lilies assaulted him. He hung back, inside the door, observing a group of workers at the end of the hall. His years working in New York City had taught him how to judge when someone was on the take.

He spotted his man right away. Middle aged with a slight paunch. His uniform looked clean but his pants were frayed at the cuff and his shoes were badly worn. Probably married; supporting a big family— knows he's not going anywhere with his job. That was his guy. He'd be willing to bend a few harmless rules for a wad of cash in his pocket.

He watched until the worker moved away from the others and started down the hall toward him. "How can I help you?" the worker asked.

"I'm here to pick up my brother's body," the man said, wringing his hands and trying to look distressed.

"Oh, yes? They can help you in the office." The worker pointed to a door further down the hall.

"I don't think the office will want to help me," the man ventured.

The worker stopped. "Why is that?"

"I want to take his body."

"Are you his next of kin?"

The man shook his head. "He's married. His wife is having the body returned to their hometown for cremation."

The worker looked away.

He inhaled slowly. He'd been right about the worker. "That's why I want the body. We don't believe in cremation in my family. My brother didn't want to be cremated. He should be buried in the family plot."

"That's up to his wife, I think. You need to talk to her."

"I have, but she won't listen." He twisted his hands. "We haven't been on the best of terms with her for years. In fact, my brother was planning to divorce her when he got back home. Our mother is frantic at the thought of his body being burned up. I think his wife is insisting on it just to spite us."

"I'm sorry to hear this. I agree with you." The worker shuddered. "I'm not going into that furnace."

"Then will you help me, please? Help me and my family?"

The worker shook his head. "I don't know what I could do."

"You could let me take the body."

"There's paperwork for that, sir. I can't help you."

"I'm not talking about doing it with paperwork. Can't you find a way to get the body to me? You could put a different body in the casket to send to his wife."

The worker's spine stiffened.

"She's going to have him cremated as soon as he arrives in New York. No one will ever know the body has been switched."

The worker didn't back away.

I've got him, the man thought. "Let's move out of the hallway to somewhere we can talk privately."

The worker led him to a storage shed at the back of the property. He unlocked the shed and they stepped inside. Rows of flower vases and folding chairs lined the walls.

He continued. "I read online that your funeral home services a lot of indigent, homeless people. Surely you have a body that you could substitute for my brother—someone without family interested in him."

The worker's demeanor changed. "I could do this, yes, but why would I?" he demanded curtly.

"I can think of a thousand reasons," the man said, removing a roll of bills from his pocket.

The worker eyed the wad of cash, then nodded. "I'll make the switch and you can pick up your brother tonight. I'll leave this shed unlocked. Be here at one ten. Don't be early and don't be late. I'll be back here at two to lock the shed."

"Good. It's settled. I'll give you half now and I'll leave the other half tonight. Right here in this vase." He picked up a stone vessel.

"You wouldn't want to cross me. If you don't leave the rest, I'll find you."

"When I take the body, you'll have the rest. You can count on that," he said, handing the worker five one-hundred-dollar bills.

He hung in the shadows and watched the back door of the funeral home. He'd been in place, observing, for almost an hour. He hadn't seen anyone near the premises. If they employed a night watchman, he wasn't in evidence. He checked his watch. It was eight minutes after one. It was time.

He clung to the shadows as he made his way around the perimeter of the property to the storage shed. He grasped the handle and pulled slowly. The door rattled and stuck in place. He cursed under his breath and lifted the door on its hinges. It swung open noiselessly.

Using the flashlight on his cell phone, he found the zippered body bag in the center of the room. He drew the door shut behind him and tied a handkerchief over his nose.

He positioned the flashlight on the shelf to illuminate his work area and removed the stiletto from his jacket pocket. He only needed a few body parts. Three to be exact.

He took the jar of mentholated rub from his pocket and smeared a liberal amount under his nose. He checked the time again. It was now one twenty. He wanted to be far away from here when the worker came back at two to find that he had the body to deal with after all.

He grasped the zipper pull and drew it down. The corpse lay stiff in its enclosure. He took hold of his knife and began his task. When he was done, he zipped the body bag shut.

He took the remaining five one hundred-dollar bills from his money clip and hesitated. He peeled off another two hundred in twenties and added them to the stack. The extra would compensate the worker for adding the now mutilated body to the stack of corpses of the indigent.

He switched off the flashlight on his phone. It was now one fifty. He needed to get out of there. He concealed the Ziploc bags with their grotesque contents under his coat, exited the shed, and disappeared into the night.

CHAPTER 3

He returned to his hotel room. The tiny slip of paper he'd positioned in the door frame remained in place. No one had entered while he was gone. A television blared from the adjacent room.

He turned on the overhead light, threw the privacy bolt into place, and walked to the small dresser along the wall. He placed the three Ziploc bags containing the body parts on the dresser, taking care that no fluids escaped their seals.

He stood back and admired his ghoulish work. He'd carved off a foot, a hand, and an ear. Clever choices. He wondered if the irony of them would ever be appreciated.

Fatigue washed over him. He looked wistfully at the bed. He couldn't allow himself to think about sleep now. He needed to be out of the post office by ten the next morning. He had work to do, tonight, to get his packages ready to mail.

He crossed to his closet and retrieved the cubes of dry ice, plastic trash bags, mailing boxes, and sealing tape he'd purchased that afternoon when he'd left the funeral home. Three gift boxes in the iconic blue of the famous luxury jeweler lay on the bed. He'd retrieved the gift boxes from where they'd been abandoned next to the trash receptacle by the elevator. Some woman must have bought herself fancy crystal pieces from the jeweler and not had room for the boxes in her luggage. The signature color was recognizable everywhere. The recipients of his packages would undoubtedly think they were getting something special when they pulled one of these boxes out of the brown paper parcel. They'd soon find out how unique their gift would be.

He'd thought his plan through a dozen times. The dry ice would keep the contents odor free for several days, especially since it was winter at the destination location for each package. He'd mail them Priority Mail and no one would ever suspect their contents.

He worked quickly, lining each blue box with a plastic bag and making sure that each zip-locked body part was surrounded by dry ice. He'd used the computer in the hotel's business center to type out the address of each recipient. He snickered when his eyes fell on the return address he'd used.

He'd printed out a sheet of paper for each one and now folded and taped each label in place. He gathered up his unused supplies and stuffed them into the clear plastic liner he'd removed from the bathroom wastebasket.

He opened the door to his room slowly. The corridor was deserted. He exited his room, double-checking that the door closed and locked behind him. He walked swiftly to the end of the corridor and the overhead illuminated sign announcing "Stairs." He couldn't risk being seen.

The man proceeded down the four flights to the first floor. He was glad that he'd requested a room on a lower floor—he couldn't imagine navigating thirty-six flights if his room had been on the top floor. He emerged on the ground floor at the back side of the main hotel building. By the odors emanating from his right, he knew that the kitchen was close at hand.

He turned in the direction of the smells and soon found himself looking at the back side of the dumpster right outside the kitchen door. This would be perfect. Kitchen dumpsters at a large hotel like this would be emptied every day.

He lurked in the shadows until he was sure that no one was around. He stepped forward and launched his excess packaging supplies over the side and into the dumpster.

He stepped back quickly and listened. Even here, he could hear the hubbub from the distant street. He scanned the view of the back of the hotel as it rose above him. There were no windows into the kitchen. He hadn't been seen.

He clung to the shadows as he made his way back to the stairwell and cursed when he found the door locked. He looked for a keypad that he could open with a swipe of his room key but found none.

He had no other choice—he'd have to go back in through the main lobby.

He made his way around the considerable breadth of the property to the front. He was relieved to see a group of young tourists staggering toward the entrance. He waited as they approached and slipped into the hotel with them.

He peeled off toward the elevator as one of the tourists asked the bellman where the lobby restrooms were located.

His elevator arrived and he quickly got on and punched the number for his floor. Now all he had to do was get some sleep and head out in the morning with his three packages stowed safely in his suitcase.

He pulled into the parking lot of the post office branch closest to his hotel. He cursed as he looked at the clock on his dashboard. It was nine fifteen. He'd overslept and would have to hurry or he'd miss his flight.

He opened the trunk and paused as a middle-aged man slid his car into the spot next to him. His neighbor got out of his car carrying an armload of business-sized envelopes and hurried inside without a glance at the man.

He turned back to his trunk, unzipped his suitcase, and removed the three packages. He entered the lobby. The only other customer was an elderly man checking for mail in his post office box.

He stepped to the self-service kiosk in the corner. A piece of copy paper was taped to the front of the kiosk. He quickened his pace until he could read the letters scribbled in black marker: Out of Order.

Damn it. He turned toward the area with full service windows manned by postal employees. Did he dare hand his parcels to someone who might be able to identify him if the contents were discovered?

He couldn't risk it. He spun toward the entrance and retraced his steps to his car.

He placed the packages gingerly onto the seat next to him and slid behind the wheel. He tapped the screen on his phone and accessed the search engine. The nearest post office branch was thirteen minutes away. If he hurried, he should have time to get the packages into the self-service bin and still make it to the airport in time for his flight.

Google maps sent him to his destination and he got the last open spot in the parking lot. The branch was humming with activity. He juggled his packages as he waited his turn at the kiosk. "You can set your packages down over there," the woman in front of him said, pointing to a work table in the middle of the lobby.

He turned away from her without comment and retained his hold on his packages.

He finally approached the kiosk's touch screen at five minutes after ten. He followed the directions on the screen for each package, affirming that it didn't contain anything flammable, hazardous, or dangerous.

When the payment screen appeared, he removed the stolen credit card that he'd lifted for this purpose. He held his breath as he ran the card through the reader and waited as the screen indicated the payment was being processed. The screen flashed the word Approved. He couldn't suppress his smile.

He grabbed the shipping labels from the kiosk as it spitted them out and affixed them to the packages. He took the receipt with tracking numbers from the kiosk and moved aside to allow the person in line behind him to step to the screen.

He went to the worktable. The only other person in the lobby was now accessing the kiosk. When he was sure the person was concentrating on their transaction, he took a handkerchief out of his pocket and ran it across the labels and over each box.

He returned to the kiosk and grasped the metal handle to open the slot. Using the handkerchief in one hand and the cuff of his jacket to cover the fingers of his other hand, he ferried each package to the slot and deposited them into the kiosk.

He was closing the metal handle when a door into the post office workroom opened and a uniformed employee stepped into the lobby, pushing a large canvas basket in front of him.

"You two made it in time for the first pick up," the employee said to him and the woman behind him who was affixing a label to her package.

"Will these go out today?" she asked.

"They will. We take them over to the main in about an hour," he heard the employee reply as he exited the building and headed for his car. He threw the stolen credit card into the trash can at the entrance as he walked by. If the lines weren't long at security, he'd make his flight.

CHAPTER 4

Things had looked much differently just a few months earlier. A chilly and damp autumn had given way to a cold and wet early winter. The holiday season was approaching and vibrant lights and decorations stood as jarring slashes of color against the gray skies.

Jill Porzek picked up her shoulder purse from the floor. She hugged it to her body as she inched carefully past her closet door in the narrow space between it and the end of her bed. She didn't want to snag the lace of the vintage wedding dress that hung from a hook high up on the back of the door. She cast a loving glance at the dress.

Jill had seen it hanging in the window of a vintage clothing shop she passed regularly on the way to her subway stop. The shop was expensive and this dress had been no exception, but it had been perfect—the complete embodiment of everything she'd dreamed of in her wedding dress. She'd walked by that window at least a dozen times before she'd entered the shop to try it on. She'd told herself that if it fit, without the need for costly alterations, she'd buy it.

The dress had fit like it'd been designed for her. Hadn't the sales clerk said as much? It had cost her every penny she'd saved over the years from her modest wages as a sixth-grade teacher, but it had been worth every penny. When Robert saw her in it, he'd realize he'd make the right choice. And they were going to be married. He'd said so—just as soon as he could untangle himself from his wife.

She shook herself out of her reverie and checked her watch. She needed to get going. She skipped the elevator and ran down the stairs from her fourth-floor apartment, quickly crossing the small lobby and emerging onto the sidewalk. She headed for her subway stop and arrived on the platform just as the train arrived. She jostled for position as she pushed her way into the car and grabbed an overhead bar to steady herself where she stood. The rocking of the train was familiar and soothing as the car propelled her to her destination.

Jill sprinted up the subway steps and joined the throng on the sidewalk in this busy SoHo neighborhood. She checked the street number on an adjacent business, then turned right and began to walk. She cautiously stepped into the street to get around a long line of parents and children. She glanced at the storefront as she passed. A handwritten sign in the window announced that Santa Claus would be making a stop there that very afternoon. "Frosty the Snowman" blared from a speaker set up by the open door and two elementary-aged school children sang along. A lump formed in her throat. Maybe she'd be one of those mothers in that line in a few years' time.

She soon came to her destination and stepped out of the flow of pedestrian traffic. She absently picked at the cuticle of the thumb on her left hand. She stood on the sidewalk and huddled into her parka against the spitting sleet as she kept her eyes trained on the door to the building.

What in the world am I doing here? I must be out of my mind. She told herself that she should turn around and get back on the subway. She'd probably misconstrued the text that she'd seen on Robert's phone when he'd left it in the hotel room. She really shouldn't have snooped in his messages.

She wouldn't have known that his phone lay tangled in the sheets but it had pinged to alert him to the incoming text. *The other woman's text.* He'd rushed out not five minutes earlier, tossing over his shoulder that he would be late for a meeting across town. He hadn't even looked at her, much less kissed her goodbye. As busy as Robert was, she'd gotten used to that.

If she was going to be his wife—when he left the frigid Elizabeth and married her instead—she wouldn't have to satisfy herself with quick encounters in out-of-the-way hotel rooms. They'd have cozy dinners and romantic evenings at home. He'd said as much, hadn't he? He was looking forward to their future life as much as she was. She was sure of it.

Jill stuffed down the rising panic she felt whenever she thought about Suzanne Brooks. The text had been from Suzanne, confirming their "sitting"—as she called it—the next afternoon at the same hotel where Jill and Robert frequently met.

She'd googled Suzanne and learned that she was a successful artist whose works had been favorably reviewed and were displayed in a fancy gallery across town. Everything she'd read referred to Suzanne's sculptures, but perhaps she was also a painter? Maybe she was working on a portrait of Robert. Surely that would explain the use of the word "sitting." It was probably innocent. But why would his sitting be in a hotel room?

Jill's mouth felt like cotton. She had to find out if her fears were justified or not. She'd come here—to this woman's studio—to do just that.

Jill flinched as she tore off a strip of cuticle. She touched the bloody quick to her tongue until the blood stopped flowing. She thrust her hand into her glove and marched up to the entrance.

She stepped off the street into an inner vestibule. A row of boxes along the wall announced the names of the tenants. She located S Brooks and pressed the intercom.

Jill held her breath, waiting for Suzanne to respond. She was about to give up and head back out onto the street when the intercom crackled and a woman's voice responded with a breathless, "Yes."

The simple word was delivered in a refined tone that spoke of boarding schools and good breeding. Jill's knees wobbled.

"Yes," the woman uttered again. "Who's there?"

"Ms. Brooks?" Jill forced herself to face the intercom. "May I see you for a moment?" She hesitated, then continued. "It's about Robert Jensen. I'm a friend of his."

"A friend of Robert's?" The line went silent, then, "Alright. Come on up. I'm in C7. I'll buzz you in."

The woman clicked off the intercom and the buzzer sounded, releasing the lock on the inner door. Jill stepped through the doorway to the elevator. She pushed the button to summon the ancient contraption.

The elevator inched its way to the third floor. Jill began to perspire and thought about returning to the first floor as soon as the doors opened. I've come this far, she told herself. *I may as well finish what I've started.*

She forced herself to walk down the short hallway to the door marked C7 and was raising her hand to knock when the door was flung wide. A tall, slender woman stood in the opening, her silver-gray hair pulled into a ponytail and her aquamarine eyes dominating a complexion riddled with tiny lines. Her body was draped in a loose white linen tunic. She was at least fifteen years older than Jill but her every pore spoke of latent sexuality. Jill recoiled involuntarily.

"You said you're a friend of Robert's?" the woman asked. "Come on in."

Suzanne moved to one side and Jill stepped past her.

"Sit wherever you like," Suzanne said, sweeping her arm across the room in front of her. "I don't often have guests. Move some of those magazines aside," she said, pointing to the one upholstered chair in the room. "I'm Suzanne," she said, extending her hand.

Jill took off her gloves. "Jill," she said, shaking hands. She moved the stack of old *Architectural Digests* onto the floor and sat in the chair. The earthy aroma of modeling clay permeated the space.

Suzanne pulled up an ottoman. She looked at Jill and raised an eyebrow.

Jill cleared her throat and looked away. "I'm engaged to Robert Jensen." She turned back to the woman to gauge her response. "Did you know that?"

Suzanne breathed in slowly and she ran her eyes over Jill. "He never mentioned it," she finally replied and shrugged. "Maybe it didn't seem too important since he's already married."

Suzanne reached into a pocket of her tunic, took out a cigarette, and lit it. She uttered the words "Do you mind?" as a formality—it was clear she didn't care if Jill minded whether she smoked or not. "Did you know he was married? Before you got engaged?" Suzanne looked pointedly at the ring finger of Jill's left hand—the naked ring finger.

Jill shifted uncomfortably in her chair. "Of course I knew he was married. He told me about his wife right away." She knew as she said it that this wasn't true. Robert hadn't confessed to being a married man until Jill had confronted him after seeing a photo of him with his wife in the society pages.

"He's going to divorce her and marry me. Just as soon as he gets this year's bonus payment in March. So they can't screw him," she replied. The words sounded lame to her own ears.

Suzanne threw back her head and laughed. "That's the oldest line in the book," she said. "He told me he had a naive young thing on the line. That must be you."

Jill bristled. "You're making that up. Why would he tell you anything? What's he got to do with you?"

"The same thing he's doing with you, sweetie. And probably lots of other women, too. Who knows?" She took a drag on her cigarette and let the smoke curl slowly into the space between them.

Suzanne stared into Jill's eyes. "He's screwing us, honey. Plain and simple. No frills. Just sex—without any side orders of love or marriage."

Jill recoiled.

"He's not going to marry you; he's got no intention of trading in his wife for another model."

"So you're having an affair with him? You're not painting his portrait... or anything?"

Suzanne's laugh exploded into the room. "No—I'm not painting his portrait. Is that what he told you? Naughty boy." She clicked her tongue against her teeth. "I wouldn't even call it an affair. There're no dinners and not much conversation. Just athletic sex every Wednesday afternoon at three."

"Doesn't that bother you?" Jill choked on the words.

"Not one little bit. In fact, it suits me to a tee. I'm too busy with my work," she waived her hand over her shoulder at a work in progress on a table in the far corner of the room, "to have time for a boyfriend. I still have 'needs', however, and he does just fine in that department.

But I guess you already know that," she said with a malicious gleam in her eye.

Jill fumbled in her pocket for a tissue and brought it to her nose. "You're not going to stop seeing him? Even now that you know about me?"

Suzanne stubbed out her cigarette in a soda can on the floor and stood. "Of course I'm not going to stop seeing him. He's absolutely perfect for me. But if you're looking for Mr. Right, honey, you've got the wrong guy."

Jill shook her head in denial. "I know he loves me. You need to stay away from him."

"And if I did, there'd be someone else to take my place in a heart-beat. Robert will never be monogamous."

Suzanne took Jill's elbow and pulled her to her feet, steering her to the door.

Jill shuffled along behind and stepped over the threshold. She turned back to the older woman and drew a ragged breath. "I'd appreciate it if you wouldn't say anything to Robert about my visit."

"I know that this hurts," Suzanne said, her tone softening. "I'm sure you and I are just part of a larger group. When he tires of one of us— or if we tire of him first—we just move on. It's the best way to think of it."

Jill looked at Suzanne with eyes rimmed with tears.

"I won't mention this to Robert," Suzanne said as she shut the door.

"Sorry I'm late," Daria Guzman said as she rushed into the classroom that served as the after-school program pickup area. "Come on, Max. Get your backpack. We need to let Ms. Porzek get out of here."

"This is the fifth time in a row that you've been late." Jill looked up from the stack of construction paper that she was sorting by color. She pointed to the clock on the wall. "Almost thirty minutes, today." She fixed Daria with a stare. "I only work the after-school pickup on Thursdays. Are you late every day?"

"No. Just Thursdays."

"You're a personal trainer, aren't you? Can't you schedule your appointments so you can be here on time? This can't continue."

"I know," Daria said. "It's not work." She leaned in to Jill and lowered her voice. "I've met someone really wonderful. He works out at my gym. We can only see each other on Thursday afternoons. At least for now."

A shiver ran down Jill's spine.

"Why is that?" She realized the question was impertinent, but she had to know.

"Well… I'm not proud of this… but he's married. For now. It's complicated. And he's got some crazy woman after him, too." Daria moved closer. "Actually—she's an elementary school teacher somewhere in the city. He says she's obsessed with him and he might have to get a restraining order. You just never know, do you?"

Jill took a step back. *Could it be?*

"I'll let it go this one last time. If you're late again next week, I'll turn in the paperwork for a late pickup fee."

"Thank you," Daria said. "I really appreciate it. Max's dad has been late on his support payments and I'm strapped at the moment. I'll tell Robert that I have to leave on time next week."

Jill swiveled her head to stare at Daria.

Max dragged his backpack along the table and the hard plastic fasteners clattered along its length.

"Pick that thing up, Max. You're making quite a racket," his mother said. "Thank you again, Ms. Porzek. I'll be on time next week."

Jill nodded but couldn't find her voice. She studied Daria as she walked away from the classroom with Max in tow. This tall, trim woman was her replacement. Just like Suzanne Brooks had predicted.

Jill shut the classroom door and locked it, leaning her back against it. Tears cascaded down her cheeks. She stretched out her right hand and fumbled for the row of light switches, knocking the cover off of the wall-mounted pencil sharpener and sending a cloud of graphite and shavings into the air. She pressed further, found the switches, and flicked them off. The room went dark except for the scant light of the Exit sign above the door. Jill bent her knees, sliding down the door into the puddle of shavings on the floor, and wept.

CHAPTER 5

Elizabeth Jensen pushed open the door to Porzek Meats. The shop was busy with patrons making selections for their evening meals. The glass-front cases were crammed full of trays of bright red beef and cuts of pork. An entire section offered chicken, turkey, duck, and game hens. Fish and seafood ranging from the ordinary to the exotic enticed from cases that lined the back wall. The line moved slowly as each customer considered their options.

Elizabeth had arrived at Ackerman Funding at six thirty that morning so she could leave work early to do her shopping. Ira Ackerman had grumbled when she stuck her head into his office to tell him she was leaving. He pointed to the mountain of invoices and checks stacked on the corner of his desk that needed to be reconciled, but she'd stuck to her guns. Today was her wedding anniversary and she and Robert were going to share an intimate dinner in front of their fireplace. He'd promised that he'd be home tonight.

She stepped in line behind a woman wrangling two bickering adolescent boys. Elizabeth would pick up a pricey piece of beef tenderloin here and stop for fresh vegetables at the Whole Foods that was a block from her subway stop. She wanted to be home in time to drag their tiny dining table to the hearth and set it with their wedding china and crystal. With any luck, she'd be able to take a bath and reapply her makeup before Robert got home.

The elderly couple at the counter were engaged in a lengthy conversation with the butcher, oblivious to the growing line behind them. The bell on the door tinkled as another customer entered the shop. Elizabeth stepped forward. The shop was now becoming crowded. She checked her watch: three ten. *Why don't they have someone else working the counter?*

As if reading her thoughts, the man on the other side of the counter rocked back on his heels, turned his head to the doorway to the back room, and hollered, "Help up front!"

Elizabeth sighed in relief.

Joe Porzek, her childhood classmate from their days in Brooklyn, parted the louvered vinyl curtain that shielded the doorway and stepped to the counter.

"Next, please," he said.

The woman in front of Elizabeth stepped forward as one of the boys shoved the other into a display of gourmet crackers. The woman lunged at the cardboard display as it teetered, but not before its contents scattered across the floor. She grabbed both boys by the arm.

"See what you did? You two are a disgrace." She looked at Elizabeth over her shoulder. "You go ahead; take my place. I've got to make these two pick all of this up." She shook her finger at the boys. "Just be glad you didn't break anything. Now get busy and replace everything exactly like it was. And I'm not going to buy steaks anymore. Not after the way you've behaved."

Elizabeth stepped over a box of crackers and smiled at Joe. She'd thought Joe was a nice kid when they were in school together. She was pretty sure that he'd had a crush on her back then. She wondered if he had married and had a family. She was certain that he gave her the best cuts of meat in the case, and when they were out of something up front, he always found what she wanted in the back. He was still a nice guy.

He beamed back at her. "How are you today?" he asked. "We don't usually see you in the middle of the afternoon."

"Today's my wedding anniversary." Elizabeth's eyes shone.

"Congratulations," Joe said dryly. "I expect your husband is taking you out tonight to celebrate?"

"No. He actually didn't remember until I told him this morning. He's not good with dates," she added hastily. "I'm going to make his favorite meal for a cozy dinner at home."

"That's very nice," Joe said. "He's a lucky guy." He looked at Elizabeth steadily. "What are you fixing?"

"Beef Wellington," Elizabeth replied.

Joe nodded. "Good choice." He moved to a long strip of tenderloin. "How much would you like?"

"Two pounds, I think," Elizabeth replied. "That'll guarantee that the center will be nice and red—like Robert likes—and I'll have leftovers for my dinner tomorrow night."

"If you get a bit extra, you'll have leftovers for both of you."

Elizabeth sighed. "Robert's rarely home for dinner. He's making a big effort to be there tonight. There's no way he'll make it home two nights in a row."

Joe nodded as he removed the large piece of tenderloin from the case, picked up his knife, ran a sanitizer rag across the blade, and sliced off a portion. In one practiced motion, he tore a sheet of butcher paper off a roll, placed it on the scale, and set the meat on top of it.

"Two pounds one ounce," he said to Elizabeth across the counter. "Is that alright?"

"Perfect," Elizabeth said. "I don't know how you can be so accurate just by looking at it."

"Years of practice," Joe said as he rolled the meat into a neat package and affixed the price label. "Anything else to go with this? We have some giant lobster tails over there," he said, pointing. "Just got them in this morning. You could make it surf and turf."

Elizabeth sidled along the case to the section he pointed to. "That's not a bad idea," she said as "Bad to the Bone" blasted from her purse. She shoved her hand into the opening and brought the phone to her ear, mouthing the words 'It's Robert. Just a sec,' to Joe.

"Hi, sweetheart," were the only words she uttered. She listened in silence and dropped her gaze to the floor. "No. I understand," she said quietly into the phone. "Okay. I won't wait up. We can do it another time." Her shoulders slumped. "Happy Anni—" she began but abruptly stopped.

Joe leaned toward her, his forearms resting on top of the glass case. Her eyes were brimming with tears when she brought them to his.

"He can't make it," she blurted out. She swiped at a tear that made its way down her cheek. "I knew this was going to happen. I could tell this morning that he was agreeing to come home just to placate me; to prevent me from asking too many questions." She swallowed hard. "Sometimes I think he's having an affair."

Joe stood still, ignoring the hustle and bustle around them.

"What's wrong with me, Joe? You've known me most of my life."

Joe leaned across the counter to her and opened his mouth to speak the words he'd been longing to say to her: that she was lovely inside and out and that her husband was incredibly lucky to have her. That any man who cheated on Elizabeth was a fool. Instead, the man in line behind her pushed himself between them.

"Excuse me. Do you mind if I get in here to look at these lobsters?" the man said.

Elizabeth stepped aside and brushed a strand of hair out of her face. "Sorry," she murmured. "How much do I owe you?" She gestured to the wrapped package of tenderloin on the counter.

"You don't have to take this," Joe said. "You don't want it now."

Elizabeth nodded mutely. "Thank you," she said in a whisper before she turned to the door and exited without looking back.

CHAPTER 6

"The Brandon Institution. How may I direct your call?"

"Robert Jensen, please," Elizabeth said. She didn't recognize the voice of the woman who answered the phone. Maybe they had hired a new receptionist. Or maybe it was just that Elizabeth rarely dialed in to the main switchboard. She usually called her husband on his cell or his direct line. He wasn't answering either. She was determined to wish him a happy anniversary. He had disconnected their call so abruptly earlier that she didn't think he'd heard her. He needed to know it was their anniversary; he was choosing *work* over *her* on their anniversary.

"I'll put you through to his voice mail," the woman responded curtly.

"No," Elizabeth said in a rush. This new receptionist certainly didn't have a friendly voice. She'd mention it to Robert. "I need to speak to him."

"Honestly, Jill. Mr. Jensen has directed me to send all of your calls to his voice mail." The woman was silent for a beat. Her voice softened when she continued. "I'm sorry for you, honey, I really am. But he's not going to talk to you. You've got to stop calling here."

Elizabeth gripped her phone with icy fingers. It was true; her suspicions must be right. Robert was having an affair.

"Jill?" came the voice on the other end of the line.

Elizabeth opened her mouth but was unable to speak. She drew a ragged breath as tears stung the back of her eyes. She listened as the woman disconnected the call.

Elizabeth stood in their tiny living room, pressing the phone to her ear, frozen to the spot. She'd suspected this before—on numerous occasions over the years—but she was certain of its truth this time. Her stomach churned and the arm holding the phone started to tremble. She brought her hand to her side, then raised it up and hurled her phone across the room. It ricocheted off the bookcase and skittered to the floor.

Her head dropped to her chest and she released her tears. She stood in the center of the room, shoulders sagging, and sobbed. When she was spent, she dropped to her knees and crawled to where the phone lay, screen side down, on the floor.

Elizabeth reached for the phone and turned it over. The expensive case had done its job; the screen wasn't cracked. She pressed the button and her login screen came into view. She released the breath she had been holding. At least she hadn't broken it.

She pushed herself to her feet, turned out the light, and made her way to her bed through the dark apartment.

Elizabeth heard the click of the lock as Robert inserted his key and opened the door to their apartment. She hadn't been able to sleep since she'd lain on the bed, fully clothed. Sometime after eleven, she'd kicked off her shoes and crawled under the covers.

She checked the time on the bedside clock. It was almost one in the morning. She'd been lying there, alone in the dark, for seven hours. She'd spent the time reliving her marriage and rehearsing what she would say to Robert. She'd wondered if she'd have the nerve to go through with it. Robert always managed to get the best of her—to win every argument. And now here he was.

She propped herself on her elbows and waited.

Robert shuffled slowly into the room.

Her eyes were accustomed to the dark and she could make out his movements. He was weaving.

He caught his foot on the leg of the bed and stumbled. He reached toward the nightstand to deposit his wallet and keys but missed his mark. They clattered to the floor. He dropped into bed and exhaled heavily.

Elizabeth smelled the alcohol on his breath.

"Happy Anniversary," she said quietly in the dark.

"You awake?"

She could tell that he was making a concerted effort to speak without slurring his words.

"I am."

He remained silent and she waited.

"Sorry if I woke you. Happy Anniversary. Did you have a good day?"

"Not as good as you've evidently had."

"Business meeting," he replied. "Foreign dignitaries…"

"Bullshit! Enough of your lies and bullshit, Robert." Elizabeth whipped back the covers and leapt to her feet. She lunged at the switch for the overhead light and the room jumped into illumination.

Robert visibly cringed and brought his arm over his eyes.

"You weren't at a business dinner. You were out with another woman." Her voice cracked. "On our anniversary, no less. You cheating asshole."

Robert sat up and tried to stand but plopped back onto the bed. "S'not true. Why would you think that?"

"Was it Jill?"

Robert's head jerked up.

"I know about her. Is she the one? Or is she old news? Are there others?"

"No." He turned to face her. "You're being ridiculous. That time of the month?"

"Don't you dare say that to me!" Her voice rose several decibels. "Tell me the truth. For once in your life, have the guts to tell me the truth!"

"You're hysterical and irrational."

"And you're drunk." She was yelling now.

"I may have had one too many." He clawed his fingers through his hair. "I have to be at the office early tomorrow. I'm not going to have this conversation with you until you calm down."

"I've sacrificed everything for you. I quit school to put you through grad school. We agreed that I'd go back to get my degree when you got a job. It was supposed to be my turn. But my turn has never come." She stomped around the room. "Everything is always—has always—been about you."

"You're delusional. Ever since you started on those fertility drugs, you've been crazy. You never acted like this before. They haven't worked, anyway. Maybe you should get off of them."

Elizabeth recoiled as if she had been slapped.

Robert continued. "You were never going to get a degree. You're not smart enough." He laughed derisively. "You've been hanging on to my coattails, trying to drag yourself up." He put his face close to hers and she shrank back from his fetid breath. "You're lucky to have me."

"You ... selfish ... bastard!"

"Go screw yourself," he screamed.

A series of thuds sounded on the other side of their bedroom wall. "Keep it down in there or I'm calling the cops," their neighbor yelled.

Robert and Elizabeth stopped and stared at each other. Elizabeth's spine stiffened.

Robert yanked his pillow and blanket from the bed. "I'll sleep on the couch tonight."

"We're not done with this conversation," she hissed as he stalked out of the room.

Elizabeth sagged onto the bed and drew the covers up to her chin. Her pillow grew damp from her tears before she finally succumbed to a fitful sleep.

CHAPTER 7

Jill held her large green tea latte with extra unsweetened almond milk carefully as she exited the shop and stepped out onto the sidewalk. The morning was clear and bright. She squinted into the sun but didn't reach into her purse for her sunglasses. At eleven dollars for this indulgence, she didn't want to spill it. She'd spent all day the prior day—Saturday—in her apartment crying, watching television, and obsessively typing emails to Robert. Unlike the Saturday before that, she hadn't sent any of them.

When she'd finally fallen asleep, she'd slept fitfully. When she'd gone into the bathroom and caught her reflection in the mirror, she'd barely recognized the sunken eyes, ringed in dark circles, that stared back at her.

She was out of Mr. Darcy's favorite cat treats and her refrigerator was bare. She had promised herself that if she showered and got dressed, she would allow herself to indulge in the treat she now held in her hand. Robert had introduced her to it and the coffee shop. There was no reason she couldn't continue to enjoy it. She didn't want to acknowledge that part of her was hoping she'd run into him at the shop.

Jill idled along the front window of the shop and hunched over her cup. She raised the spout to her lips and took a tentative sip, making sure the liquid wouldn't scald the inside of her mouth. Satisfied that it had cooled off enough, she was tilting her head back to drink when she heard a woman call her name.

Jill turned in the direction of the voice and saw a woman with shiny dark hair styled into a precise bob and a large pair of sunglasses closing in on her. She didn't recognize the woman. Jill began to smile, the words "Do I know you?" on her lips.

Jill watched in disbelief as the woman's expression morphed from serious to hateful and her hand swung up from her side. The woman was holding a large Styrofoam cup. In one swift motion, she hurled the black coffee it contained into Jill's face.

Jill recoiled as passersby jumped aside, shooting annoyed glances at the two women.

Nicole Mills leaned in toward Jill, bringing her face so close that droplets of spittle landed on Jill's lips. "He was mine, you little slut. He was happy with me and we were going to move to London together. I was going to get my PhD at the Royal Academy of Music. We were planning our wedding. All we needed was for him to save a little more money and then he was going to file for divorce." Her breath was hot and sour. "Then you came along and took him away." She pushed her glasses up on her nose. "I hope someone does to you what you did to me."

Jill stumbled backward, dropping her latte and bringing her hands to her chest in a defensive gesture. Her reflection, eyes wide and mouth agape, stared back at her—in duplicate—from the shiny black surface of Nicole's sunglasses. The angry woman didn't move.

Jill turned and fled. Mr. Darcy would have to get along without his treats.

Jill wove her way through the jumble of tables and chairs to a spot at the back of the pub, across from the bar. She began to set her purse on the table but hastily stopped and shoved the strap back onto her shoulder. Even in the dim light of the bar, she could see the sticky rings from glasses and greasy swaths from God-knew-what on the table top. She glanced around her. None of the other tables had been wiped clean.

She checked her watch. It was two fifty-five and she'd had to rush out of her classroom the minute the last bell had sounded at two thirty. Robert was always very cross if someone made him wait. She'd seen how he'd upbraided inattentive waiters or sales clerks. She shuddered. Now was not the time to antagonize him.

Why had Robert insisted they meet so early? And why had he chosen such a sleazy spot? She'd double-checked the address he'd given her when she'd arrived a few minutes ago. She was in the correct place.

The only other people in the room were two old men nursing beers at the bar, and a short, squat bartender with a bulbous nose and a florid complexion. He glanced in her direction and she thought he looked surprised to see her in a place like this. He grabbed a well-used bar rag and a stack of paper napkins and approached her table.

"What'll it be, miss?" he asked as he swiped haphazardly at the table top, knocking crumbs into her lap. He stuck a napkin into the wet trail he'd left on the table.

Jill hesitated. She wasn't going to consume anything from a place as unhygienic as this.

The man stared down his nose at her.

"I'm waiting for someone," she said.

The bartender grunted. "What'll ya have while ya wait?"

Jill understood. She wasn't welcome to sit here without ordering. "Coffee. Do you have coffee?"

"Yeah. I got coffee. Cream and sugar?"

Jill shook her head and the man moved off. She fixed her gaze on the door and waited.

The bartender brought her coffee at three ten. "I had to brew a fresh pot," he said as he set the too-full mug on the table, its contents sloshing over the side.

"Thank you," Jill murmured as he retreated to the bar. She slid the mug to the middle of the table and mopped up the spill with the cocktail napkin. The odor of scorched coffee made her nostrils twitch. He hadn't made a fresh pot. The coffee had been sitting on a burner for hours. She returned her attention to the door.

Robert stepped into the pub at three twenty. Jill waved at him as he stood inside the doorway, allowing his eyes to adjust to the low light.

Her smile froze on her lips as he approached. She started to rise.

"Sit," he commanded as he yanked out the chair opposite hers and threw himself into the seat.

Jill lowered herself back into her chair.

"I was afraid I'd gotten the wrong address," Jill began, gesturing to the room with her hand. "This isn't your type of place. And you're never late."

Robert sat in stony silence.

A chill ran down Jill's spine. What in the world had gotten into him?

"What's going on?" She swallowed hard.

"What's going on? Like you don't know?" Robert hissed.

Jill stared at him, wide-eyed.

Robert leaned across the table. "You've been going around town, talking to people about me. That's what's been going on."

"I ... I just ..." Jill stammered.

Robert cut her off. "You wanted to find out what I've been doing. You wanted to tell people to stay away from me."

His face was inches from hers.

"None of it is any of your business."

Jill felt the blood pounding in her temples. She reached out and grasped his arm. "We're going to be married. I think it is my business—if you're still seeing your old girlfriends." She straightened and forced herself to look him in the eye. "It's not right, Robert. You need to stop seeing them."

He barked a derisive laugh.

The color drained from her face. Jill felt dizzy.

Robert gripped her hand and removed it from his arm, throwing it onto the table. He sneered at her. "We were never going to get married."

Jill choked. "Yes we were. You told me you were going to tell Elizabeth you were leaving her; you wanted to be with me." Her voice trailed off in a whisper.

"I'd never marry a controlling, nosy bitch like you." He pushed his chair back.

"Wait." Jill lunged at him. "You're right. I'm sorry. I never should have contacted that woman. I'm so sorry. It won't happen again..."

"You're damned right it won't happen again. We're done."

"No!" Jill's voice rose and the bartender turned a disapproving eye toward them.

"I can change. We can go back to the way we were."

Robert shook his head. "This is it. Don't contact me—or anyone near me—ever again." He turned and strode out the door without a backward glance.

Jill collapsed into her chair, knocking her cup of coffee to the floor as she brought her outstretched arms to her side. She fumbled in her purse for her wallet. Her vision was blurred by the wall of tears spilling down her cheeks.

The bartender approached with a mop to clean up the spill. "No charge," he said. "Only cowards break up with someone in a bar."

Jill nodded her thanks. She made her way to the door and fled into the cloudy afternoon.

CHAPTER 8

The sense of unease that Joe shouldered on the bottom step swelled to palpable dread as he rounded the turn onto the third landing. He tucked the iPad firmly under his arm and ran up the remaining stairs. He hadn't thought anything of it when she'd left her precious iPad at his place earlier in the week. He'd been expecting a frantic call from her, checking to make sure that she'd left it with him and making arrangements to pick it up as soon as possible. But when she hadn't called him or returned any of his calls to her, he'd become concerned. When he'd finally placed a call to the school where she worked and learned that she'd called in sick three days earlier and hadn't been heard from since, his concern had turned to worry.

He strode down the hall to apartment 4D and rapped sharply on the door. Sweat soaked the collar of his flannel shirt and he tore open the snaps of his down jacket. He held his breath, willing Jill to answer the door. *Come on, Jill. Answer the damned door.* His gut told him his younger sister was incapable of doing so.

Joe knocked again, louder this time, as he fished the duplicate key out of the pocket of his jeans.

"Hey—people are trying to sleep in here," yelled the neighbor in the next apartment. Joe knew they worked the night shift at the front desk of a business hotel just off of Wall Street.

Joe inserted the key in the lock and the door creaked open. The complete silence made the hair rise on the back of his neck. *Where's Mr. Darcy?* His sister's vocal tabby never failed to greet him at the door. Hadn't he and Jill always joked that the cat was part dog? Joe stepped into the apartment and kicked the door closed behind him. Mr. Darcy was not in evidence.

Joe's skin prickled and his saliva tasted brackish. Something was definitely amiss. He set the iPad and key on the kitchen table and crossed the small room that served as living room, dining room, and kitchen, to the door at the opposite end.

"Jill?" he called, fearing she wouldn't answer. He grasped the handle and turned, but the door wouldn't give. Locked from the inside. "Jill!" he yelled as he twisted the handle first one way and then the other. The only response was the tick of the antique mantle clock that he'd gotten Jill when she'd graduated from college. She'd loved that clock. *My first real, grown-up possession*, she'd told him proudly.

Joe pummeled the door with the sides of his hands. The only response was the curt "Hold it down over there," from the neighbor. Joe stepped back, brought his right foot up, and struck at the door with the heel of his heavy work boot. The frame splintered on the third kick. The door swung open until its progress was stopped by the body on the other side.

Joe choked as he screamed Jill's name. He thrust his shoulder into the opening. *Shit!* He was too big to slip through.

He forced his eyes to travel over the body of his sister, lying slumped and motionless in front of him. *She's dead! Jill is dead!* The words hammered in his head.

He had to get to her; had to cut her free. Maybe he'd find a pulse?

Joe pulled out the pocket knife that he'd carried since his Boy Scout days decades ago. He flipped open the long blade and slid it under the length of red silk scarf that led from the door knob to Jill's neck. He regularly sharpened this blade along with the knives at his butcher shop. It cut through the fabric with one swift upward thrust. Jill's body toppled forward and she sprawled onto the floor, her left arm flung wide and her neck at an unnatural angle.

Joe fell to his knees and crawled through the door into the bedroom. He grasped his sister's shoulders and turned her onto her back. Her lips were blue and her eyes stared at him, unseeing. He shuddered and brought shaking hands to her bruised neck. Her flesh was cool to the touch. He pressed his fingertips into the skin covering the carotid artery, already knowing what he would find. There was no pulse. Jill was dead.

He dropped his chin to his chest and a guttural moan escaped his lips. He moved his hand to grasp hers. A tear slipped down his cheek and trickled onto their hands. He watched as it slowly coursed its way across their fingers before disappearing into the rug below.

"Why?" he whispered. "Why did you do this? Why didn't you come to me? I could have fixed it. I'd have fixed anything for you."

His heart hammered in his chest. He knew he should call 9-1-1. He should do it now.

Joe took a deep breath, and then another, as his heart rate returned to normal. Still holding Jill's hand, he retrieved his phone from his jacket with his free hand. The home screen appeared and he tapped the phone icon, then inserted the digits 9-1-1.

Joe brought the phone to his ear with a shaking hand and sucked in a deep breath while he waited.

"My sister's dead," he stammered when the dispatcher came on the line. "My sister hung herself."

Joe heard footsteps in the hallway. He knew he should go to the door. Instead, he clung to his sister's hand.

Someone knocked firmly on the door.

Joe remained at Jill's side.

"Mr. Porzek? This is the police. Open up, sir."

Joe heard the neighbor's door creak open. "What the…?" the man said.

"Go back inside, sir," the officer at the door instructed.

"What's going on?" the man asked.

"Someone will question you. For now, we need you to go back inside."

Joe rose to his feet, still holding Jill's hand.

The officer pounded on the door again. "Mr. Porzek," he called.

Joe cleared his throat. He took one last look at the lifeless form of his sister and carefully placed her hand on her stomach. He stood and his eyes fell on a long white lacy dress hanging from a hook on the back of her closet door. He was no expert on such matters, but it looked like an old wedding dress. His brows knit together. What in the world was Jill doing with a wedding dress?

"Mr. Porzek!"

Joe turned and started for the door. His awareness of his surroundings seemed peculiarly heightened. His sister's usually immaculate apartment was disheveled. Mail spilled from the kitchen table and onto one of the chairs. The sofa pillows were scattered on the floor. He glanced into the kitchen. The sink was full of dirty dishes and a Styrofoam cup from her favorite coffee shop sat on the counter.

He knew his sister. This was not how she usually lived. And where was Mr. Darcy? She'd never have left the fate of her beloved cat to chance. Had she given him away?

He stopped when he reached the door. Had she left a suicide note?

"Mr. Porzek, can you hear me?" the officer bellowed. "We're going to have to use force to get in."

Joe turned and quickly scanned the scene in front of him. There was no note on the coffee table or either of the end tables. Likewise, for the kitchen counters or on her tiny dining table. If she'd left a note, it must be in her bedroom. He started to retrace his steps.

The door frame shook as someone applied force to the door.

Joe stopped. *What am I doing?* He looked reluctantly back at the door to her bedroom. He cleared his throat. "I'm here… I'm coming," he yelled. He swept his eyes around the apartment one last time. The iPad that was nestled with her spare key caught his attention. On impulse, he scooped it up and secured it in an inside pocket of his jacket. He stepped to the door and let the police enter the scene where his beloved sister had drawn her last breath.

Joe stood at the far end of the living room in the spot Officer Jackson had directed him to. He cradled his head in his hands, trying to still his racing thoughts. He snuck occasional glances at the body of his sister, now neatly zipped into a rubber body bag placed atop a gurney. He couldn't believe she was gone, but every time he looked at the hideous black pouch skimming the form of his slim sister, the reality of it felt like a kick in the groin.

He was staring at the carpet when Officer Jackson laid a hand on his shoulder.

Joe jerked and dropped his hands.

"I'm sorry to startle you, sir," the officer said.

Joe shook his head. "I was lost in my own thoughts." He gestured to the room in front of him. "This is all so surreal. I can't believe it."

"It's shocking, I know. Is there anyone you'd like us to call? You said that your sister wasn't married but that your parents are still alive. Have you let them know?"

Joe shook his head no.

"Would you like us to notify them?"

Joe straightened his shoulders. "I'll do it. They should hear it from me."

Officer Jackson nodded.

"I don't want to do it on the phone. I need to deliver this news in person."

"I understand," the officer replied. "Those two men that just arrived are from the coroner's office. They'll take the body to the morgue. The medical examiner will perform an autopsy and sign the death certificate."

Joe drew back suddenly. "Why is the medical examiner getting involved? Why are you doing an autopsy? This is a suicide, plain and simple. You said so yourself." His voice began to rise.

"We believe it's a suicide but we can't be sure. The ME's autopsy is standard procedure." The officer paused as the men began to push the gurney toward the door. "You say the door was locked when you arrived here?"

"Yes. I used her duplicate key to get in." He pointed to where it lay on the kitchen table.

Officer Jackson nodded. "There are no signs of forced entry." He and Joe stood and watched in silence as the gurney exited through the doorway and was steered toward the elevator that serviced the apartment building.

"Did you find a suicide note?" Joe asked in anguished tones.

Officer Jackson shook his head. "No note. At least not yet. We don't always find suicide notes. Sometimes people mail them or email them." He looked at Joe intently. "You say that the two of you were very close. Have you checked to see if she sent you a text or an email?"

"Nothing. I looked while I was waiting for you to finish up."

"Something may still turn up," the officer said. "I know this must be very confusing for you."

Joe brought his hands to the sides of his face and nodded.

"Did your sister suffer from depression, anxiety disorder, or any form of bipolar?"

"No… not that I know of." He swallowed hard. "It appears I was wrong."

"Do you know if she was taking any medications?"

Joe shrugged. "I don't think so."

"Was she addicted to drugs or alcohol?"

"No," Joe replied firmly.

"Had anything happened—at work or in her home life—that caused her undue stress?"

"You mean that might have pushed her over the edge?"

"I wouldn't refer to it like that." He looked at Joe. "The absence of any of these factors is the reason we need to investigate the possibility of a homicide."

"Alright," Joe said. "I don't know of anything that was upsetting her."

"We're almost finished here. The ME should have her report out within a week. This apartment will be sealed off until we've confirmed the cause of death."

"What does that mean?"

"No one other than the police will be allowed in here. And the body won't be released for burial or cremation until then."

"That'll be hard on my parents," Joe said.

"We'll do our best to expedite things," the officer said. "In the meantime—if anything turns up or if you remember anything—please contact me." He pressed a card with his phone number into Joe's hand. "I know this seems like a lot of red tape, but it has to be done."

Joe looked away. "I understand."

"We found her smartphone and are taking it into forensics. Assuming the ME's report establishes that this was a suicide, her phone will be released to the family."

"Okay," Joe replied.

"Did your sister have a computer? It's odd that we didn't find one in here anywhere." He gestured around the room.

Joe shrugged. "Not that I know of." Should he mention her iPad?

Officer Jackson looked at him quizzically. "Any sort of computer?"

Joe swallowed hard and shook his head no. That iPad would be the best place to learn what caused his sister to do this to herself. He wasn't going to turn it over to the police. Jill's death came by her own hand—that was clear to him. The police had everything they needed to reach that conclusion. Officer Jackson had asked about a computer. In Joe's opinion, an iPad wasn't technically a computer. They called them *tablets* didn't they? Officer Jackson hadn't asked about a tablet.

An officer standing just inside the door gestured to Officer Jackson with his chin. The officer acknowledged the gesture and turned back to Joe. "We're done here. For now." He started toward the door.

Joe remained standing by the sofa.

"You'll have to leave with us," the officer said. "No one—other than an officer—can enter until further notice. I'll need to take the duplicate key with me," the officer said. "As I said—until further notice. You'll get the key back."

Joe swiveled his head and took one last look around the apartment. His gut told him he had what he needed on Jill's iPad.

CHAPTER 9

Maureen and Fred Porzek sat at the kitchen table in their modest home in Brooklyn. Fred picked at a chip in the Formica tabletop while Maureen clutched a sodden wad of tissues. Joe sat on the opposite side of the table, his younger brother Paul next to him. He stared at the red cherries and vibrant green leaves of the kitchen curtains which had remained unchanged in this room that was the heart of his childhood home. This kitchen had seen celebrations and sorrows over the years, but nothing like this.

"I can't believe this, Joey," his mother choked on the words. "Our Jill's gone?"

"I know, Ma. I can't believe it either."

"Why didn't any of us know that something was so wrong with her?"

"People don't always tell what they're feeling inside. Especially their families," Paul said quietly.

"Did you have any idea she was unhappy, Joe? She was closest to you," Fred said.

Joe shook his head. He'd decided the existence of the iPad would be his secret. At least until he'd had time to go through it to see if it held any clues to his sister's recent mental state.

"It's a mortal sin." Maureen sobbed again. "She was a good Catholic girl. She knew better than that."

"She was obviously suffering from serious depression. The Church recognizes that," Joe said.

Fred and Maureen turned hopeful eyes on their oldest son. "But the burial…"

"She can be laid to rest with Grandma and Grandpa in the family plot," Joe continued. "I've already checked with Father O'Toole. The Church allows it now."

"And her soul?" Maureen asked in a quivering voice.

"Will go to heaven. She won't be doomed to eternal hell," Paul said.

45

Maureen lowered her gaze to the table and pressed her tissues into her eyes. "She was such a kind girl. To us and to her students. She deserves to be with the angels."

"She does," Joe agreed. *What she deserves is to still be alive. I have to find out why she killed herself.* He pushed his chair back. "Father O'Toole will be here soon. Paul," he turned to his brother, "will you stay with Mom and Dad? I have something I need to do."

Paul raised an eyebrow at his brother but nodded without question. "I'll be right here."

Joe trudged up the worn stone steps of the modest brownstone in Brooklyn not more than a mile from his parents' place—where he'd just left his devastated family sitting at the kitchen table, trying to make sense of news that was incomprehensible.

He turned the key in the lock and entered the vestibule. He'd always taken great satisfaction in coming home to the house that he'd paid a king's ransom for the prior year. The fact that he'd branched off from his family's butcher shop ten years ago to launch his own shop on the upper west side, and had been successful enough to pay over two million dollars for this place, usually filled him with pride. He felt nothing tonight.

He tossed his keys toward the wooden bowl on the table in the entryway and didn't care when they missed their mark and skittered to the tiled floor. The only thing on his mind was Jill's iPad.

He walked past the kitchen on his way to the stairs and realized he hadn't eaten since before he'd left for work at three fifteen in the morning. The clock on the landing chimed ten—hours past his bedtime. He was hungry but didn't think he could keep anything down.

He took the stairs up one level to the room at the front of the house that once had been a parlor but now served as his office. Joe switched on the overhead light. He pulled the iPad out of his jacket pocket.

Why didn't I ask her about this? She was always protective of her possessions. The modest salary as a sixth-grade teacher imposed a rigid financial discipline on his sister. She never asked anyone for money and she didn't borrow money for her possessions. He'd admired her for her financial tidiness and often told her so. She'd been so proud when she'd saved the money to buy herself this iPad and she was never without it. Leaving it behind with no attempt to verify it's whereabouts should have been a red flag. *Why did I miss the sign?* Because he was busy and preoccupied with his own problems at the butcher shop. *I knew something was off with Jill—I should have talked to her.*

Joe took it to the recliner that sat in front of the tall window overlooking the street. He drew the thick curtains and switched on the floor lamp.

He opened the iPad and noted that the battery was at 23%. He'd have to buy a charger cord tomorrow.

The "Enter Passcode" screen was staring him down. He had no idea what her password would be. If she'd written it down anywhere, it would be in her phone or her apartment. He didn't have access to either of them.

Joe took a deep breath and typed in *password*. The box jiggled and returned him to "Enter Passcode". She wouldn't be so stupid, he thought. How many times were we warned not to use "password" as our password?

He typed it in again, this time with an uppercase 'P'. Again, the box jiggled. Joe set the iPad on his lap. This was ridiculous. He would never be able to hack his way into his sister's iPad.

The clock chimed the quarter hour. He was exhausted and should go to bed. He needed to be at his shop again in the morning. He'd forgotten to make arrangements for someone to cover for him. The trucks would be arriving with his twice weekly delivery of fresh fish. He had to be there to receive it and see it safely stored in the cooler.

Joe hesitated, then brought the iPad up for one more try. He punched "MrDarcy" into the passcode box and the home screen jumped into view.

Joe got out of the recliner and positioned himself at his desk, the iPad in front of him. He stared at the screen full of icons and apps. His computer expertise was limited to email and Excel. He recognized the icons for Facebook and Gmail, but the rest were unfamiliar to him. It would take hours to go through all of this.

He tapped the icon for Facebook and Jill's picture appeared in a circle on the upper left side of the screen. He began scrolling through the pictures. Were these what they call posts? They seemed entirely random to him.

Joe ran his hand across his eyes and yawned. He'd have to deal with this when he had the time and energy to understand what he was looking at.

He returned to the home screen. The clock in the hall bonged three times. Quarter to eleven. He really should go to bed. He'd barely be able to function the next day as it was.

Joe clicked on the gmail icon. He had his own account and was familiar with email. He noted the long list of unread messages and scrolled through them. Jill followed a lot of bloggers that focused on elementary education. He opened an evite, reminding her that she'd accepted an invitation to a baby shower next Saturday. Joe inhaled sharply. Instead of celebrating a new life, she had taken hers.

He continued scrolling. He rolled past an email from a local vintage clothing store bearing the subject line You'll Look Perfect for the Wedding. Did this have anything to do with the dress hanging on the back of her closet door? Their uncle had teased Jill with the old refrain "Always a bridesmaid; never a bride." Joe had known it bothered his sister and that, as the years rolled by, it had struck Jill as a cruel taunt. *Why hadn't I insisted that he quit teasing her?*

Joe returned to the email and clicked on it. He read the message—blinked—and read it again:

Ms. Porzek,

The wedding dress you selected looks like it was made for you. I had fun helping you find the perfect gown for your wedding. You'll make a beautiful bride. Thank you, again, for shopping local.

What the hell? Why in the world had Jill bought a wedding dress? As far as the family knew, she wasn't even dating anyone. Had she lost her mind or had she been planning to marry someone the family wouldn't have approved of?

The clock's Westminster chimes sounded, followed by eleven bongs. There was no way he was going to bed now. Joe picked up the iPad and headed for the coffee pot in the kitchen.

Joe pushed the button on the coffee pot and pulled a tub of margarine out of the refrigerator while the coffee brewed. He was glad that he'd resisted the urge to buy one of those new coffee makers that used those pricey pods. He needed an entire pot of coffee tonight.

He opened the lunch meat and reached for his loaf of bread. The heel and two remaining slices were covered in green fuzz and he threw the lot in the trash. He didn't need the carbs anyway.

The coffee finished brewing and he brought a full cup to the table. He took a swig and began a careful review of Jill's email inbox. The seventh page of emails contained a message that would change the course of his life.

The email was a terse message with a subject line reading: STOP.

Joe clicked into the message. It read:

It's over. Stop contacting me. You're delusional. And leave the others alone. If I have to get a restraining order, I will.

The message was from the email account of rbtj42. The sender did not sign the email.

Who the hell is rbtj42? Joe assumed it was a man. Was rbtj42 the person that Jill had bought the wedding dress for?

Joe continued scrolling further down into her inbox. He was about to give up when, two months earlier, he found another email from rbtj42. This one bore the salacious subject line:

On FIRE to see you.

Joe hesitated. Did he really want to click on this email? Would he learn things about his sister he really didn't want to?

He had to know. There was no turning back now.

Joe opened the email:

They're holding the room for us. I'll be there as soon as I can. I won't be able to stay for long—the b$#%^ is expecting me—but it'll be long enough. Don't keep me waiting…

His blood pounded in his temples. *Who was this bastard rbtj42, talking to his sister like that?* The implications of the email were clear to him. Jill had fallen for a married man and was having a clandestine affair.

Jill knew better than to carry on with a married man. That must be why she hadn't told the family about him. Joe swore under his breath. The bastard must have made the clichéd promises to her: that he'd leave his wife and marry Jill. That had to be why she'd bought a wedding dress. And then rbtj42 must have dropped her.

Joe took another swig of his coffee, then spat the now cold liquid back into his cup. He entered rbtj42 in the search box and isolated all of the messages between Jill and whoever this was.

The results confirmed what Joe expected. Jill had been carrying on an affair with a married man for the last nine months. Her emails to the bastard were hesitant at first whereas his were full of flattery and seduction.

He gathered that they'd met at a chance encounter in Central Park. She'd been chaperoning a field trip and he'd seen her phone fall out of her purse. He had retrieved it and chased after her to return it to her. A simple coffee date to thank him had turned into more.

It was clear that Jill was head over heels from the start. By the third month of their tryst, Jill was pouring out her hopes and dreams in heartbreakingly poignant emails. Rbtj42 never responded with anything of substance, confining his replies to logistical details of which hotel and when they would meet again.

How could Jill have been so stupid? This was classic married man behavior.

Three and a half weeks earlier, however, the predictable email exchanges had changed. Jill had confronted him about affairs with other women: a personal trainer named Daria and an artist named Suzanne Brooks that he met on Wednesday afternoons for sex. At the same hotel that he and Jill met at. He had accused Jill of prying and meddling—even stalking the artist and forcing a meeting with her. Jill had recounted what must have been a horrible encounter outside of their favorite coffee shop with an opera singer. The emails had stopped on a dime with his terse message ordering Jill to STOP and threatening a restraining order.

Jill had sent dozens of emails to rbtj42 after that. One day during the week following the STOP email, she'd sent him hourly messages—all to the effect that she was sorry; she wouldn't do it again; she had to see him; they could go back to the way they were; and she loved him. Her final email contained only a subject line: "Robert, I can't live without you."

Joe pushed the iPad away as he heard the alarm clock from his bedroom on the floor above signal it was time for him to get up. The coffee and tragic news about his sister caused his stomach to churn. Saliva pooled in his mouth and he swallowed hard. He didn't have time to get sick.

Joe headed to his bathroom to shower and start his day. He wasn't done with rbtj42. He'd find the bastard and make him pay.

CHAPTER 10

Joe pulled the printout of the first page of Suzanne Brooks's website from his jacket pocket. He unfolded the well-worn paper and glanced at the numbers above the door not more than twenty feet from where he stood on the sidewalk. This was the place.

He checked his watch. It was almost two o'clock. He hated to miss the late afternoon rush at the butcher shop, but it couldn't be helped. He needed to follow Suzanne Brooks to her three o'clock rendezvous on Wednesday afternoons at the hotel with Robert. He could think of no other way for him to identify Robert. And he needed to know exactly who this Robert was. This evil Robert who had broken his sister's heart and spirit; this hideous man whose absence in Jill's life had caused her to take her own. *I have to know.*

Joe studied the photo of the artist posted on her website. Sometimes these photos were decades old. Would he recognize her? If she still sported that mane of long white hair, he thought he would. Now all he had to do was wait.

He turned up his collar against the stiff breeze and paced in front of the tall glass window of a garish souvenir store, crammed with hundreds of items, all bearing the initials "NYC". He pretended to inspect the items on display while he kept an eye on the door to Suzanne's building. He imagined Jill lingering on the sidewalk, as he was doing now. He felt her anxiety as she rode the elevator to apartment C7 and her anguish as she confronted Suzanne and confirmed her suspicions about Robert.

The door opened. Two men clothed in long black overcoats exited the building, deep in conversation, and headed in the opposite direction. Joe turned aside to shield his face from the chill wind.

He almost missed the tall, slender woman who slipped out the door, clutching a hooded parka at the throat. Was this Suzanne? He didn't think so. He would continue to wait.

She was turning the corner at the end of the block when the wind blew her hood back revealing a mass of white hair. Joe cursed as he shoved his way through the crowd to catch up with her.

He turned in the direction she had gone. The street was devoid of pedestrians; there was no tall woman in a parka. She couldn't have disappeared into thin air. He moved forward, then stopped and swiveled his head, searching for her.

The entrance to a subway stop was on his left. Had she gone down to the platform? That seemed the most likely explanation. Should he go down to see? He hadn't even considered the possibility that she'd take a subway to the hotel. Following her on the subway would be difficult.

Joe was staring into the distance at the far end of the block, trying to decide what to do, when the door to a small market on his left opened and the woman emerged, carrying a bag. The neck of a bottle of wine protruded from the lip of the bag. She glanced at Joe and gave him the polite half smile that New Yorkers give to strangers on the street.

It was her; without a doubt, it was Suzanne Brooks. Joe spun away from her. *Now she's seen me. Can I still follow her to the hotel?*

Suzanne walked on, fumbling to replace her wallet in her purse. She zipped her purse and hurried on her way without another glance at the stranger on the street.

Joe's heart hammered in his chest. He'd have to risk it. He knew of no other way to expose the identity of his prey. He kept to the inside of the sidewalk, close to the shops and businesses. If she turned around or acted alarmed at being followed, he could always duck into one of the doorways. Suzanne, however, was in a hurry and never looked back.

The hotel was another four blocks away. This section of the street was busier, with restaurants occupying most of the storefronts. Joe melted himself into the swell of pedestrians. His heart rose when Suzanne raised her hand over her head in welcome to a dark-haired bare-headed man in a business suit. He appeared to be in his early forties.

The man raised his arm in response and stopped on the street in front of the hotel, arms outstretched to her now, waiting for her to fold herself into his embrace.

Robert's face was fully exposed. Joe brought his cell phone to his face, tapped the photo button, and snapped as many photos as he could until the couple turned and went into the hotel.

Joe stood, rooted to the sidewalk, as passersby flowed around him like a rock protruding from a stream. He stared at the happy couple until the revolving door into the hotel swallowed them up. *I've done it. That must be him. The man that destroyed my sister.*

Joe turned and pushed against the crowd until he reached the subway entrance. He propelled himself down the stairs and arrived on the platform just in time to get on a train that would take him home. He'd originally planned to capture Robert's photo and return to work, but the butcher shop would have to get along without him this afternoon.

Joe stationed himself by the door to the train as it took him closer to home with each stop. When he reached his destination, he brushed past an elderly couple moving cautiously out of the train. The man had an expensive-looking camera slung around his neck and the woman was unfolding a map. He ignored their attempts to solicit his attention—tourists needing directions, he thought—as he hurried past them, averting his gaze. He took another step away from them, then stopped and turned back. What if his parents were traveling and needed help; wouldn't he want someone to stop for them?

The couple thanked him profusely for coming back.

He answered their question and headed for the exit. He took the stairs two at a time getting out of the subway station.

Joe had researched online sites he could use to identify Robert based upon his photo. All he needed to do was transfer the photos he'd just taken to his computer and upload them to one of the sites.

He went straight to his computer when he got home. He logged in, transferred the photos, and opened the site he'd saved to his bookmark bar. While Robert's photos were uploading, Joe removed his down jacket and tossed it across the recliner in the corner. He paced while the small wheel spun in the center of his computer screen.

After what seemed like an eternity, the computer screen flashed a professionally produced photo of Robert Jensen, 42, of New York City. Joe stared at the image. It was him.

Below the photo were a few descriptive sentences. Robert was VP and Director of Economic Studies at the Brandon Institution. He held a PhD in economics from Columbia University. His wife's name was Elizabeth and he had no children. *The description fails to report that he's a cheat and philanderer; that he's a heartbreaker without a conscience.* Links to his LinkedIn account and Facebook page followed the brief description.

Joe forced himself to pull out the desk chair and sit down. He clawed his fingers through his hair, then clicked on the link to Robert Jensen's Facebook page. The message invited him to send Robert a friend request; he didn't think so.

Joe scrolled through the items posted on Robert's timeline and realized they all featured Robert volunteering in the community. Robert on a Habitat for Humanity site; Robert reading to children at a library; Robert serving a meal at a food bank; Robert coaching a soccer team for indigent children. Based upon his Facebook page, you'd think Robert was a philanthropist and all-around good guy.

Joe shoved his chair away from his desk and began to pace. No wonder Jill fell for the guy. He had quite the act going for himself. Funny that he omitted cheating on his wife as one of his accomplishments.

Joe crossed to his desk. He'd seen enough. He was about to click the red button in the upper left corner of his screen when his eye fell on the photo visible at the bottom of Robert's timeline. The woman standing behind Robert in the shadow seemed vaguely familiar.

He scrolled until the image was in the center of the screen. He used keyboard shortcuts to enlarge it. He knew that woman. His eyes flew to the text above the picture. It stated that the photo was of Robert and his wife at a gallery opening.

He rested his elbows on the desk and put his head in his hands. Robert Jensen's wife was named Elizabeth. She was his Elizabeth—the Elizabeth Newbury from his childhood—the one he had a crush on then and still had a crush on now, if he were honest with himself.

This monster that had destroyed his sister was now hurting his Elizabeth.

CHAPTER 11

Elizabeth nodded to the familiar older woman who worked behind the counter at Porzek Meats.

"What can I get you today?" The woman smiled at Elizabeth.

"Actually, can I speak to Joe, please?" Elizabeth looked around the woman, toward the curtained opening to the back room.

"Is there something you need that isn't in one of our cases? I can help you with that."

"No. I didn't come in to buy anything today." She turned her attention back to the woman. "I came in to talk to Joe."

"He's usually very busy in the mornings." The woman eyed her curiously. "If you have a complaint, I'll be happy to pass it along."

"It's nothing like that." Elizabeth swallowed her impatience. "I want to talk to Joe. It's personal. And I won't take long."

The woman nodded. "Let me see if he can come out." The woman knitted her brows as she retreated to the back room. She emerged a moment later, with Joe in her wake. "She's over there, by the window," the woman said, pointing to Elizabeth.

"She's an old school friend. It's fine," he said to the woman. He wiped his hands on his apron and went to the window where Elizabeth gazed out on the street.

"Elizabeth—hi—you asked to see me?"

Elizabeth turned grave eyes on him and nodded. "I just heard that Jill died. I'm so sorry."

Joe inhaled deeply. "Yes… thank you." He cocked his head to one side. "How did you find out? We didn't have a funeral—under the circumstances. Family only."

"I saw it online last night. I'm Facebook friends with one of her friends. I feel terrible that I didn't say anything to you. You must think I'm horrible."

"Not at all." He shook his head. "We kept it very quiet."

Elizabeth leaned close and caught his eye. "I understand she took her own life?"

"We think so."

"That's so hard on you and your family. How are your parents coping with this? I didn't know them well but they were always very friendly to me. They seemed like such a happy couple."

"They're devastated, as you can imagine. We all are." He passed his hand over his eyes. "They're also ashamed that she would have done this. My mother still calls it a mortal sin and makes herself suffer, worrying that Jill's soul is doomed to hell."

Elizabeth brought her hand to her heart. "Surely the parish priest has told her otherwise?"

"He has, but it doesn't seem to sink in with my mother." He stared past her, out the window. "Old beliefs are hard to break. And Jill didn't leave a note so my parents are consumed with trying to understand why she would do such a thing."

"I get that—wanting to understand it. But sometimes the black cloud of depression can be overwhelming. You can't see any way out." She turned her head aside. "The only way to get relief from the pain you're feeling is to end it all."

Joe put his hand on her elbow. "Are you speaking from personal experience?"

She looked into his earnest eyes. "Let's just say my life is at low tide right now."

"How was your anniversary? Did he make it up to you for having to work late?"

Elizabeth's jaw set. "He wasn't working late. He was out with another woman. My marriage is in trouble."

"That's terrible." He paused, wanting to tell her what he knew about Robert but knowing he could not.

Elizabeth dropped her eyes to the floor. "We had a huge fight and haven't spoken to each other since."

"What do you plan to do now?"

"If I could just have a baby, I think things would get better."

"Bringing a baby into a troubled marriage doesn't fix things. In fact, it usually makes things worse."

"I think our troubles getting pregnant made things worse. We went through all of the fertility tests." Her voice cracked. "Robert's not the problem. It's me."

She glanced up at him.

"I've been taking fertility drugs and I know they've made me moody. I feel the change in myself. I really want a baby. If I can just get pregnant, I'll go off of the drugs and we can rebuild our marriage. I've got to try. I've been brought up to believe that divorce is a last resort."

Joe looked into her eyes and blanched at the pain he saw there. "Just don't let despair overcome you, like it did my sister."

"Do you have any idea why she was so depressed?"

Joe shrugged. "I have my own theories—nothing definite."

Elizabeth nodded and reached into her purse. "I'm sorry that I missed her funeral. Will you give your parents this condolence card?" She handed him a cream-colored envelope.

"I will," he said. "And if things get worse for you, promise me that you'll reach out for help."

Elizabeth nodded slowly.

"You can always come to me, you know. I'm here for you."

Joe turned and walked into the back room of the butcher shop. He picked up his razor-sharp knife and resumed slicing the steaks that he'd been preparing when he'd gone out front to talk to Elizabeth. His movements were rapid and sure, but his mind was elsewhere. He was looking at the beef loin on the table in front of him but the only thing he could see was Robert Jensen's face as he'd captured it with his camera.

"Hey… slow up, Joe," said the journeyman meat cutter who had been with him since he'd started the shop. "We're not in that big a hurry."

Joe rocked back on his heels and looked at the man.

"That's how you lose a thumb," he said. "I know you've done this thousands of times, but you shouldn't work that fast."

Joe set his knife on the table and leaned forward, resting on his knuckles.

"Something's bothering you. You're acting like you did right after we found out about..." the man paused. "Jill."

Joe remained silent.

"Why don't you get out of here? You're due for a day off. I can put in a couple of extra hours—cover the afternoon rush."

Joe raised his eyes to the man and nodded slowly. "Thanks. I've got something I need to do." He reached for the steaks he had just cut.

"I'll take care of all that." The man gestured to the back door. "Take off your apron and get out of here."

Joe untied his apron, lifted it over his head, and threw it into the hamper on his way out the door.

He knew what he had to do. He had to confront Robert. He'd wanted to accost the man from the moment he'd identified him; he'd wanted to beat the shit out of the asshole. He'd been restraining himself until he cooled down. Winding up in jail would shine a spotlight on his sister's affair with a married man, which would only upset his parents even more. And it wouldn't bring Jill back.

Elizabeth, however, was another matter. She was still here; still suffering at the hands of this asshole. He hadn't been able to help Jill but he might be able to help Elizabeth. He was going to try.

Joe turned south out of the shop's back door. He pulled the slip of paper out of his wallet that held the address of The Brandon Institution. By now, he had it memorized, but he checked it again. Joe stepped to the curb and hailed a cab.

He sat rigidly in the back seat of the cab, cracking his knuckles over and over, as the cab inched its way through traffic to the financial district. When it finally pulled to the curb, he had no better idea of what he was going to say to Robert than when he'd started on his mission thirty minutes earlier.

I'll have to wing it. What was it his mother always told him? Quit planning everything and let God guide you? He hoped God was real and was with him now.

Joe rode the elevator to the nineteenth floor and pushed through the double glass doors with The Brandon Institution emblazoned on them in bold block letters.

A pretty young redhead looked up from the reception desk. "May I help you?" she asked.

"I'd like to see Robert Jensen."

"Certainly. Do you have an appointment?" She turned to her computer screen and brought a calendar into view. He noted that she wasn't wearing a wedding ring and wondered if Robert was involved with her, too.

"I don't."

"I believe Mr. Jensen's calendar is booked this afternoon."

"Just call him," Joe said. "Tell him Joe Porzek is here… P-O-R-Z-E-K," he said, spelling the name out. "Jill's brother. Just tell him that."

The woman's brow furrowed. She reached for her keyboard and placed the call.

"That's right. Joe Porzek. I told him you were booked all afternoon." She paused, listening. "Alright, I'll tell him." She punched a key to end the call.

"Mr. Jensen will be right with you."

"Not here," Robert said tersely as he approached Joe in the reception area of The Brandon Institution. He thrust his arms into his coat as he ushered Joe out the double doors.

Robert stepped to the elevator bank and pushed the button. "We can go to the park across the street."

Joe remained silent as they rode to the ground floor and crossed the street.

"I don't have time for this," Robert said as they made their way into the park.

Joe felt the skin prickle at the back of his neck. *This asshole doesn't have time?*

"I can't believe she sent you to me," Robert spun on Joe as soon as they were out of earshot of the handful of people in the park on the blustery afternoon. "We're done. I made that perfectly clear to her."

Joe heard a steady ringing in his ears as his blood pressure rose.

"I told her if she didn't stop contacting me—stalking me—and my friends, I'd get a restraining order against her. I thought she understood that." He leaned toward Joe, oblivious to the bead of sweat forming on Joe's upper lip and the streaks of red rising from his collar. "That includes sending you to find me. I can take one out against you, too."

Joe's upper lip curled back as he grabbed Robert by the lapels and held him fast, their faces inches apart. "Listen to me, asshole. You won't be getting a restraining order against Jill."

"I most certainly will..." Robert sputtered, pushing against Joe's chest.

"You won't." Joe's voice was a growl as he tightened his grip. "Because she's dead."

Robert stopped struggling. "What?"

"She hung herself."

Robert gasped. "I didn't know."

Joe waited, expecting a show of sadness or regret from Robert. It didn't come.

"That explains a lot." Robert's eyes narrowed. "I thought she was becoming unbalanced."

"You complete prick." A fleck of Joe's spit landed on Robert's lip. Joe shoved Robert backward into a light post and pressed him into it until Robert winced. "Her death is on your hands."

Robert gulped. "I'm sorry. I truly am."

Joe cut him off. "No, you're not, asshole. The only person you care about is yourself. What do they call that? Narcissism? You're a god-damned narcissist, aren't you?"

Robert remained silent and motionless.

Joe pressed harder. "You are. But I'm here to tell you what you're also going to be: you're going to be a good and faithful husband to your wife."

Robert's eyes widened. "What do you know about my wife?"

"That's none of your business. I'm the one doing the talking here. And I'm giving you an order. Get rid of the girlfriends. The artist, the trainer, the scientist. All of them."

Joe took pleasure in the look of amazement mixed with terror that played across Robert's face.

"And anyone else. From now on, you keep your pants zipped and go home every night to your wife. You treat her right."

Robert stared at the man, slack-jawed.

Joe moved one hand up to Robert's neck and pressed against his windpipe. "If you don't do as I say, I'll know. And I'm not gonna like it—but you're gonna like it even less. Are we clear on this?"

Robert nodded.

Joe shoved Robert as he released his grip, sending him to his knees on the asphalt walkway. Joe turned and left the park without a backward glance.

CHAPTER 12

Elizabeth rolled over and looked at the bedside clock. Two fifteen. She hated waking up in the middle of the night—she could never get back to sleep. Had she forgotten to take her melatonin? She turned to the other side of the bed. She and Robert hadn't spoken to each other since their recent fight but he had come home right after work each night and had been sleeping with her in their bed.

She patted his side of the bed with one hand, then propped herself on her elbow. Robert wasn't there. He must be in the bathroom. She lay on her back and listened for the sound of his footsteps. Sleep evaded her. Robert didn't return to bed. Was he sick? Maybe he needed her. She should get up to check on him.

Elizabeth swung her legs over the side of the bed and ran a foot along the floor in the dark, searching for her slippers. Where in the world had she left them now? She finally gave up and padded to the bathroom over the icy floor.

The room was dark and silent. Where was Robert? She walked to their bedroom door and found it slightly ajar. She squeezed her slim frame through the opening and noticed a sliver of light from under the coat closet door.

Was Robert in the closet? What in the world would he be doing in there in the middle of the night?

She crept noiselessly toward the closed closet door. When she was almost upon it, she heard him speak in a whisper.

Elizabeth halted and leaned forward until her ear touched the door.

"I told you," he was saying, "I'll tell her after I get back from the conference in Las Vegas."

He grew silent. *He's listening to someone on the phone.*

"I know that's a month away, but it can't be helped."

Silence again.

"Of course I want to be with you all the time. But things with Elizabeth have gotten … well … odd. I told you about that creep in the park?"

Elizabeth clamped her hand over her mouth.

"I'm just thinking of you. I don't want this guy to come after you. I need to keep you safe."

Bile was beginning to rise in her throat.

"Keep the faith. It'll be soon. And in the meantime, we need to be more careful than ever. We shouldn't see each other as much."

She heard him inhale and his tone hardened. "This is the only way. I've got to go. We don't want to get caught."

Elizabeth drew back from the door and made her way swiftly back to the bedroom. She stumbled over one of her slippers as she came around the foot of the bed. She cursed under her breath and climbed under the covers.

She was pulling them up around her when she heard the creak of the hinges on the closet door. Her heart hammered in her chest and she wondered if she would be sick. *Robert is leaving me! He's found someone else!*

Robert entered the room and walked to his side of the bed. She heard him fumble with something on his nightstand. He must be plugging his phone into the charger. Just another routine night for Robert, she thought bitterly.

What am I going to do? I have to get pregnant. Surely he won't leave me if we're having a baby.

She felt his weight settle into bed beside her. Within minutes, he was snoring.

Elizabeth stared at the ceiling. She needed to figure out how she was going to hold her marriage together.

Ira Ackerman walked to the window of his business on the fifth floor. Ackerman Funding had been operating a factoring business out of this space in the garment district for over fifty years. His father had started the business and Ira had taken it over and grown it tenfold. If his father were alive today, he'd be very proud of what his son had accomplished.

Today was not a day to celebrate his success, however. He was having trouble collecting payments from one of his biggest accounts and his precise bookkeeper had made some uncharacteristic errors. And now the scrupulously punctual Elizabeth was late for work. What was going on with her?

She wasn't answering her phone. He leaned his head against the glass to view the street below through the grime of a window that hadn't been washed in decades. From this distance, he wouldn't be able to make her out on the sidewalk even if she was approaching the building.

He began to pace. This was damned annoying. He needed her here and needed her to do her work accurately. She'd been making mistakes lately. It wasn't like her.

Ira plopped down into his chair with such force that it rolled away from the desk. Maybe it was time to replace Elizabeth. That's what his father would advise. He always said that you had to fire your staff every few years and start over. They all got lazy and took advantage of you. Or worse—they embezzled from you. Maybe only a few bucks here and there, but it was still your money they were taking, his father had said.

As he thought this, Ira knew he wouldn't fire Elizabeth. She'd been with him for more than twenty years. He'd hired her during her freshman year of college and she'd learned the factoring business from the ground up. Her work was flawless—until recently—and she knew how to handle his diverse clientèle.

Ira rubbed the stubble on his chin. She also put up with his frequent outbursts of profanity and his short temper. Not to mention running errands in the city for his demanding wife. Anyone who could satisfy that woman was a saint. Elizabeth did all of this without complaint. Truth be told, he cared for Elizabeth. She was nicer to him than his own daughters who, now that they were married to a prominent lawyer and a surgeon, treated him like he was an embarrassment.

Ira drummed his fingers on his desk. He was the kind of embarrassment that provided six-figure weddings for both of his ungrateful girls. Elizabeth, on the other hand, thanked him profusely for every bonus he'd ever given her.

She wouldn't be getting any bonuses now—not with being late for work without calling him and not with the quality of her work lately—but he wasn't going to fire her. Not yet. He'd have it out with her the minute she walked through the door. He'd find out what was going on with her and he'd fix it. He couldn't tolerate the disruption to the one area of his life where he felt successful.

The heavy wooden door groaned on its hinges as Elizabeth hurried into the office at half past ten. Her desk sat across from the door, in front of a tall window. The door to Ira's office opened to the right. It stood ajar and she snuck a glance at him, seated at his desk, as she tossed her coat onto her hook on the wall and made her way to her desk.

She heaved a sigh of relief. Ira was on the phone. She'd log into her computer and get busy. Maybe he wouldn't even mention her being late.

Elizabeth pulled up the list of overdue accounts receivable and frowned. Something was definitely wrong. Had she made a mistake? She scrolled down. *Oh, God, I've made a mistake! Has Ira noticed?*

Elizabeth was sorting through the stack of invoices that she'd filed the day before when she heard Ira hang up his phone. "Elizabeth," he bellowed.

Elizabeth's skin prickled. He never called her that. Ira was the only person on the planet who regularly called her "Lizzie". She wouldn't tolerate the nickname from anyone else, but she thought it showed affection from her irascible boss and she liked it. Being called "Elizabeth" by him was unsettling.

"You need me?" came her familiar reply.

"Yeah. Come in here."

"Now? I'm working on the receivables."

"Yeah, now. That's what I wanna talk to you about."

Elizabeth drew in a deep breath and rose from her chair. It looked like the gig was up. She knew Ira wouldn't be pleased with her error. She might as well take her medicine.

Ira turned to her as she stepped into his office. "What the hell do you think…" he began, but the words froze on his lips. The pretty girl with the rosy complexion and neatly styled hair was almost unrecognizable. Her hair hadn't seen a comb and dark bags underscored her eyes.

Ira motioned for her to sit in the chair opposite his desk and came to stand next to her. He worked his hands nervously back and forth. "Are you alright? You look sick."

"I'm fine."

"You're not fine. You look like hell. I've never seen you like this."

Elizabeth shrugged.

Ira knelt down on one knee and peered into her face. "Something's wrong. You've been making mistakes and you've been late to work. And now you look terrible."

Elizabeth turned away from his gaze.

"You need to level with me. I deserve that. Are you sick?"

Elizabeth shook her head emphatically.

"What then? You're not yourself."

Elizabeth stared at her hands clasped in her lap. She had to tell someone. She didn't have anyone else. She knew Ira cared for her—in his odd, Ira sort of way. Maybe he'd know what to do.

"Robert is having an affair and is planning to leave me." A sob escaped her lips. "He's going to divorce me."

"What?!" Ira exploded. "That's complete bullshit." He stood quickly. "Why do you think that? Did he tell you he wants a divorce?"

"No. Not yet. He plans to tell me when he gets back from a business trip to Las Vegas next month."

"Then how do you know about it?"

"I overheard him talking to his girlfriend on the phone last night… in the middle of the night. That's why I look so terrible. I didn't get much sleep."

Ira paced around his desk, stroking his chin.

"I can't believe this. You're a great wife. Believe me, I know about 'difficult' wives." He spun to face Elizabeth. "And after all you've done for him. You quit college and put him through school. He wouldn't be where he is today without you." He slammed his fist on his desk. "Ungrateful bastard."

Tears streamed down Elizabeth's face. She made no attempt to restrain them.

Ira reached into his pants pocket and pulled out his old-fashioned monogrammed handkerchief. "Here," he said, pushing it toward her. "It's clean."

Elizabeth brought it to her streaming eyes.

"Let me talk to Robert," Ira said. "Yours isn't the first marriage to go through this sort of hiccup and it won't be the last."

"I… don't… know," Elizabeth choked out the words. "What… would you… say?"

"I'll remind him of his marital duties and obligations. Man-to-man. Sometimes that's all it takes." He cleared his throat and looked into Elizabeth's eyes. "I'm sure that's all it will take." He wouldn't let this spoiled Ivy League bastard husband of hers make her miserable and ruin the best bookkeeper in the history of his business.

CHAPTER 13

"She's here." The woman stepped away from the counter and leaned through the vinyl slats into the back room of Porzek's Meats. "Joe," she said, raising her voice.

He turned in her direction.

"That customer you wanted me to tell you about when she came in? She's out here, now."

Joe nodded, put the knife he'd been using on the table, and hastily wiped his hand on one of the ubiquitous sanitizer rags. He followed the woman into the front of the shop and walked over to where Elizabeth stood by the register.

"Good to see you, Elizabeth." He quickly took in the pallor of her complexion and the sag in her shoulders. "What can I help you with?" He moved toward the case filled with fresh fish, displayed on ice. "Maybe some Atlantic Salmon?"

Elizabeth stayed in place and shook her head. "I'm not here for me." She held up a scrap of paper. "My boss's wife is giving a dinner party and gave him this list to drop off." She gave a half smile. "So— of course—I'm doing it. I don't think he could find this place if he tried."

Joe took the paper from her. He whistled through his teeth. "This is going to be quite some dinner party. I'd like to be invited, myself." He slipped the paper into his pocket. "Will you be picking her order up, too?"

"No," Elizabeth replied. "I draw the line there. Can you deliver it to their apartment?"

"For an order this size, we most certainly can." He stepped from behind the counter and put his hand on her elbow, pulling her aside.

"I've been thinking about you a lot. I've been worried about you."

Elizabeth patted his hand. "Don't worry. I'm doing fine."

"Honestly, Elizabeth, you don't look like you're doing fine."

"I'm just getting over a cold, that's all," she lied.

"So things are going better with your husband?"

Elizabeth forced a smile onto her lips. "I think they're about to get better. Ira's going to talk to him. Robert's going to Las Vegas to an international economic development conference next month. Ira feels sure that when Robert's had time to think about things, we'll be fine."

Joe opened his mouth to continue questioning her, but thought better of it. What good would it do to upset her? "Good to know," is all he said.

"I'd better get back to the office. We're really busy right now."

"Tell your boss 'thanks for the order'."

"Do you have their address?"

"I think we've delivered to them before. I can find it in our files."

"No need to do that." She pulled a folded piece of paper out of her oversize purse. "I'll jot it down for you now."

Joe handed her the pen that he kept stuck behind one ear.

Elizabeth scribbled the address onto the back of the paper and handed it to him before she rushed out the door.

Joe was stapling the paper Elizabeth handed him to the order when he noticed the text on the reverse side. He brought the paper to the window. It was an itinerary containing flight and hotel information for Las Vegas the next month.

Joe blinked. It had to be. He now knew when and where Robert would be.

Ira stood and waved to the man who entered the coffee shop, collapsing his umbrella and brushing the rain from the lapels of his Burberry trench coat. Robert acknowledged the older man with a jerk of his chin and made his way through the cue of people waiting to place their orders.

"Would you like something?" Ira asked, pointing to the counter. "I can wait."

"I really don't have time, Ira," Robert said, jerking out the chair opposite Ira and dropping into it. Robert looked at his watch. He had someone else he wanted to be with on Wednesday afternoons and she was a lot more fun than Ira Ackerman. "What did you want that couldn't wait?"

Ira bristled. Why did this young buck think he could talk to him like this? Didn't anyone respect their elders anymore? He took a deep breath. He was doing this for Elizabeth—it wouldn't help if he got mad.

"I want to talk to you about Elizabeth," he began.

"Is everything alright with her at work? She isn't messing up, is she?"

Ira's brows furrowed. "No—she's a great employee—best bookkeeper I ever had."

"Well, then …"

Ira leaned closer. "Although she *has* been distracted lately, and it's been reflected in her work. And she looks terrible—like she hasn't slept in a week."

Robert squirmed in his chair.

"I finally asked her what was wrong." Ira pinned Robert with his stare. "She said that things aren't good between the two of you. She thinks you're having an affair and are going to leave her."

Ira scrutinized the young man. Robert clenched his teeth and looked away. Ira had hit his mark.

"She's right, isn't she?"

"That's none of your damned business, Ira. This is between Elizabeth and me."

"That's where you're wrong, Robert. If it affects Elizabeth, it affects me. And if stress and heartbreak interfere with her performance as my bookkeeper, it affects my business." Ira placed his hand on top of Robert's wrist and pinned it to the table. "I don't let anything interfere with Ackerman Funding."

"That sleazy little factoring company that you inherited from your rich dad? Some of us had to make our own way to the top."

"That wouldn't be you, Robert, in any event. Your wife sacrificed her own education to put you through school. And this is how you repay her? That's pathetic."

"What do you want from me?"

"I want you to get rid of all of your other women—permanently—and be good to your wife. She's a gem and you don't deserve her, but for some reason she's crazy about you. Try to be at least half as good as she deserves—that'll be a big step up for you."

"Go to hell, you crazy old coot. You have no business poking your nose in here. I won't tolerate it."

"You don't have a choice."

Robert leaned close to Ira. "But I do have a choice. Elizabeth's told me about how some of your most delinquent accounts miraculously pay themselves current. She thinks that when you 'talk' to them, you're giving them solid business advice. I think you're sending your enforcer friends after them. Rumors of mob connections among the factoring companies in this city have been circulating for years. Maybe it's time for some in-depth investigation into Ackerman Funding."

Robert leaned back and looked into Ira's eyes. "I can make it happen, you know. I have contacts at the US District Attorney's Office. One word from me and you'll have all sorts of attention you don't want."

"You're one cocky bastard," Ira said quietly. "Elizabeth would be better off without you."

Robert shot to his feet, grabbed his umbrella, and strode out of the coffee shop into the rainy afternoon without another word.

Ira shook his head. Dumb bastard thinks he knows about my friends? Maybe it's time he met one of them. Ira smiled a mirthless smile. It was time to make a call to one of those friends.

"I'd like you to visit someone for me," Ira said into the burner phone he'd purchased earlier, with cash.

"Sure thing," Artie Savio said. "One of your regulars or somebody new?"

"New. Not one of my clients. Somebody new."

"Yeah? What's the deal?"

"He's the husband of Elizabeth that works in my office."

"That looker that keeps your books?"

"That's the one. Seems he needs some reminding about his marital duties."

"Shit, Ira. What do you care about that?"

"I care because he's making her unhappy. When she's unhappy, she's late to work and messes up my books. That makes me unhappy."

"Gotcha."

"Seems he's got women on the side."

"Who doesn't?"

"Seems he thinks it's time to leave Elizabeth high and dry and move on. That's what's making her—and me—miserable."

"So you want me to explain to him that he's not goin' anywhere?"

"Exactly."

"Who is this guy?"

"Robert Jensen. He's an up-and-comer at a think tank. Economic development guy."

Ira heard Artie suck in his breath. "Not the kinda guy I usually deal with. Why don't you talk to the bastard?"

"I already did."

"And it didn't go so well?"

"It didn't."

"You lookin' for a little more?"

"I am. Not too much. My bet is that he'll scare real easy."

"You want a light touch with this Robert Jensen?"

"I do."

"Any idea where I'll find him?"

"He's going to Las Vegas next month. A business meeting. I was thinking I'd send you there to do the job."

"I used to go to Vegas all the time. Lots of business dealings." He chuckled. "Haven't been for a while. Doing more important work, now. Still—a trip to sunny Vegas this time of year? You can have a break on my fee."

"You've got a deal. Stop by here later tonight to get the details of his trip. I'll be working late. Wait until after Elizabeth leaves at six."

"Will do. Can you give me some details about the guy? A photo? I'll do some surveillance on him before I get there."

"I'll give you all that tonight."

"I'm looking forward to this vacation, care of Robert Jensen. What sort of proof do you need that I've taken care of the problem."

"Just make sure he comes back a good husband."

Ira pressed the buzzer to unlock the door for the delivery of sea bass for tonight's dinner party. They were hosting his daughter and son-in-law and his son-in-law's insufferable parents. His wife left the house early to get her hair and nails done so she could be home in time to let the house cleaners and cook in.

Why they needed a cook for dinner for six people, he'd never know. Why he had to suffer through an evening with these pretentious people was beyond him.

Ira checked his watch. The delivery was early, which suited him to a tee. He was anxious to get to his office.

Ira stood in the door of their apartment and beckoned to the man as he got off the elevator. The man approached and extended his hand.

"Joe Porzek," he said.

"Your name is on this invoice," Ira said, waving it over his head. "Is this your shop?"

"It is."

"I thought Porzek's was in Brooklyn."

"That's my dad's butcher shop. I opened on the upper west side seven years ago."

Ira nodded as he motioned Joe inside. "Business good?"

"It's been very good." Joe smiled. "Thanks to customers like you. This sea bass is the best in town."

"At this price, it better be," Ira grumbled. He led them into the kitchen and opened the refrigerator. He pointed to an open spot on a shelf.

Joe placed three packages, wrapped in butcher paper, on the refrigerator shelf. "There's also filet mignon and pâté." He handed Ira another package. "I brought you some lox. Gratis. I know that fish is ridiculously expensive."

"Thank you." Ira headed back to the door. "How come you're making your own deliveries? Don't you have a minimum wage kid to do that?"

"I wanted to talk to you, Mr. Ackerman. Without being overheard by Elizabeth."

Ira's brows shot up. "Do you know Elizabeth?"

"We went to school together. I consider her a good friend."

Ira stopped and looked at Joe.

"I'm concerned about her." Joe took a deep breath and continued in a rush. "I'm afraid that she's depressed about her marriage. I know that her husband is cheating on her. He's an idiot…."

"He sure is," Ira broke in.

"I'm worried that if things get worse, she might do something to hurt herself. My sister recently committed suicide and I can't stand by and watch someone else sink into that kind of despair."

"You care about her, don't you?"

Joe turned aside and stared at a spot on the wall. "I do. The last time I saw her—when she dropped off this order," he pointed over his shoulder to the kitchen, "she said that things were going to get better, but she looked worse than ever. I'm frightened for her." He ran a hand through his hair. "Maybe I'm just being paranoid. Jill's death has knocked me for a loop."

"You're not being paranoid—and you're not wrong. Elizabeth doesn't want to admit it, but things are getting worse."

"Does she confide in you?"

"Not really." He sighed heavily. "I took matters into my own hands and talked to Robert. Thought I could talk sense into him."

"It didn't work?"

"No. It didn't. I think he's going to come back from his business trip to Las Vegas and file for divorce."

"Shit," Joe said. "She'd be better off without the bastard, but I'm not sure she'll survive the breakup. Meanwhile, this husband of hers keeps wreaking havoc in people's lives."

"It may not come to that," Ira said.

Joe brought his head up. "I'm sorry—what did you say?"

"It doesn't matter."

"Will you let me know how Elizabeth is doing? Call me if there's anything I can do for her?" Joe took a business card from his pocket and handed it to Ira. "My cell phone number is on the back."

Ira nodded and ushered Joe to the door. The butcher seemed like a nice young man. Elizabeth would be much better off with him than that creep of a husband of hers.

CHAPTER 14

"I'm fine, Ma." Joe reassured his mother. "You don't need to worry about me, okay? The shop is doing well."

"But you're not married and you don't have a girlfriend," Maureen said. "I want you to be happy."

"I'm happy, Ma."

"I don't know." She cupped his face with her hands and bent it to hers. "You may be a foot taller than me, but you're still my baby. After Jill, I need to be sure. She wasn't married and didn't have a boyfriend, and she…" Maureen broke off with a sob.

"I'm not Jill. Nothing's going to happen to me."

"I just wish we knew why she did it." Maureen hung her head.

"Maybe it's best this way," Joe said quietly. Knowing that Jill had been involved with a married man wouldn't comfort his parents.

Maureen nodded slowly. "I don't know if this pain will ever go away."

Joe drew his mother close and held onto her while she cried. He didn't think the pain would ever go away, either.

Not only had Robert ruined Jill's life, he'd destroyed his parents' lives as well. And now he was on track to wreck Elizabeth's. The bastard was headed for a week in the sun in Las Vegas. Joe curled his hands into fists and his nails dug into his palms. Robert Jensen couldn't get away with this.

Joe threw off the covers and launched himself out of bed. There was no point in lying there, staring at the ceiling. He'd decided—sometime after midnight—what he needed to do. He had plans to make.

He padded into the kitchen and flipped the "on" switch on the pot of coffee that he'd set up before going to bed. He retrieved the slip of paper with Robert's itinerary on it from his jacket pocket and brought his laptop to the kitchen table.

The pot hadn't stopped brewing but he quickly switched out his mug for the pot, allowed it to fill, and then replaced the pot. Cup in hand, he sat down in front of his laptop.

He smoothed the crumpled paper. Robert was scheduled to arrive on a flight from JFK to Las Vegas at 3:12 pm, the Monday after next. It listed his hotel and that he was scheduled to fly home the following Saturday.

Joe drained his cup and got up to refill it. He'd never been to Las Vegas. He'd take a trip to Vegas to attend to business of his own— with Robert Jensen. A private chat with the slug while he was away from home and out of his comfort zone might make more of an impact. He'd conduct a private "visit" with Robert, then take a day or two to see the tourist sights before returning home.

Joe spent the next hour searching for flights. He didn't want to be on the same plane with Robert. This close to his departure date, flights were expensive. He finally settled on a red-eye that would arrive at dawn on that Monday morning. He'd return the following weekend.

Joe googled the hotel that Robert was staying at. The website showed that the hotel had no available rooms. What had he overheard in his shop when two of his customers were discussing their travel plans? It was always good to call the hotel in such situations; they might have had a cancellation.

Joe leaned over his computer screen to read the toll-free number. He punched the digits into his phone and waited while the call was connected. He gave the operator his requested dates and sipped his coffee while he listened to her clicking on her keyboard.

"You're in luck, Mr. Porzek. We've just had a cancellation. It's an upgraded room, however, so it'll be thirty dollars a night more than our standard room. Will that be alright?"

Joe hesitated.

"Sir?"

"That's fine." He'd never been to a resort hotel, much less stayed in an upgraded room. Being in the same hotel with Robert would make his mission much easier to achieve. He read his credit card number to the woman at the other end of the line.

"Here's your confirmation number, sir."

Joe grabbed a pen and jotted the number on the paper with Robert's itinerary. He tossed the pen on the table as he ended the call.

He'd done it. He was taking action.

Joe listened to the hall clock chime twice. It was two thirty in the morning. There wasn't enough time to go back to bed now. He headed for the shower and an early start on his day.

Elizabeth stepped to the counter. "Is Joe here, by any chance?"

The woman eyed her up and down, noting the thin gold band on the ring finger of her left hand. "He's in the back but he's busy. Can I help you?"

"I want to order something special for a week from Saturday."

The woman picked up a small rectangular order pad. "What would you like?"

Elizabeth sighed. "I'd like…" she began as Joe stepped through the curtain and into the front of the shop, carrying a tray of neatly trimmed pork chops.

"Elizabeth," he greeted her as he slipped the tray into place in the case. "What brings you here?"

"I want to order a tenderloin for the Saturday night when Robert returns from his business trip," she said. "He'll be sick of eating out by then and a home-cooked meal will be perfect."

"That's nice of you," he said stiffly. *Nicer than the bastard deserves.* He'd have to make the man understand his duty to Elizabeth.

"I thought I'd re-create the dinner for our anniversary that we didn't get to have—when he had to work late."

Joe nodded silently and looked at the woman behind the counter.

"I've got the order," she said, tapping the pad with her pen.

"Great," Elizabeth said. "I'll see you then, Joe."

"I won't be here that day," Joe said.

Both women stared at him.

"I'm going on vacation," Joe said.

The woman stepped back. "I've never known you to take time off, Joe. In all the years I've worked for you, you've never taken a day for yourself."

Joe shrugged. "I'm overdue."

"You certainly are, if that's true." Elizabeth smiled at him. "Are you going somewhere fun? Somewhere warm?" She drew her coat close around her and made a mock shivering motion.

"Don't know yet," Joe said, leaning his elbows on the counter. "I've got one thing planned but I'll play it by ear the rest of the time."

Elizabeth turned serious eyes on him. "I'll bet that's exactly what you need, after the year you've had. I'm glad to hear it, Joe." Elizabeth reached up and patted his arm. "Have a good time. Safe travels."

CHAPTER 15

Elizabeth pushed through the throng of pedestrians crowding the sidewalk in front of The Brandon Institution. She was determined to see Robert before he left for the International Economic Development Conference. He was scheduled to be gone for the entire week.

He'd slipped out of their apartment before she'd woken up. She'd thought about calling him to wish him a safe trip, like she usually did. After overhearing his phone conversation to God-knows-who, however, she wanted to see him in person.

She'd flat-ironed her hair, allowing it to cascade around her shoulders, and carefully applied makeup before she'd left Ackerman Funding. She'd checked herself in the mirror; she looked good. She'd give him a hug and the sexiest kiss she could muster before he got on that plane. Elizabeth would leave him wanting her.

She was twenty-five feet from the building's revolving door when she spotted the familiar figure of her husband stepping onto the pavement, wheeling his suitcase behind him. He crossed quickly to the curb and signaled to the Uber driver waiting there.

Elizabeth called his name. The Uber driver opened the trunk of his car and loaded Robert's suitcase as Robert grasped the handle of the rear passenger door.

She cupped her hands around her mouth and shouted his name again, this time as loudly as she could, as she shoved her way toward him. Robert turned to her and paused by the open door.

Elizabeth recognized the flash of irritation that crossed his face.

"Elizabeth. What are you…"

She caught up to him and pressed herself against him.

He released his grasp on the door and reluctantly brought his free hand to the small of her back.

"I had to see you before you left," she said. "You didn't even kiss me goodbye."

"I didn't want to wake you," he said, pulling back from her. "I really have to get going."

"Your flight doesn't leave for almost three hours."

"I have a stop to make on the way to the airport."

Elizabeth drew a deep breath. The passionate send-off she'd rehearsed in her mind wasn't going well. He was annoyed with her, she could tell. This couldn't be happening.

She stood on tiptoes and placed her hand on the back of his head, guiding his lips to hers. Elizabeth poured her loneliness and longing into the kiss.

Robert stood rigidly in place, his lips unresponsive. A cab pulled to the curb behind the Uber and honked. Robert removed her hand from the back of his head and brought it to her side.

"I've really got to go." He sat down into the seat of the car and looked up at her.

Elizabeth swallowed hard, fighting back tears.

Robert glanced away. "I'll call you, tonight," he said as he shut the door.

Elizabeth took a step back from the curb into the path of a pedestrian walking rapidly along the edge of the crowd. He bumped her with his shoulder, causing her to stagger. The man cursed at her but she ignored him, regaining her balance as she watched the Uber bear her husband away from her.

Elizabeth turned her collar up around her ears to muffle the cacophony of midday city noise and walked the three blocks to the nearest hotel. The sharp bursts of jackhammers and car horns ripped through her swirling thoughts. She tipped the bellman to hail a cab for her. She needed peace and quiet to explore the idea that began forming as Robert's Uber pulled away from her.

"Where to?" the cabbie asked.

Elizabeth paused, the address to Ackerman Funding on her lips. She gave the cabbie the address to her apartment instead. She settled into the back seat of the cab. She knew what she had to do. She opened the browser on her phone and searched for flights to Las Vegas. She checked her watch and selected a flight that would arrive four hours after Robert's. That would give her enough time to go to the apartment to pack. Hadn't vacations always been romantic for them? If they could leave all of their recent problems behind, she was sure she would get pregnant. It was her best shot. What else could she do?

She tapped the button to place a call to Ackerman Funding. She prayed that Ira would answer the phone instead of allowing the call to go to voice mail. The phone rang until the call clicked over and her voice came on the line, thanking the caller for calling, supplying their address, fax number, and hours of operation, and inviting the caller to leave a message. She disconnected and placed the call again.

Ira answered on the fourth ring. "Ackerman Funding," he said gruffly.

Elizabeth grimaced. Ira had the least friendly telephone voice on the planet. It was a good thing that she handled the phones.

"Hello?" came his voice again.

"Ira," Elizabeth began, wondering what she was going to say to him, knowing he would not approve of her chasing Robert to Vegas. Her mind seized on the first idea that came to her. "You know my aunt? The one that lives outside of Buffalo?"

Ira didn't recall Elizabeth ever mentioning her aunt, but then he wasn't a particularly good listener. Hadn't his wife always harangued him about that? "I do," he lied.

"She's in the hospital. A heart attack."

"Oh... I'm sorry to hear that," he said, wondering what that had to do with him.

"It's bad," Elizabeth embellished, "but they think she'll be okay. She'll have to go to a rehab hospital before she goes home." She drew a deep breath, searching for the next thing to say. "I'm her only family. I've got to go to help make the arrangements. And to have stuff done at her house before she comes home. Install grab bars and panic buttons... that sort of thing." She smiled smugly. That sounded plausible.

"Of course," Ira replied.

"I'll need to be gone from work, Ira," Elizabeth said, not sure he was putting two and two together.

"Ah… sure. How long will you be gone?"

"Just a week," Elizabeth said quickly. "I'll be back in the office next Monday."

"That'll be fine," Ira said, without meaning it. It would not be the least bit fine to have her gone this week but he knew that he had to approve this emergency vacation. What kind of a boss would he be if he didn't?

"Thank you, Ira. I really appreciate it."

Ira took a deep breath and forced himself to say, "Take care of your aunt and don't worry about things here. If you need more time, just let me know."

Elizabeth felt a pang of guilt. She knew him well enough to realize that his largess in the face of an inconvenience to his business was a big concession for him. And here she was—lying to him. "You're a kind man, Ira. I appreciate this more than you know."

Ira swallowed the lump in his throat as they hung up.

Elizabeth inserted her key in the card reader on Robert's hotel room door and held her breath until the light on the reader turned green. She turned the handle and stepped into the room. She couldn't believe that the clerk at the reception desk had believed her story and made her a key for Robert's room. The addresses on their driver's licenses matched and she'd shown the woman the same credit card that Robert had used when he'd checked in. The fact that they were short-staffed at check-in and the line behind her was a dozen deep must have also worked in her favor. Things were falling into place; that had to be a good omen for her plan.

She rolled her suitcase into the room. Robert's shaving kit was in place on the bathroom counter but his suitcase stood in the center of the room. He hadn't unpacked his clothes. He must have been in a hurry to meet up with someone, she surmised. Her husband was the consummate networker.

She smiled. She'd give him something worth coming back to the room for. He'd find her waiting for him in the negligee he'd bought her for their first anniversary. She'd order champagne and his favorite appetizers from room service. The lights would be dimmed and she'd have classical music playing from her phone.

She spun around in place. The room was lovely. The setting was perfect. The confidence in her plan that had ebbed and flowed during the long flight to Vegas was at high tide. Things were going her way; she was sure of it.

CHAPTER 16

Robert turned in the direction of his name. He eyed the other people in his vicinity in the generous lobby of the hotel. His gaze lingered on an attractive brunette that he'd met at previous industry conferences. He'd made subtle advances to her before. She'd always declined, proffering her status as a happily married woman. Maybe that had changed—he'd have to check. As awkward as the send-off from his wife had been, he'd been aroused. He never liked spending the night alone when he was out of town and he was determined to find a companion for the night.

A male voice had called his name and he forced himself to keep searching. The only person in his vicinity was a short, squat man with a greasy pate and a crooked nose.

Artie Savio raised the cell phone in his left hand and used it to motion for Robert to follow him.

Robert paused. Did he know this guy? He didn't think so.

Artie stepped toward him and took his elbow, propelling him forward. Robert wrenched his arm free.

"What the hell do you think you're doing?"

"I'm gonna have a few words with you. Over here." Artie pointed to a pair of marble columns . "Right out in the open. You'll be nice and safe."

"I'm not going anywhere with you." Robert stepped back.

Artie lunged at him and hooked his arm in a vice-like grip. "Relax. Enjoy that glass sculpture on the ceiling. I was readin' up on that Chihuly guy while I waited for you. Always tryin' to improve myself." Artie snorted and steered them both to the columns. "Mr. Ackerman sent me to have a few words with you."

Robert threw his head back. "That pompous old geezer? Are you here to preach to me about my marital duties?"

"I believe you need some reminding. I've done some checking—you've been spreading it all over town. Artists—trainers—opera singers. Even a teacher, until she offed herself."

"Ira's already talked to me. I'll tell you the same thing I told him: It's none of your @#$%ing business!"

"Mr. Ackerman thinks it is his business. You're messing with one of his assets—his bookkeeper. She's unhappy, so Ira's unhappy. And I'm not happy when Ira's not happy. Can a Columbia grad understand that?"

"So you've done some digging about me?"

"I know all about you, buddy boy."

"And what's that supposed to do? Scare me?" Robert snorted. "He sends a goon that could be straight out of central casting for *Get Shorty* and he expects me to listen to you?"

Artie's eyes bulged. "You're a buffoon."

"You'd do well to keep a respectful tone, asshole."

"Respectful to you? Not a chance. This sort of shenanigan," he drew a circle on the man's chest with his finger, "might impress the half-witted folks you all deal with, but it won't work with me. You can't touch me."

Robert put the fingertips of both hands on Artie's shoulders. "You're in the wrong neighborhood up here." He looked at the Chihuly ceiling. "The strip clubs and brothels are down the street." He pushed Artie.

Artie didn't move. The vein in his temple throbbed. He felt like he had when he was in the fourth grade. A boy in the class ahead of him had ripped his lunch box out of his hands and strewn the contents on the playground, grinding his heel into his sandwich and tossing his apple high and out of sight. The boy had been taller, older, and stronger than Artie, but none of that had mattered. After ten-year-old Artie had finished with him, he'd never gone near Artie again.

He watched as Robert crossed the lobby and greeted a leggy brunette in a formfitting dress. She turned to Robert and Artie saw a smile spread across her face. She offered her hand to Robert but didn't resist when he pulled her into an embrace that lasted too long for a business hug. Robert lifted his face from her shoulder and smirked at Artie across the lobby. Robert tucked the woman's hand into his arm and led her toward the bar.

Artie knew what Robert was doing. He was going to have a fling with this woman and was throwing the fact in Artie's face. Artie might not be a kid anymore, but he was feeling the familiar rage he experienced on the playground. He didn't need to even this score, he told himself. He took a deep breath. He *wanted* to even the score. Maybe no one had ever taught this asshole the lessons of the playground. Better late than never, Artie told himself.

CHAPTER 17

Elizabeth punched the pause button on her phone to stop the audio-book she had been listening to while she waited for Robert to return to his room. She propped herself up on her pillow and allowed one of the spaghetti straps to slip off her shoulder.

The door latch clicked and the door opened, only to slam quickly shut.

Elizabeth swung her feet over the side of the bed and got up. Maybe his hands were full and he needed help opening the door. She rounded the end of the bed and was heading for the door when the latch turned again. The door banged open as Robert and a brunette woman tumbled in from the corridor.

Elizabeth froze as the pair staggered to regain their footing.

The woman's hair hung in her face and a pair of strappy stiletto sandals dangled from the index finger of her left hand. "I gotta pee first," she began as Robert put up a hand to silence her.

"What?" she asked as she tossed her hair out of her face. "Oh, God," she said as she followed Robert's gaze to Elizabeth. "We in the wrong room?"

"You're in the wrong room," Elizabeth spat out the words. "This is my husband."

The woman swung her head to Robert. "You said you were divorced. What the hell's the matter with you?" She straightened and Robert reached for her. She slapped his hand away. "Wait until I tell the others. You'll be the laughing stock of this conference." She crammed her feet into her sandals and stormed out the door.

"You complete bitch," he hissed at Elizabeth. "Now look what you've done."

"Look at what *I've done*?!" Elizabeth threw her hands in the air. A couple paused at the open door and glanced at the spectacle within. Elizabeth shrank back, conscious of her scanty attire.

"Everything okay in here?" the man asked.

Robert spun on the man. "We're fine," he spat, slamming the door. He turned back to Elizabeth. "You're making a scene."

"This isn't my fault. You're the one who brought another woman to your room!"

"She didn't mean anything to me, but my job does. And now she's going to make trouble for me. We've got to keep our reputation squeaky clean at The Brandon Institution. God knows what she'll be saying about me."

Elizabeth felt her color rise. She stepped closer to Robert. "That's all you're concerned about? Your reputation at The Brandon Institution? What about our marriage? *What about us?!* How could you do this to me?" She waved her hand around the room and began to cry.

"I didn't invite you here. You put yourself in this situation."

"You're despicable. You don't deserve me. I came out here…" Elizabeth began as Robert moved to the door.

"I don't have time for this shit now. I have to find her and explain before my career is ruined." He stalked out and slammed the door behind him.

Elizabeth stared at the back of the door and her pulse throbbed in her temples. *How dare he?* She turned and kicked his suitcase. He wasn't going to do this to her; he wasn't going to control the timing of everything anymore. They were going to have this discussion and they were going to have it now.

She grabbed her jeans from the back of the chair and stuck her legs through the openings. She let her negligee hang like a tunic on the outside and pulled a sweater over her shoulders to cover herself. This was Vegas. No one would turn a head at her appearance. She snatched her purse from the nightstand and stuffed her feet in her shoes. She checked the time on her phone. It was ten forty. She headed out after Robert.

Joe took his newspaper and water bottle to a chair in the corner of the hotel lobby. If he scooted the chair a foot to the left, he'd have an unobstructed view of the entrance. He made the necessary adjustments and checked his watch. It was ten o'clock. Robert would be out partying. Joe was anxious to accomplish his mission. He'd rehearsed what he was going to say to Robert. He was ready.

Joe scanned the lobby. No Robert. There were plenty of people coming and going. Vegas really did come alive after dark. A short, squat man lingered on the other side of the lobby, by two marble columns. Joe opened his newspaper and began to read. Jet lag caught up with him. His head sunk to his chest and he dozed off.

Elizabeth darted off of the elevator and raced to the lobby. The dark-haired man striding through the automatic door was her husband. She ran across the lobby, keeping her eyes fixed on the point where she'd last seen Robert.

Joe jerked himself awake. *Damn it.* This was no time to fall asleep. He brought the newspaper to his lap and sat up straighter in the over-stuffed chair. He swiveled his head in time to glimpse Robert exiting the hotel through the front entrance.

Joe dropped the newspaper to the floor and strode across the lobby. A woman wearing a negligee and jeans sprinted for the front door. The squat man he'd seen earlier cut in front of him. Joe attempted to side-step quickly but clipped the man with his shoulder, spinning him around. Joe continued on his way without offering an apology.

Joe followed Robert, losing sight of him periodically as groups of tourists stepped between them. He pressed on and caught sight of Robert at the edge of the property by the famous dancing fountain. Robert was standing to one side, arguing with a tall brunette woman. Joe hurried toward them and stopped twenty feet behind, observing the escalating disagreement.

The short, squat man from the hotel was ten feet in back of Joe and closing fast. Robert never turned around; never knew he was being followed.

The brunette turned away from Robert and he grabbed her elbow, swinging her around to face him. She drew her right hand back and brought it up to slap his left cheek with a resounding thwack. A couple standing next to them put their heads together, whispering and pointing at them. Robert stepped back and she stalked off.

Robert followed her and picked up his pace as he approached the stoplight ahead. He stepped around a group of pedestrians and spotted the brunette at the front of the crowd at the curb. He pushed his way through to her.

Traffic jammed the street when Joe arrived at the corner. Joe stretched his six-foot, four-inch frame to its maximum height and searched the sea of people in front of him as he waited for the light to change. He caught sight of Robert to his left. The woman in the weird attire and the short, squat man from the hotel were between Robert and himself.

He moved toward Robert.

The high-pitched squeal of brakes being applied with full pressure split the air, followed by screams—both male and female—of distress. Traffic in the street came to a standstill. A large tour bus was pulled to the curb. Lettering on the side proclaimed the best in luxury Las Vegas tours. The driver stood on the top step, gesturing wildly with his hands and grasping at his chest. Most of the people around him had their cell phones to their ears. A group huddled around something in the road another twenty-five feet ahead.

Joe swiveled his head in search of Robert. A trickle of sweat ran along his collar. The woman in the negligee was walking rapidly back toward the hotel.

An emergency siren sounded in the distance, approaching fast. He followed the swell of the crowd to a group shielding the object in the road. He didn't notice the man from the hotel lingering in the crowd on the opposite side. When he got close, everyone was standing still, heads down. He inched his way forward. The Mexican food he'd enjoyed for lunch rose in the back of his throat. Saliva began to pool in his mouth and he swallowed rapidly. He leaned forward and stood on tiptoes. His height afforded him a clear view.

Joe recognized the figure splayed on the pavement, his arms and legs in impossible alignment and his glassy eyes staring into the sky. A widening circle of blood framed his skull. Robert Jensen lay on the concrete and was most certainly dead.

CHAPTER 18

He noticed the wallet that lay against the curb. Was it the dead man's wallet, thrown free by the impact with the bus? The noise of the sirens was quickly growing louder. If he wanted that wallet, he'd have to act fast.

He inched his way along the curb until his right foot rested on the wallet. Although his view was obstructed by the crowd, he knew that the body was spilling blood into the roadway not more than ten feet from where he stood. The man bent his knees and squatted, pretending to tie his shoe. He palmed the wallet and opened it quickly.

The man removed a credit card from one of the slots. He already knew what he'd do with the card. His plans were falling together beautifully. He also removed a thick stack of bills. He'd count it later, when he was alone. The bill on the outside bore the likeness of Benjamin Franklin. The man smiled.

He stood and wove his way through the sea of people to the body. He allowed the wallet to drop from his hands and nudged it with the toe of his shoe. He'd want them to identify the body; to notify the next of kin.

He shrunk back but remained in place as the first police officer arrived on the scene. The officer was immediately surrounded by people who had witnessed the unfortunate event. Some were weeping; some were gesturing; some were attempting to show the officer where they'd been standing at the time. Everyone's story seemed to agree on one point: the dead man had voluntarily stepped off the curb and into the path of the bus. The driver could not have stopped in time; the death was unquestionably an accident.

Elizabeth's red-eye flight back to JFK landed at five forty-five the next morning. The captain had apologized for the bumpy flight but had said that the strong tailwinds had delivered them to their gate thirty minutes ahead of schedule. She was glad to be home; glad to be away from Robert and that woman. The images of them together had played over and over in her mind the whole way home. She'd give anything to be able to erase them.

She knew one thing; she was furious with Robert. She'd even imagined his violent death—and taken satisfaction in the thought. How had she sunk so low? She'd have to find some way past all of this.

She waited in line for a cab into the city. She retrieved her phone from her purse and switched off airplane mode. She had a missed call and a voice mail from an unfamiliar number starting with the area code for Las Vegas. She deleted the message without listening to it.

The phone rang and the readout displayed the same number with the Vegas area code. She hesitated, then swiped at the screen. "I don't want to talk to you—" she began.

The unfamiliar voice cut her off. "Elizabeth Jensen?"

"Yes." Elizabeth brushed her hair out of her eyes.

"This is Detective Bateman of the Las Vegas Police Department."

Elizabeth sat up straighter.

"Are you Robert Jensen's next of kin?"

"Yes." Her stomach clenched. "I'm his wife."

"I'm sorry to have to tell you this, ma'am, but your husband has been killed in an accident."

Elizabeth doubled over and brought her free hand to her forehead.

"Mrs. Jensen?"

Elizabeth heard the voice calling her name as if it were coming from a thousand miles away.

"Are you there?"

She opened her mouth and a muffled sob escaped.

"I know this is a lot to take in. Is there anyone with you that I could speak with?"

Elizabeth rocked herself back and forth. "No," she croaked.

"Alright." He paused before continuing. "Take a deep breath. I'm going to give you my phone number. Do you have something to write with?"

Elizabeth nodded her head, then spoke. "Give me a minute." She churned through her purse and withdrew a pen and a credit card receipt for the snacks she had bought at the Las Vegas airport. She found a blank space to record the number. Elizabeth forced herself to breath in and out slowly. "I'm ready."

The officer gave her his phone number, repeated it, and made her read it back to him. "I'm going to give you some information now but want you to call me if you have any questions."

"Robert's de… dead?" She gasped. "What happened?"

"He stepped off the curb into the path of a bus."

Elizabeth gasped. Her anger at her husband evaporated. Tears pooled in her eyes and spilled down her face.

"He died at the scene. There was nothing anyone could do."

"He was always so careful when he traveled," she choked out.

"Anyone can make a mistake like this. It's easy to do. The sidewalk was packed. A lot of people saw it happen."

"So he didn't suffer?" she asked in a small voice.

"No. He was killed on impact."

"Where is he now?"

"He's at the morgue." Officer Bateman cleared his throat. "That's one of the reasons I'm calling. You'll have to make arrangements to transfer his body."

"I see," she said, even though she didn't. "How do I do that?"

"Any of the funeral homes here can help you. They'll collect the body. Do you live here?

"No. We're in New York City. Robert was in Las Vegas for business."

"You can have your husband sent home for burial if you wish."

"I'll have his memorial service here." She drew a ragged breath. "I'll come get him."

"You don't have to make the trip. Your funeral home can handle all that. You'll need the case number I'm about to give you."

Elizabeth continued to cry softly.

The officer paused. "Let me know when you're ready."

"Okay," Elizabeth sniffed. "I'm ready." She took down the information that the officer provided.

"I'm terribly sorry, Mrs. Jensen," the officer said. "Have you got a friend or family you can call to be with you?"

Elizabeth thought about this. Did she? She did not.

"Please call someone to help you," he advised. "You've had a terrible shock."

"I will," she said, automatically saying the words he wanted to hear.

"You've got my number if you have any questions."

"Thank you." Elizabeth tapped the button to end the call and cradled her head in her hands. Robert was dead.

Elizabeth's head ached from crying in the cab all the way to the apartment. She padded into the bathroom and found the bottle of Ibuprofen in the medicine cabinet. She shook two tablets into her hand and washed them down with water she drank directly from the faucet.

What had the policeman said? What was she supposed to do now? She pressed her palms to her temples. She needed to call a funeral home to have Robert's body sent home.

The room swam around her and she bent over the toilet and retched.

The officer was right; she needed help. The only person she knew to call was her boss. Ira would know what to do.

She picked up her phone. The screen told her it was seven thirty in the morning. She punched in her passcode and tapped on contacts. She scrolled until she came to the one for Ira.

She paused, her finger poised over the screen. She rarely called Ira on his cell phone. She hugged herself with her free hand. If this wasn't a good reason to call him outside of the office, nothing was.

Elizabeth punched the call button and held her breath while the phone remained silent and then began to ring.

"Hello," came the voice on the other end of the line.

"Ira …" Elizabeth began before emotion rendered her speechless.

"Lizzie?" Ira was fully awake now. "What's wrong? Has something happened with your aunt?"

Elizabeth moaned.

"Are you alright? Breathe deeply," he said. "I'm here."

"It's … it's Robert," she managed to choke out.

"What about Robert?"

"He's… he's dead." She wailed.

"What do you mean he's dead? What happened? I thought he went to Las Vegas yesterday."

"He did." She breathed deeply and continued. "He stepped off a curb and got hit by a bus. He was killed instantly."

Ira was momentarily silent. "I'm so sorry, Elizabeth. I'm so very sorry."

Elizabeth held the phone to her ear and cried.

"Are you alone? Do you have anyone you can call?"

"Just you," she said in a small voice.

Ira's heart took an unexpected jolt. Had anyone—ever—relied on him for comfort?

"I'll book you a flight from Buffalo and pick you up at the airport. You can stay with us while you sort this out."

"I'm back here… at my apartment."

"Oh…," Ira said. "How did you get back so—"

Elizabeth interrupted him. "I need to bring Robert home."

"Of course." What difference did it make how she got home from Buffalo? "We can have the body…" He grimaced—why hadn't he said *Robert* instead of *the body*? "…sent here."

"That's what the officer told me," Elizabeth said.

"Would you like me to call a funeral home for you? I can make all the arrangements."

"Would you?"

"Of course."

"Thank you," she said in a whisper.

"I'll be on my way to get you as soon as I get dressed. I'll be there in thirty minutes."

"No," she said. "You don't need to. I just want to be by myself right now. If you can make the arrangements with the funeral home, that will help." She heard a door open on his end of the line.

"I'm just going to my study. Can you give me whatever information you have?"

Elizabeth recited what the officer told her.

"I'll let you know when I've made the arrangements." He cleared his throat. "There'll be other things to contend with, too. We don't need to think about them right now. Just know that I'm here for you and I'll help you."

"Thank you," she said in a voice soaked with tears.

"You're going to get through this, Elizabeth. I promise."

She disconnected the call.

Ira shook his head, amazed at his paternal feelings for this girl.

Ira walked back down the hall to his bedroom and crossed silently to the bed. His wife remained on her side, her sleep mask squarely in place. He watched her rhythmic breathing. Elizabeth's call hadn't disturbed her.

He returned to his home office, shutting the door. He removed the top right-hand drawer from his desk and inserted a letter opener into the tiny slot at the top of the false back of the drawer. He removed the wooden slat, retrieved a burner phone from the stash he kept hidden there, and took a seat on the leather sofa that ran underneath the tall window. He looked out on the city and traced the progress of a truck on the street below—some hardworking delivery man making an honest living to support his family, he thought idly. Probably a much more decent man than this schmuck that his bookkeeper was now mourning over.

He placed the call.

Artie answered on the eighth ring. "Yeah?" he asked, stifling a yawn.

"It's me," Ira said.

"Hey, boss. You heard?"

"I did. How'd you know?"

"Why else would you be calling me at this hour? Who'd you hear it from?"

"His wife. She got the call from the police. Didn't know who to turn to."

"She upset? Seems to me she's better off without the little bastard."

"I agree with you, but she's devastated."

"She'll get over it."

"I expect she will. I'm not calling to talk about the grieving widow." Ira drew a deep breath. "I want to ask you how it happened."

"I didn't see it, but I heard he stepped in front of a bus. Got knocked at least twenty feet."

"Were you close to him?"

"I was tailin' him. Arrived on the scene right after it happened. Before the police got there."

"So it was an accident?

Artie paused. "As far as I know."

"Had you had your talk with him yet?"

"We'd started it but hadn't finished. That's why I was tailin' him."

"And you didn't have anything to do with this?"

Artie sucked in his breath. "Pushin' bastards in front of buses ain't my style. Besides, I was only here for conversation with this bastard."

"Okay," Ira said. "I just wanted to make sure you didn't have anything to do with this."

"Relax. It's all taken care of."

CHAPTER 19

Ira waited in the cab outside of Elizabeth's apartment building. Transportation of Robert's body had been easily arranged. Once the funeral homes had been contacted, all he had to do was supply his credit card number. They had made all the arrangements. Robert's memorial service had been scheduled and his body was now prepared for a private viewing. He'd offered to take Elizabeth to the funeral home for this purpose and desperately hoped he wouldn't have to go into the viewing room with her. He never understood the tradition of open caskets.

His thoughts were interrupted when Elizabeth opened the door of the cab and slid into the seat next to him. She wore no makeup and her face was pale. Her hair was pulled back into a neat bun at the nape of her neck.

She turned to him and forced a smile onto her lips. "Thank you for coming with me, Ira. And for making all the arrangements. You've been so helpful."

He reached over and patted her hand. "It's the least I could do. How are you feeling this morning? Did you get some sleep?"

Elizabeth shrugged. "I'm okay. I dozed on and off."

"You should see the doctor. Get something to help you sleep."

"Maybe. It's just that my mind's a jumble. I've got such mixed feelings about Robert. He was definitely cheating on me and I'm still furious about that. Sometimes I think I'm glad he's… he's dead."

"You don't mean that."

"I'm not so sure."

"Now's not the time to think about all of that. Get through today and the memorial service and go from there." Ira wondered if his advice was well-informed or not. "And return to work when you're ready. You don't have to rush back." He really hated this last bit; the truth was that he needed her back at Ackerman Funding yesterday.

"I appreciate that, Ira, I really do. I think I'll be better off if I quit thinking about all of this. I'll never learn the truth now, anyway. I plan to come to work the day after the memorial service."

Ira practically had to sit on his hands to keep from clapping in glee. "If that's what you think is best," he replied.

"I do," Elizabeth said as the cab pulled to the curb.

Ira paid the driver. He put his arm around Elizabeth's shoulders as he ushered her into the lobby of the Haven Funeral Home. The heavy aromas of flowers, beeswax candles, and furniture polish filled the space. "We're here for Robert Jensen," he said to the receptionist.

She consulted a journal on her desk and nodded. "We're expecting you," she said, glancing up and giving Elizabeth a reassuring smile. "I'll call your funeral director. He'll be right out. If you'd like to take a seat over there," she said, pointing to a row of chairs lined up against the paneled wall across from her desk.

Ira was helping Elizabeth with her coat when the funeral director, a tall man in his late fifties with rigid posture and a precise haircut, approached.

"Mrs. Jensen," he said, extending his hand. "I'm very sorry for your loss."

Elizabeth shook his hand and nodded.

"I understand you're here to see your husband before we complete his preparation for the memorial?"

"Yes," Ira interjected. "Before he's cremated." He faced Elizabeth. "You don't have to see him, you know, if you don't want to, Elizabeth." Ira ran a finger around his collar. "Robert was positively identified in Las Vegas, wasn't he?"

"He was." The funeral director turned to Elizabeth. "We've prepared your husband for viewing, before cremation, as you requested, but you don't have to see him if you don't want to. You can change your mind. It's entirely up to you."

"You see, Elizabeth." Ira broke in. "It's not necessary."

"I understand." Elizabeth found her voice. "I'd like to see him. One last time."

Ira wiped his palms on his trousers.

"You can wait here, Ira," Elizabeth said, eyeing him closely.

"I wouldn't dream of letting you go in there alone," Ira said. His confident tone conflicted with the unease in his eyes.

"I'd rather be alone," she said, turning to the funeral director. "Would that be alright if I had a moment with Robert in private?"

"Certainly. It's a very common request." He turned to Ira. "Would you mind waiting here, sir?"

Ira released the breath he'd been holding. "Of course. Take all the time you need, Elizabeth."

"Come with me," the funeral director said, steering her down a long corridor. Their footsteps were muffled by thick burgundy carpeting. He opened the door into the last room on the left. The lights were dimmed and the casket was positioned on a table at the far end of the room. A pair of cushioned chairs stood to the right of the door.

Elizabeth sank into one of the chairs and stared at the casket.

"Would you like me to open the lid?" he asked.

"Yes, please." She turned her head aside. "Would you leave after you've done that?"

"I will," he said, reaching under the other chair and plucking a box of tissues from the floor. He placed it in the chair next to her. "I'll be waiting right outside the door."

"Thank you," Elizabeth mumbled and she pulled a tissue from the box.

The funeral director lifted the lid of the casket and secured it in the upright position.

"Take as much time as you need," he said in a low voice. "Many people sit right here and never go up to the casket."

Elizabeth nodded her thanks.

The funeral director stepped out of the room and the door clicked shut behind him.

Elizabeth remained rooted to her chair, staring at the floor. Her mind swirled with her conflicting thoughts about this man she'd loved unconditionally for so many years. The man that she'd sacrificed so much for. And evidently the man that had been about to leave her.

She glanced at the casket, then turned away. His tall frame reposed in the Brooks Brothers navy blue suit that he'd bought the month before. He'd been so proud of that suit.

She felt guilty that she hadn't donated the expensive suit so that someone—still living—could benefit from it. Robert wouldn't consider buying a used garment, but most of her clothing had come from Goodwill—especially when Robert was in college and she was supporting both of them on her modest salary. She knew he would want to be cremated in that suit, so she'd had it sent to the funeral home. She'd inserted a small copy of one of their wedding photos in the inside breast pocket so that part of her would be buried with him.

She put her shaking hand up to her mouth and forced herself to look at the casket. His dark hair was fuzzy and parted on the wrong side—nothing like the sleek, shiny hair that he took such pride in. His hands were placed at an unnatural angle. She'd heard people bemoan the fact that the body in the casket didn't look like their loved one at all. Now she knew what they were talking about.

It was unsettling to see Robert looking so unlike himself. She didn't want to see any more. A tear rolled off her chin and onto her lap. She took a wad of tissues from the box, pressed them into her eyes, and forced herself to cast one last glance at the casket. Robert didn't look like the Robert she wanted to remember.

She rose from her chair and exited the room.

The funeral director came to her side. "Did you have a satisfying visit with your husband?"

Elizabeth nodded.

He looked at her carefully. "Are you ready to sign the papers? Acknowledging that this is your husband, Robert Jensen, and that you authorize Haven Funeral Home to proceed with cremation?"

Elizabeth stared at him through her tears. "I am."

He led her to his office at the other end of the hall.

Elizabeth sat in the chair he indicated as he slid into the seat behind the desk. He handed her a form. "This authorizes us to cremate your husband." He regarded her thoughtfully. "You had his body sent home instead of having him cremated in Las Vegas before transport here. Are you sure this is what you want?"

"I'm certain that this is what Robert would have wanted." Elizabeth breathed in slowly through her nose. "I'm ready." She picked up the pen he held out to her and scribbled her signature in the place he indicated.

He nodded and rifled through the other papers in a file that bore the label Jensen, Robert. "I see that you've made all the arrangements for the memorial service the day after tomorrow. We'll have his urn at the church by nine that morning."

Elizabeth nodded.

"There's one last thing." He took a small paper bag from his desk and removed a simple gold band. "Do you want to keep Robert's wedding ring or would you like it added to his cremains?"

She stretched out her hand and took the wedding band. What would she do with it? She already wore a matching band and they didn't have any children to pass it down to one day. She quickly thrust it back at him. "Place it with his cremains, please."

"Of course." He cleared his throat. "Is there anything else we can do for you?"

"No. Thank you."

They stood. "I believe your friend is waiting for you. I'll walk you out."

Elizabeth hesitated, clenching and unclenching the top of her purse.

"Is there something else?"

Elizabeth ran her eyes over his face. Should she tell him that they'd done a horrible job? That the body didn't look like her husband? What difference did it make—he was going to be cremated, anyway. An involuntary shiver ran down her spine. It was Robert. The only thing she wanted to do was get away from this place—away from her husband's cold body. She wanted nothing more than to crawl between the sheets to let sleep relieve her of the burden of thought for a while. "No. Nothing. I'm ready to go home."

CHAPTER 20

Joe leaned against the butcher case, balancing a tray of neatly trimmed chicken breasts on his knee. The tray began to tip and the woman behind the cash register rushed over, catching the end of the tray before the poultry slid across the floor.

"You look like you could fall asleep on your feet," the woman said, peering into his face. "In fact, that's what I think just happened here." She steadied the tray as Joe slid it into place in the case.

Joe gave her a wan smile.

"I thought you were supposed to come back from a vacation relaxed and refreshed. You look like death warmed over."

"I may have picked up a bug while I was on the road."

"Where did you go?"

Joe turned aside. He hadn't mentioned where he was going on purpose. It didn't seem to matter much now. "Las Vegas."

"You also came back early." She leaned close and lowered her voice to a whisper. "Did you lose a bunch of money gambling? My cousin lost almost all of his retirement savings. His wife divorced him over it."

Joe shook his head. "Not a dime. I didn't even play the slots."

"Did you have a nice time? What did you do?"

"I got done what I'd planned to do," he replied curtly. "But I'm beat." Whether it was a bug or the stress of the long flights and the sight of Robert's mangled body on the pavement, he needed to go home and sleep.

"It's slow this afternoon. Why don't you get out of here? I can handle the counter myself and Seth is back there if I need anything cut."

Joe caught the toe of his work boot on a chair as he removed his apron and stumbled.

The woman's eyes held great concern. "Go home now and go to bed. If you still feel under the weather in the morning, take tomorrow off too."

"I'm sure I'll be fine after a good night's sleep."

He snatched his jacket from the hook by the door and headed into the gray haze of the late afternoon. He knew he'd be fine if he could erase the images of the dead bodies of his sister and Robert Jensen from his mind.

Joe opened his eyes to a shaft of sunshine streaming through a slit in his bedroom drapes. He couldn't remember the last time he'd over-slept. He threw back the covers and snatched his phone from his nightstand. Maybe his employees were right; he needed to take the day off. He called the shop then showered and dressed and went to the cafe in the next block.

He settled into a table by the window and ordered a Denver omelet, English muffin, and coffee. The waitress brought his food and offered him the newspaper that had been abandoned by one of the other din-ers. He smiled in appreciation; he rarely found time to read the paper. He savored his leisurely meal as he leafed through the Times. He was flipping past the obituaries when his hand froze. Robert Jensen's face was staring back at him.

Joe bent over the page and read the obituary detailing Robert's ca-reer, education, and accomplishments. It reported that his memorial service would be later that day. Joe checked his watch. If he hurried, he could change into a suit and make it to the service on time. He signaled to the waitress for his check.

Two hours later, Joe hurried up the stone steps and into the narthex of the church. He took his place in line behind two men and a woman waiting to sign the guest book. From the body language of the three, he presumed they knew each other. Based upon their crisp business attire, he assumed they were Robert's colleagues. The strains of organ music filled the space with a majestic swell. The three stepped to the entrance of the nave.

Joe took up the pen and hurriedly added his name to the guest book. His eye caught a name at the top of the page: Suzanne Brooks. He took an involuntary step back. *What is she doing here?* It took a lot of hutzpah to attend the memorial service of your married lover.

His hand hovered over the page and he glanced behind him. No one was watching him. He began flipping through the pages. Both Daria Guzman and Nicole Mills were in attendance. He released the breath he didn't realize he'd been holding. Would he be able to pick them out in the crowd? He was going to try.

Joe slipped into the nave and leaned against the back wall, taking stock of the scene in front of him. Pews fanned out in a semicircle on either side of a wide center aisle. The church was full. He suspected the turnout was due to Robert's business connections in the community rather than a testament to a wide circle of friends who would truly miss him.

Elizabeth sat in the front row, at the end, with an elderly couple as the only other occupants of her pew. The man was Ira Ackerman and the woman must be his wife. A soaring stained glass window at the end of the aisle bathed Elizabeth in a golden glow as the afternoon sun streamed through it.

The front of the church held a long table bearing an urn, a large framed photo of the deceased, and seven oversize floral arrangements. A casket was not present.

Joe kept his gaze focused on Elizabeth. She sat, her posture straight and head turned to the young pastor who was conducting the service— the picture of decorum. Elizabeth wasn't wailing; wasn't carrying on. He wondered if her sorrow was equal measure shock and relief, with only a small amount of regret mixed in. The man had been cheating on her, after all, and she'd known it.

Elizabeth turned her head to Ira. Her profile was lovely. Joe hoped she'd continue to come into his shop. His mouth went dry. She needed to come into the shop; needed for him to show her how a man should behave toward a woman like her.

A hand on his elbow brought him out of his reverie. One of the ushers pointed to a vacant seat along the outside of the third pew from the back. Joe reluctantly abandoned his vantage point at the back of the church and took the proffered seat.

The officiant opened the Bible and began to read from the New Testament. Joe sat tall and scanned the crowd. He spotted a woman with a full head of white hair in the pew four rows in front of him. It was Suzanne Brooks. He'd observed her closely enough to recognize her. She sat very still and occasionally dabbed at her eyes with a tissue. She apparently had feelings for the guy. Bully for her.

He continued roaming the congregation with his eyes. Several people sat with heads angled to their laps. Looking at cell phones, he surmised.

The pastor had now moved on to a recitation of Robert's accomplishments. Joe tried to listen and glean anything he didn't already know about Robert, but soon found his mind wandering.

No one in his pew was weeping or reaching for a tissue. He turned his attention back to the congregation. The only other people in attendance who were obviously crying were two women sitting toward the back in adjacent rows on the other side of the church. He studied them. They both appeared to be in their thirties. The right ages to be Daria Guzman and Nicolle Mills, he concluded.

The congregation rose as the organ began the familiar strains of "Amazing Grace." Joe didn't join in the singing. When they sat down, the pastor intoned the final prayer and benediction.

The pastor proceeded from the altar and extended his hand to Elizabeth. She took it and he led her down the center aisle and out the back of the church. The row behind Elizabeth stood and the congregation began an orderly recession into a receiving line to pay their respects to Elizabeth.

Joe stood and waited patiently with his row. He watched the exit to the street near the front of the church and noted the quiet departures of Suzanne Brooks and the other two women he felt sure had been Robert's mistresses. He wondered if Elizabeth had taken note of them; wondered if she even knew who they were. For her sake, he hoped not.

Joe shuffled along in the cue until he finally reached Elizabeth. Her eyes widened in surprise when she saw him.

"Joe. I didn't expect to see you here."

"I wanted to pay my respects, Elizabeth. We go back a long way."

Elizabeth nodded.

"If you need anything—anything at all—I want you to call me, okay?"

"That's very nice of you, but that won't be necessary." Elizabeth pushed her shoulders back. "I'll be fine."

Damn! Had he offended her? "I didn't mean that…" he stammered. "I just meant if anything comes up, that's all."

Elizabeth gave him a thin smile.

"I'm really sorry for your loss," Joe said as she turned to the next person in line. He hesitated in the narthex, wondering whether he should get back into the receiving line to talk to Elizabeth again. Now's not the time, he told himself. He exited the church and stood on the sidewalk, at loose ends with what to do with his afternoon. He put his head down and proceeded to his shop at a brisk pace.

CHAPTER 21

Daria Guzman was trying to return to even keel on the day after Robert's memorial service. She was heartbroken and grieving, but their affair had been conducted in secret and she had no one to console her. Her son hadn't even known she was dating. He had noticed her sadness and she knew it scared him. She had to pull out of her funk.

She nudged aside the package leaning against her front door as she entered her apartment. She carried her bag of groceries to the kitchen counter and checked the time on the microwave's clock. If she hurried, she'd have enough time to put away her groceries and open the package before she needed to leave to pick up her son after school.

She quickly returned to her doorway and picked up the box, wrapped tightly in brown butcher paper. The return address listed Robert Jensen at his office address.

Daria gasped and spun around, slamming her back against the wall in the hallway. The box tumbled from her hands.

Mrs. Walker, the elderly widow across the way, opened her door and stepped into the hallway. "I brought that up from out front for you. Wouldn't want it to get stolen." Mrs. Walker touched Daria's forearm and peered at her over the top of her glasses. "Are you alright, dear?"

Daria turned a vacant stare to her neighbor. She forced herself to nod. "Yes. I'm fine."

"You don't look fine." Mrs. Walker began to stoop to pick up the package.

Daria bent and grasped the box. "Really. I just had a shock." She turned abruptly and stepped into her apartment, package in hand. "Thank you for this." She held up the package. "Don't worry about me," she said over her shoulder as she shut her door.

What had Robert sent her? She needed to see. He must have sent it right before his tragic accident. She had been unsettled by watching his grieving widow at his memorial. She shouldn't have gone; she knew she shouldn't have gone. Seeing his wife had only brought up questions that would never be answered. Surely this package would contain something that would prove his love for her. It would be her only tangible evidence of the future that would never be.

She moved into the kitchen and unloaded the milk and eggs from her recyclable grocery bag and stowed them in the refrigerator. The bread, pasta, and jar of marinara sauce that she'd bought for tonight's dinner could wait.

Daria took the package to her desk, rummaged in the drawer until she found the box cutter, and sliced through the external packaging. She removed the outer layer to reveal a gift box in a famous shade of blue. Her eyes grew moist. This has to contain something very special, she thought.

She lifted the lid of the blue box and removed the spherical contents. The package weighed too much to be jewelry, she thought. She began gingerly extricating a Ziploc bag from its casing of dry ice gel packs, humming softly. *What in the world needed to be refrigerated?*

The Ziploc was halfway out of its packing when she recognized its contents. She was looking at a set of five toes. A scream froze on her lips.

Daria dropped the bag and lurched backwards. She stood, gulping in air. She took a step forward, then bent over and retched on the floor.

She stood and wiped the back of her hand over her mouth. Staggering to the kitchen counter where she'd left her purse, she removed her cell phone and stabbed at the unlock button until it recognized her fingerprint. She punched the phone icon and, with shaking hands, typed in 9-1-1.

She brought the phone to her ear and turned away from her gruesome discovery. The voice on the end of the line spoke the familiar words "9-1-1. What is your emergency?"

Daria choked and leaned her elbows on the counter to steady herself.

"I… I got a human foot in the mail." She inhaled through her nose. "I need the police."

Nicole Mills passed the mail boxes on her way out of her building. A small parcel lay on the floor, propped against the baseboards under the bank of boxes. She couldn't remember the last time she'd received a package.

She bent and checked the name of the recipient. The package was addressed to her. She drew back in shock and snatched the box from the floor. The name of the sender was Robert Jensen. Robert was dead—she'd attended his memorial service the day before. He must have mailed this before he died.

She checked the postmark: Las Vegas, Nevada—two days earlier. Hadn't he already been dead two days earlier? What in the world was this?

She checked her watch. If she didn't leave for class now, she'd miss her bus and be late. What was it her instructor always said? As a performer, if you're five minutes early you're on time and if you're on time, you're late. He always locked the classroom door on the hour and didn't allow stragglers to enter. She eyed the package wistfully. She'd taken a week off when Robert had broken up with her; she couldn't afford one more absence. If she still wanted to get into the PhD program at Oxford, she had to pass this class.

Nicole retraced her steps to the stairwell and raced up to her fifth-floor apartment. She jammed her key in the lock and flung the door open. She tossed the package onto the small round table that stood just inside the door. She took one last, questioning look at it, then flew out the door and back down the steps.

Whatever was in that box would have to wait. Missing a week of classes and confronting Robert's new girlfriend, like some crazy stalker, were enough. She wasn't going to risk missing class so she could find out what was in that box. She'd open it when she got home.

Nicole pushed through the door of her building and caught sight of her bus barreling along 49th Street toward her stop. She clutched her satchel full of sheet music to her chest and ran full tilt, catching up to the bus as the driver was pulling the lever to close the doors.

She called out and the driver turned his head to her. He smiled and kept the door open. She stepped up into the bus.

"Thank you," she said breathlessly as she made her way to an open seat in the front. Nicole leaned into the headrest as he pulled away. She couldn't wait to get home to see what awaited her in that package.

Suzanne Brooks answered the buzzer from the lobby.

"Ms. Brooks," the familiar voice of her mail carrier came over the intercom, "I've got packages for you."

"You can just leave them, like usual," Suzanne said. "I'll be down to get them in a bit. They'll be fine; no one is going to bother them."

"One of the packages requires your signature. I can't leave it. If you don't want to come down, I can take it back to the postal substation with me and you can sign for it there."

"No... no... don't do that," Suzanne said. "I forgot that I'd ordered supplies from a vendor that always requires a signature. I'll be right down."

Suzanne shoved her bare feet into her slippers and searched for something to put on over the thin, paint-streaked nightshirt that she favored when she worked. A wool peacoat lay over the back of a kitchen chair where she'd thrown it the night before. It would have to do. She shrugged into it, grabbed her keys out of the bowl on the shelf by the door, and headed for the lobby.

The mail carrier stood, shifting his weight from foot to foot, when the elevator doors opened and she entered the lobby. Suzanne was relieved to see that none of her neighbors were there to witness her disheveled appearance.

The mail carrier handed her a green card and a pen. Suzanne signed for the package. "Thank you," she said. "I'm sorry I held you up." She moved toward the elevator, anxious to get away before she ran into anyone.

"You've got another one," the carrier said, nodding to the package he'd set down at his feet. He bent, picked it up, and held it out to her.

"Oh… I wasn't expecting anything else." She glanced at the return address: Robert Jensen. Sadness washed over her. Robert was dead. She'd said her goodbyes at his memorial service. Had Robert sent her this before his untimely death?

The mail carrier cleared his throat.

She took the package. "Thank you." Suzanne turned and hurried into the elevator. When she got to her apartment, she deposited the package of paint that she'd ordered on the floor. She'd open it later.

She took Robert's package into her kitchen and rummaged in a drawer for her heavy-duty scissors. "Damn it," she muttered, when she came up empty-handed. She was the only person who lived here—she really needed to keep better track of her things. Now she'd have to use a kitchen knife. She'd just had them sharpened. Hadn't the man scolded her about using her good knives outside of the kitchen? There was nothing for it; she needed to find out what was in that box.

She selected her best paring knife and set to work on the layers of tape that secured the package. By the time she'd pried open the lid, the blade was coated with sticky residue. Suzanne took the knife to the sink and reached for the sponge, then set the knife in the sink. Cleaning the blade would have to wait.

She returned to the package and lifted out a glossy blue gift box. She smiled to herself. She'd mentioned to Robert that she'd always shopped at Tiffany & Co. for really special gifts. He must have remembered. She opened the lid and untwisted the wire tie from a plastic trash bag that enclosed the contents of the box. She looked for an envelope with a note from Robert but didn't find one.

Suzanne removed a spherical package of dry ice gel packs, secured with more tape. She pursed her lips. What in the world was he sending her that required all of this? Surely not something from Tiffany & Co.

She retrieved the knife from the sink and sawed through the tape on one side. She set the knife on the table and wedged the fingers of one hand through the opening. Holding contents of the box against her chest with the other hand, she tugged the dry ice away from a Ziploc bag in the center.

She blew an errant strand of her silvery hair out of her eyes and set the mangled ball of dry ice gel packs and tape on the table. She reached for the exposed corner of the Ziploc bag and pulled it free.

Suzanne stared at the gnarled mass of pink flesh at the end of a bloody stump. She jumped to her feet, knocking her chair to the floor. Her scream reverberated around her apartment.

The package from Robert contained a human hand.

CHAPTER 22

Officer Derek Stanley was the first to respond to the call from dispatch about a human hand being delivered in the mail to a Suzanne Brooks. This would make a nice change from the usual robberies, burglaries, and domestic violence calls that were daily fare for the 1st Precinct.

Brooks sounded suitably rattled when he'd buzzed from the entrance to be allowed into the building. He waited a moment for the elevator but had grown impatient and took the stairs, two at a time, to her apartment on the third floor.

He knocked on the door marked C7. "Ms. Brooks, this is Officer Stanley, NYPD," he called.

Suzanne threw the door open. She stood, wearing the nightshirt and coat, her green eyes wide and rimmed in red.

"May I come in?" Officer Stanley asked.

Suzanne stepped aside and pointed to the table. "It's in a Ziploc bag."

Derek walked around the table, viewing the bag from different angles. He turned to Suzanne. "Why don't you take a seat over there." He indicated the end of the sofa. "I've got to call this in. We'll need a photographer and someone from the medical examiner's office to take charge of this."

"It's a human hand, isn't it?" Suzanne asked, knowing the answer.

"It appears so."

Suzanne sank into the sofa while he made his calls.

"I'll take your statement while we wait for the others to arrive," he said, pulling up a kitchen chair and removing a small tape recorder from his pocket.

Suzanne nodded mutely and turned her head to stare out the window. "I can't stand to look at it," she said, gesturing with her head to the table.

"I understand," the officer said. "I'm going to record this. Is that okay?"

Suzanne shrugged. "Sure."

"Is that everything, over there? All of the packaging—you didn't discard anything?"

"That's all of it," Suzanne said in a small voice.

"Okay. Good." Derek cleared his throat. "Let's start at the beginning. When did you take possession of the package?"

Suzanne cradled her head in her hands and began her recollection of the bizarre events of the afternoon.

"The return address lists a Robert Jensen with an address at The Brandon Institution here in Manhattan. Do you know this Robert Jensen?"

"Yes."

"How do you know him?"

"We were having an affair—had been for more than a year."

"You talk about it in the past tense. Had your relationship come to an end?"

Her voice cracked. "Robert died last week. I attended his memorial service yesterday."

Derek furrowed his brows. "What was the cause of death? Do you know?"

"He stepped off the curb in Las Vegas and got hit by a tour bus." She swallowed hard. "Accidental. I understand he was killed instantly."

Derek breathed in slowly. "I'm sorry for your loss."

Suzanne stared at her hands, clasped in her lap.

"I've got a few more questions. Are you able to continue?"

Suzanne nodded slowly.

"Had you been hoping to make it more than an affair?"

"No. Never. Robert was married."

"That didn't bother you?"

Suzanne shook her head. "Not in the least. I'm fifteen years older than he is—was. I have no intention of getting married again. It was a consensual, casual affair. We met at a hotel near here every Wednesday afternoon at three."

"Did his wife know about you and her husband?"

"I don't think so," Suzanne said. "We didn't talk about her, though, when we were together." She coiled a strand of her hair around her index finger. "We had a physical relationship. That's all it was. Nothing deep."

"I see."

Suzanne leaned forward in her chair and rested her elbows on her knees. "Robert wouldn't send me a body part. He didn't do this."

"The postmark on the package is Las Vegas, Nevada. Last Thursday."

"He was already dead by then."

Derek cocked his head to one side. "Do you have any idea who might've done this? Who would want to discredit Robert or hurt you?"

"None," Suzanne said, then squeezed her lips into a straight line.

The officer raised an eyebrow at her.

"Except he was having other affairs. I wasn't the only 'other woman'. Maybe one of them wasn't as," she paused, searching for words, "philosophical as I am."

"Can you give me the names of any of these other women?"

Suzanne shook her head no. "I only met one of them."

"Tell me about that."

"She came to see me. Here." Suzanne swung her hand around the room. "Mousy little gal. Midthirties. Surprising, really. I wouldn't have thought she was his type."

"What did she want?"

"She wanted to find out if Robert was sitting for a portrait." She barked a laugh.

"What did you tell her?"

"The truth. That we were having a purely sexual affair."

Derek leaned toward her. "How did she react to that?"

"Started to cry but she didn't seem surprised. She suspected the truth before she came to see me."

"What else did she say?"

"Just that he loved her and to stay away from him." She stared at her hands, clenched in her lap.

Derek remained silent.

"I told her that I would do no such thing—that even if I did, he'd replace me with someone else." She sighed heavily. "I told her that if she was looking for 'Mr. Right', Robert wasn't it. He wasn't the kind of man that would ever be faithful."

"How did she take that?"

Suzanne ran a hand through her hair. "I think it broke her heart."

"What happened then?"

"She begged me not to mention her visit to Robert. I agreed. She left."

"And did you mention it to him?"

Suzanne nodded slowly. "I thought he should know. Men can have stalkers, too. Frankly, the visit was a bit unnerving."

"What did he say when you told him?"

"He laughed, but not in a way that meant he found it funny. More derisive. Said that he was surprised that she was resourceful enough to find me."

"Was he worried about her?"

Suzanne pursed her lips. "I'm not sure. He was annoyed. I could tell it upset him."

"Did he mention her name?"

"Something with a *J*. 'Janet'? 'Jill'?" Suzanne narrowed her eyes. "I think it was 'Jill'."

"No last name?"

Suzanne shook her head no.

"Did he say anything else about her?"

"Just that he'd never get involved with a teacher again."

"Did he mention the school?"

"No."

Derek inhaled slowly. "Any idea whose hand you received?"

Suzanne sunk into the back of the sofa. "None."

It was four hours later when the ME and forensic team finished photographing, tagging, and collecting the evidence. Suzanne sat, rooted to her sofa and staring out the window in stony silence the whole time.

Derek approached her. "We're done, now, ma'am."

Suzanne turned to face him.

"We've taken everything with us," he said. "Is there someone you can call? Somewhere else you can go for a while?"

Suzanne nodded slowly. "I'll call a friend. I can't stay here."

"If you remember anything else—anything at all—please call me." He handed her his card. "We're going to find out who did this."

"Don't you need to figure out whose hand it... was?"

"Yes."

"How are you going to do that?"

"Forensics has a lot of tools at its disposal—DNA evidence and the like."

"Don't you have to have some idea of who you're looking for first? How can you tell from one hand?"

"We're just beginning our investigation, ma'am. There's a long way to go from here." Derek reached for the door handle. "Be careful, Ms. Brooks. There's a deranged person out there and he or she has your name and address."

Nicole boarded her bus at eleven o'clock that night. Rehearsal had run long and she was anxious to get home—to open the posthumous package from Robert. The memorial service had left her feeling fretful and depressed. Maybe this package would bring her some sense of closure.

She pulled out her cell phone to check the news since she'd be home too late to tune in on her TV.

The lead story began to play. The US Post Office had delivered a package to a woman in the city that contained a severed human hand. A shiver ran down her spine. She didn't want to listen to another story about the macabre—especially when she was about to walk home from the bus stop late at night. She hunched over her phone and was searching for her Instagram icon when the reporter continued with the information that the package contained the return address of the late Robert Jensen, at his business office at The Brandon Institution in Manhattan.

She gasped. Her package was from Robert, at his business address. Could she have a box with a body part, too?

She rocked back and forth in her seat, thinking. She knew one thing for sure: she wasn't going to go home and unwrap that package.

Nicole scrolled to her phone icon and placed her call to 9-1-1.

CHAPTER 23

Elizabeth felt the vibration of her phone and slid her hand under her pillow, skimming it back and forth on the sheet. It connected with something solid and she wrapped her fingers around her phone, bringing it to her face.

She pushed her sleep mask back onto her forehead, opened one eye a crack, and peered at the screen. Four fifteen. The display showed Unknown Number. She pushed the button on the side to send the call to her voice mail.

Elizabeth turned onto her side. Who in the world would be calling her at this hour? It was the day after her husband's memorial service.

Thanks to the sleeping aids from her doctor, she'd been able to get some rest. Without them, she couldn't quiet her mind and relax. They knocked her out, however, and left her feeling groggy in the morning. Like now. Her brain felt like it was sinking in quicksand. She lay back on her pillows and was about to close her eyes when her phone vibrated again.

This time the screen showed the incoming call was from Ira. He'd been her rock during the ordeal of Robert's death, helping her cope with the paperwork and the details. She'd never known him to call her at this hour.

Elizabeth swiped the screen and answered with a groggy "Hello".

"Elizabeth," Ira said. "I've been trying to reach you. Are you alright?"

"I was asleep. I took something and didn't hear my phone. Did you try to call?"

"Did I try to call?" He paused. When he continued, she knew he was making an effort not to sound exasperated. "I've been worried about you. Did you see the news? Did the police contact you?"

Elizabeth leaned forward, propping herself up on one elbow. "I went to bed before nine. If the police called, I didn't wake up. I had my phone on vibrate."

She heard his sharp intake of breath.

"Why? What's wrong?"

"I don't know how to say this, except to say it."

He paused again and Elizabeth's mouth felt chalky. "Go on."

"A woman in SOHO received a package in the mail that contained a human body part."

Elizabeth rubbed her hand across her forehead. "That's gross, but what's that got to do with me?"

"They… they," he stammered, "the package bore the return address 'Robert Jensen.' At his office address."

Elizabeth bolted out of bed. "What? Robert mailed a body part?"

"No. They don't think so. The package was mailed from Las Vegas after he died."

"But why would the package say it was from him?"

"That's what they've got to figure out."

"Who was this person that received it?"

Ira cleared his throat. "The news reporter said that the woman had had a long-standing romantic relationship with Robert."

Elizabeth's knees crumpled and she slipped to the floor. "A woman he was having an affair with?" Her voice was a whisper.

"I wanted you to know—to hear it from me. The police have probably been trying to contact you. If not, they'll want to interview you this morning."

A moan escaped her lips.

"Are you up to talking to them?"

"I… I don't know."

"I'll call my lawyer. He'll be there with you."

"Do you think that's necessary? I don't know anything about this…" her voice broke into a sob.

"I think it's wise," Ira told her. "Don't talk to anyone until you hear from me. Promise?" Ira asked insistently.

"I promise."

Detective Adam Harnet and Officer Derek Stanley climbed the last flight of stairs to Elizabeth's fourth-floor apartment. "You did a nice job questioning Suzanne Brooks," Adam said. "Your report was very helpful."

Derek felt a flush creep up his neck. He'd been trying to make detective for the past two years. Maybe this case would be his chance to prove himself.

"I'm glad you could come with me. I'll do the questioning. If you feel that I haven't covered something, slip me a note. Otherwise, just observe Elizabeth Jensen."

"Is she a suspect?"

"Not at this time. This is such an unusual case that everyone that's connected to Robert Jensen is a suspect."

Derek nodded as Adam consulted his watch. "We're a few minutes early." Adam raised his hand and knocked.

Jay Goldstein answered the door at five minutes before eleven. The officers held out their credentials. The attorney scanned them quickly and stepped aside, motioning for them to enter Elizabeth's apartment.

"I'm Jay Goldstein," he said, extending his hand to each man, in turn.

"We're here to talk to Elizabeth Jensen."

"She's right this way," Jay said, leading the way down the narrow hallway to the tiny living room.

"We'd like to talk to Mrs. Jensen alone," the detective said.

"I'm her attorney. I'll be staying."

"Her attorney? We're not charging her with anything. We've just got a few questions," Adam said.

Jay nodded. "Even so. We thought it wise that I be present."

They entered the room to find Elizabeth perched on a small sofa. The only other seating in the room was a straight-backed chair.

Jay settled next to his client and Adam pulled the chair to a position opposite Elizabeth. A narrow coffee table stood between them. Derek leaned against the wall behind Adam.

Derek noted the geometric patterned drapes at the windows and the narrow bookcase against the wall. They all looked like items with strange sounding names from the behemoth Swedish furniture retailer that specialized in furnishings for small spaces. Although neat and stylish, this couple was living on a tight budget, he thought. A wedding photo in a silver frame was displayed prominently on the bookcase. No other photos adorned the room.

"Mrs. Jensen," Adam began, "thank you for seeing us this morning."

Elizabeth nodded, her eyes somber. The dark circles underneath and the gray cast to her makeup-less face were consistent with her status as the grieving widow.

"We'll be taping our conversation," he said, placing a small tape recorder on the coffee table. He glanced at Jay.

The attorney nodded. "It's standard procedure," he said to Elizabeth.

"I understand that your husband was killed in a tragic accident in Las Vegas last week and that his memorial service was yesterday," Adam said.

Elizabeth brushed a stray strand of her uncombed hair out of her eyes.

Adam cleared his throat and continued. "I believe you heard the news report that a human body part was mailed to a woman in SOHO."

"Yes," Elizabeth said.

"And that the return address on the package was from a Robert Jensen, at your husband's work address at The Brandon Institution."

"She's aware of all that," Jay broke in.

Adam held up a hand. "I'd like to hear from Mrs. Jensen, please."

"I heard that. Why…"

Goldstein put his hand on her arm. "Let the detective ask his questions."

"The package was posted after Robert's death, so he couldn't have mailed it himself. Dismembering bodies is a crime and we have to find the person or persons responsible. That's why I'm here."

"I don't know how I can help you."

"The person who received the package is a sculptor who lives and works in SOHO. Her name is Suzanne Brooks. Did you know her?"

"No."

"Did your husband know her?"

Elizabeth shrugged. "Not that I know of."

Adam searched her face as he asked his next question. "Would it surprise you to know that Ms. Brooks told us that she and your husband were having an affair?"

Tears pooled and hung in Elizabeth's eyes. Her shoulders dropped, and Adam had his answer before she spoke.

"I …" She choked on her words and swallowed. "I suspected my husband was having an affair. I didn't know who the woman was."

"Had this happened before? Had Robert had other affairs?"

Elizabeth moaned and dropped her head to her hands.

"Is this necessary?" Jay asked. "She just buried him yesterday."

"I'm sorry that these questions are upsetting for you, Mrs. Jensen. I wouldn't ask them if they weren't important. We need to find out if someone held a grudge against your husband."

Elizabeth turned her face up to his.

"Maybe someone who felt jilted by him?" Adam continued.

"I don't know of anyone." Her voice was a whisper.

"Did any of his colleagues at work bear him ill will?"

"No. He was very well-liked and respected at The Brandon Institution. That's why he was selected to go to the conference in Las Vegas."

"So he got along with everyone?"

Elizabeth nodded. Maybe too well with some, she thought, remembering his assistant that she suspected had a crush on Robert. Weren't crushes on a boss common? Especially one as good-looking and charming as Robert? She paused and studied her hands. What good could come of mentioning her unfounded suspicions to this officer? It would only make trouble for a young woman that didn't deserve it. "Yes. Everyone."

"What about family members?"

"Robert was an only child and his parents passed away years ago. He wasn't in contact with anyone that I know of."

Jay began to rise. "I think that's…"

Adam raised a hand to motion him back to his seat. "I just have a few more questions."

Jay resumed his place on the sofa.

"Where were you when your husband was killed?"

Elizabeth lowered her gaze to her hands. "I was in Las Vegas."

Jay swung his head to her and narrowed his eyes.

She wondered if Ira had told Jay her story about taking care of her aunt in Buffalo.

"Did you accompany him on his business trip?"

She shook her head no.

"You need to answer audibly."

"No," Elizabeth said. "I flew out separately to surprise him."

"And… did you surprise him?"

Tears pooled in Elizabeth's eyes and dripped off her chin to her knees.

"Tell us what happened in Las Vegas."

"I wanted to have a romantic getaway. The hotel gave me a key to his room and I was there when he came back." She paused and Adam waited for her to continue. "He didn't come back to his room alone," she said in a small voice.

"Who was with him, Mrs. Jensen?"

"Some woman he picked up there."

"Were they … ?"

"Going to have sex?" Elizabeth blurted out. "Yes … If I hadn't been in the room and spoiled it for them."

"So they walked in and found you there?"

"Yes."

"What happened then?"

"She was pissed. Said she didn't know he was married. She walked out, threatening to bad mouth him at the conference."

"How did he react to that?"

"Oh—he wasn't about to have his business reputation tarnished. He took off after her."

"What did you do?"

"I … I put some clothes on and chased after him."

"Did you find him?"

"I caught sight of him arguing with her by those big fountains in front of the hotel. I tried to catch up to them but there were a lot of people on the Strip and I lost sight of him. I kept going until I came to the corner. I didn't want to cross the street. I was scared to be out with all of those people late at night."

"Was that about the time that your husband was accidentally killed?"

"I think so. I didn't learn about his death until the next morning."

"Did you go back to his room?"

"Only long enough to grab my stuff and return to the airport. I got a seat on a red-eye back to JFK."

"Let me get this straight. You flew to Las Vegas and back in one day?"

"After seeing him with that other woman, all I wanted to do was to come home."

"Were you aware that there had been a fatal pedestrian accident on the Strip before you left?"

"No. I heard sirens as I was walking back to the hotel, but the Strip is a very noisy place. They didn't seem out of place."

"When did you learn of Robert's death?"

"I got a call from a police officer as soon as I turned my phone back on after landing."

"What did you do then?"

"I called my boss, Ira Ackerman. I work for Ackerman Funding."

"Did you go back out to Las Vegas?"

Elizabeth shook her head again.

"Audibly," Adam prompted.

"No. Ira made arrangements with funeral homes both here and in Las Vegas. They took care of everything."

"What is the date of your return flight to JFK? What will the airline records show?"

"Is this necessary?" Jay bristled.

"It's helpful to know that Mrs. Jensen couldn't have been in Las Vegas on the day that the package was mailed."

Elizabeth sifted through a stack of papers on her coffee table, found the one she was looking for, and extended it to Adam. "Here's my airline confirmation email."

He perused it quickly and addressed Elizabeth again. "What are your plans for the future?"

Elizabeth's brows knitted together.

"Will you stay in this apartment?"

Elizabeth nodded slowly.

"Will you keep working?"

"That's my plan. I might…" she stopped as Jay narrowed his eyes at her.

Adam noticed the nonverbal communication between them. "What do you do for Ackerman Funding?" he continued.

"I'm the Administrative Assistant to Ira Ackerman."

"Is that here in New York?"

"Yes. We're a factoring business in the garment district."

"I see." Adam made a note. "Address?"

Elizabeth supplied it.

Adam turned to Derek and raised an eyebrow. Derek shook his head.

"If you remember anything that might shed any light on why this package bore your late husband's name and address, please let me know." He handed her his card and gave one to the lawyer.

Jay rose and this time Adam followed suit. "I'm sorry for your loss, Mrs. Jensen, and for the intrusiveness of some of my questions. I appreciate your time."

Elizabeth drew a deep breath. "You're welcome. I'm sorry I don't know anything that will help." She walked them to the door and sank against it after she'd closed it on them.

She turned to Jay. "I was just going to say that I might go back to school. Now that I've inherited all that money from his life insurance policy. Why didn't you want me to say that?"

"It's none of their business. You never want to volunteer information to the police."

"But I'm not guilty of anything."

"I know that, but the police think everyone is guilty of something." He shook his finger at her. "I'm glad Ira called me and had me come over. No talking to them without me being present. Understand?"

Elizabeth shrugged. "Fine, but I don't have anything to hide."

CHAPTER 24

Derek shifted his weight from foot to foot, rocking impatiently, while he listened to Adam's side of the conversation.

"Two additional body parts?" Adam said into the phone. He looked at the officer and nodded at him as he continued to scribble notes on the pad in front of him.

Derek stepped around the desk and leaned over Adam's shoulder to read as Adam wrote. The Detective's penmanship left a lot to be desired, but he was able to make out the words "foot" and "right ear".

"The Detective Bureau will take over this investigation," Adam said. "We'll find out whose body or bodies these are from, and who dismembered them." Adam listened and nodded. "We'll coordinate with the other precincts, Captain. You can count on us."

He hung up the receiver.

"That right hand you took in the other night wasn't the only unwelcome package delivered that day." Adam motioned for Derek to sit. "Seems two other women got packages in the mail the same day."

"A foot and a right ear?" Derek pulled up a chair.

"That's right. Both packages were allegedly from Robert Jensen."

"Good God," Derek said. "We've got a sicko—or sickos—out there."

"That we do."

"Let me guess—the women who received them were also having affairs with Jensen?"

"Right again. Detectives from the other boroughs talked to both of them. Daria Guzman—a thirty-seven-year-old personal trainer—was currently having an affair with him. Guzman believed that Robert was going to leave his wife and marry her; that he was going to tell his wife as soon as he got back from a business trip to Las Vegas."

"I can't believe women still fall for that."

"Neither can I. I searched the court records—he hadn't filed for divorce. The other recipient is Nicole Mills—a thirty-one-year-old opera singer who had been jilted by him for a teacher by the name of Jill Porzek."

"Anyone contact Ms. Porzek to see if she's gotten any unwanted parcels?"

"Yep. Seems Ms. Porzek is beyond caring."

Derek cocked his head to one side.

"She committed suicide after Jensen broke up with her recently."

Derek whistled through his teeth. "He's left a lot of destruction in his wake."

"He certainly has. There were a lot of people who didn't have positive experiences with our Mr. Jensen."

"Who wanted to discredit him by sending body parts to his mistresses? Allegedly from him—after he died?" Derek asked.

"Sounds really twisted, doesn't it?"

"It sure does." Derek took a deep breath. "Do we have any idea whose body parts these are?"

Adam shook his head. "The lab has taken DNA samples to tell us if we're dealing with more than one victim. We can also learn gender. The ME can give us a rough idea of height. That's about it for now."

"Will we run the DNA through the National Combined DNA Index System for matches?"

"Yep. If this victim—or victims—have prior criminal records or other reason to have DNA records in CODIS, we'll get a name. Or if they have a close relative in the database, we could get a lead there." Adam sighed heavily. "All of that could take months."

Adam tapped his computer screen. "I'll enter this into the Violent Criminal Apprehension Network database, too. If body parts have been mailed to recipients in other parts of the county, we'll find out through ViCap."

"What do we do in the meantime? Should we talk to these other women?"

"Yes. I'll want to interview all of them. I'd also like to get a DNA sample for Jensen. We need to know if he had anything to do with the packages."

"They were mailed after he died."

"I understand. They were postmarked after he died. Maybe someone posted them for him?"

"Do you think that's likely?"

"Nothing in this case is in the realm of likely."

"Have you contacted the widow to see if we can pick up his hairbrush or toothbrush?"

Adam shook his head no. "Based upon her lawyer's actions when we questioned her, I'm assuming the answer will be 'no'. I've got the District Attorney's office working on a search warrant."

"She may be cleaning out all of his stuff. We need to act fast," Derek said.

"I agree. We should have the warrant in hand this afternoon."

"Good."

"Want to be there when it's served?"

"I wouldn't miss it," Derek said, swallowing hard to hide the grin forcing itself onto his lips. Maybe his desired move into the Detective Bureau was finally at hand.

Adam and Derek, together with another officer from Precinct #1, gathered outside the door to Elizabeth's apartment. Adam pulled the warrant out of his pocket.

"Mrs. Jensen isn't a suspect. She's just buried her husband and this is going to be very upsetting for her." Adam looked at each man in turn. "We're here to get DNA samples from her late husband. Toothbrushes; hairbrushes; a coffee cup that hasn't been washed; an old water bottle on his nightstand. You know the drill."

Derek and the officer nodded.

"This should be quick and easy. In and out in fifteen minutes. We don't need to go through the place with a fine-tooth comb. As soon as we've got enough, we're outta there."

"We understand," Derek said.

Adam turned back to the door and knocked firmly. He waited and knocked again. "Mrs. Jensen, this is Detective Harnet."

The doorknob turned, and the door opened a short distance until it stopped at the end of the security chain. Elizabeth pressed her face into the opening. "What are you doing here?"

"Please open the door, Mrs. Jensen."

Elizabeth's eyes widened when she took in the sight of Derek and the other officer. She shut the door, removed the chain, and opened the door. She stood in the doorway, staring at them.

Adam handed her the search warrant.

Elizabeth scanned the paper. Her brows furrowed. "What's this?"

"We have a warrant to search your apartment."

Elizabeth gasped and took a step back.

"We need to collect a DNA sample from Robert," Adam said. "That's all we're looking for."

Elizabeth put her hand to her forehead and raked her fingers through her hair. "Why do you need his DNA?"

"It's part of our investigation into the packages," Adam said.

Elizabeth cocked her head to one side "Packages? I thought there was only one."

Adam put his hand on the door and stepped into the apartment. "Two other packages were received that day containing body parts."

Elizabeth stumbled as she stepped back. "Two more? Both from Robert?"

Adam nodded. "From the same return address. Both sent priority mail from Las Vegas."

"Did they also go to that woman in SOHO? Suzanne Brooks?"

"No. The recipients were other women."

Her eyes grew wide as she fixed her gaze on Adam. "Did Robert... know... these women?"

Adam nodded. "Yes, ma'am. Robert was having an affair with one of them and had recently broken up with the other."

Her eyes glistened hard. "What do you need?" she asked.

"Anything that would contain physical evidence from your husband—blood, sweat, hair, saliva."

"His toothbrush is the red one in the holder on the bathroom vanity."

"Thank you," Adam said. "We'll get it. Meanwhile, Derek will wait with you in the living room."

Derek frowned slightly but followed Elizabeth to the living room. He gestured to the sofa, but she shook her head and paced in front of the window.

"Are you allowed to do this?"

"That's what the warrant is for, ma'am. That gives us the authority."

"Shouldn't I have my lawyer here?"

"You can call him if you'd like to. We don't need to wait for him to be present. We're not questioning you."

Elizabeth peered out the window.

Derek ran his eyes over the room. It was neat and tidy, with the exception of the documents strewn on the coffee table and the mountain of crumpled tissues that spilled off the end table and onto the floor. He noted the absence of the wedding photo of the couple that had been on display the last time he'd been in the room.

Elizabeth remained with her back to him, her arms crossed over her chest, hugging herself.

Derek sidled to the coffee table and peered at the documents. A letterhead bore the name The Equitable Life Insurance Company. The widow was evidently the beneficiary of one or more life insurance policies. That wouldn't be surprising. Life insurance would be one of Robert's employee benefits.

He leaned forward, searching for an amount. His eyes came to rest on a figure: $2,000,000. He straightened and brought his eyes back to Elizabeth as she turned to him.

"His gym bag," she said.

Derek raised his eyebrows.

"Would his gym bag be helpful? For DNA?"

"It might be," Derek said. "Do you have it?"

Elizabeth nodded. "It's in the hall closet, on the floor. That's where he kept it."

"Adam," Derek called over his shoulder.

"Have you touched anything in that bag?"

Elizabeth had gone through it, looking for clues of Robert's extra-marital affairs. She'd found a note from a woman who signed her name "Daria"—with a whole string of x's and o's. The bitch. The note expressed Daria's disappointment that Robert hadn't shown up for their planned rendezvous at a hotel.

She'd destroyed the note in a fit of pique and slung the bag into the back of the closet. What would be the point of telling the police about the note now? They already knew about Robert and his affairs. She wondered if Daria was one of the women who had received a body part in the mail. Elizabeth's lips flattened into a hard line. The cheating slut would have deserved it—no matter how disgusting it would have been.

Derek was staring at her, his eyebrows knotted.

Elizabeth forced her mind back to the topic of Robert's gym bag. Did she have to humiliate herself further by telling the police about the note? Elizabeth shook her head no.

Adam rounded the corner and stepped into the living room.

"Elizabeth tells me that Robert's gym bag is in the hall closet," Derek said.

"Found it!" He addressed Elizabeth, "Thank you. I think we've got everything we need."

Elizabeth took a deep breath. "Will I get his stuff back?"

"When we're done with it, yes," Adam said. "We'll be in touch."

Derek looked at Elizabeth. "Did you have anything you wanted to tell us?"

She shook her head.

"We'll be leaving, then," Adam said, as he, Derek, and the other officer headed out the door. They listened as Elizabeth engaged the deadbolt and slid the security chain back in place.

Adam turned to Derek as they descended the stairs. "Why did you ask her if she had anything to tell us?"

"I don't know. I just had the feeling she was holding something back."

Adam shrugged. "Wouldn't be the first time someone didn't tell us the whole truth. Happens with witnesses all the time. Whatever she's concealing—we'll find it."

They rounded the corner on the second floor and continued their descent. "Did you check out those documents on her coffee table? They looked official."

"I was just going to tell you." Derek grinned. "They're life insurance claim forms. It seems that Robert Jensen left his wife very well provided for."

"Really?"

"Yep. To the tune of two million."

Adam whistled softly through his teeth. "That's more than 'well provided for'. People have been murdered for less than that."

"That's what I was thinking," Derek said.

"But we don't have a murder case on our hands. The Vegas police were very clear that Robert's death was an accident. There were a lot of witnesses."

"I know. This insurance policy simply means he was a man that took care of his wife."

"Seems out of character for the cheating bastard."

"It doesn't add up," Derek agreed. "Sometimes things don't."

They stepped out onto the street. "We need to get this stuff to the lab," Adam told the officers. "We need to find out if Robert's DNA was on any of those packages."

"And if it's not?" Derek asked.

"That will just support what we already think—that Robert Jensen didn't have anything to do with those packages. Confirmation of facts is always good. We need to be patient and see where the evidence takes us," Adam said. "Let's get going."

CHAPTER 25

Elizabeth rolled onto her back and opened her eyes. It was Saturday morning. She could lie in bed as long as she liked. Maybe she would stay in her pajamas all day, like she'd done the prior Saturday. And have another long, miserable day reliving Robert's betrayals and nursing old wounds. Elizabeth drew a deep breath and flung the covers off.

She padded to the kitchen in the fluffy socks she now wore to bed every night, without worry about the snide remarks that Robert used to make about them. She reached for the canister of ground coffee that lived on a shelf above the coffee maker. There was barely enough to make half a cup. She pulled out a box of cereal and poured a serving into a bowl. The carton of milk emitted a sour odor when she opened it. She poured the milk down the drain and slung the container into the trash.

Elizabeth braced herself against the sink and swallowed hard. She was not going to dissolve into tears over the fact that she didn't have anything to eat for breakfast. She'd allowed this to happen and she was going to fix it. She was a grown woman, for heaven's sake. She'd get dressed and go to the grocery on the corner.

She picked a notepad off of the counter and jotted down a list. When she finished, she returned to her bedroom to get dressed. She picked up the jeans that she'd dropped into a heap on the floor and sat on the edge of the bed. She swiveled her head around the room. The usually tidy space was littered with dirty dishes, unread mail, and discarded clothes. The rest of the apartment was in similar disarray. How in the world had she let herself become so slovenly?

Elizabeth shoved her feet through the legs of her jeans and dug through the stack of clothes for a sweatshirt. She was going to spend the day cleaning and doing laundry. It was time she put her house back in order. She checked her supply of cleaning products and satisfied herself that she had what she needed. She stuffed her shopping list into her purse, donned her down jacket, and headed out of her apartment.

The morning was crisp and the skies were clear. It promised to be a sunny day. If she finished her tasks early, she'd treat herself to lunch at her favorite bistro two blocks over.

She navigated the busy grocery with ease and was unloading her purchases in under an hour. She unwrapped the poppy seed bagel with strawberry cream cheese that she'd bought at the deli counter and took a generous bite. She moved to the coffee maker and opened the bag of coffee she'd just brought home. The heady aroma of freshly ground beans filled the air. She breathed in deeply and smiled. She scooped enough coffee into the basket to make an entire pot and pushed the brew button. When it was done, she took a large mug of coffee and her bagel into her bedroom. She'd strip the bed, start the laundry, and work her way around the apartment from there.

Elizabeth stacked, sorted, and scrubbed until she'd restored her apartment to its customary tidy condition. She finished in her kitchen, hanging a clean dish towel on the hook by the sink. She stepped back and turned in a circle in the middle of the kitchen, drinking in the mixed aromas of coffee and Windex. She nodded in satisfaction. The restored order in her home restored her spirits, too. She wouldn't let things get messy again.

She checked the time on her phone and gasped. It was half past two. The bistro closed at three. She found their phone number on her browser and placed a take-out order. She'd bring her French dip sandwich home to eat in her spanking clean apartment. She began to hum as she put on her coat and headed out of her apartment again.

Elizabeth was walking quickly home, her take-out bag over her arm. The bag was warm and her sandwich smelled wonderful. Her mouth watered.

Elizabeth passed in front of a quaint gift shop that she loved to poke around in. The owner only stocked items by local artists and there was always something new and interesting to see. I'll come back tomorrow, she thought. I'm too hungry to stop now.

She stepped around a row of animal carriers that stood on the sidewalk in front of the shop. A sign in the window read "Pet Adoption: All Cats Free Today." The shop owner had a soft spot for strays. One of the things Elizabeth loved about the shop was the selection of dog- and cat-themed items. Elizabeth remembered that the owner allowed Home Fur Good to hold adoption clinics in her store when the shelter got too full. If they were giving away cats, that must be the case.

She slowed her pace and looked into the carriers. A sweet feline face peered at her from the last carrier on the end. A pair of big brown eyes locked with hers. She stopped and knelt. The eyes took on a pleading note. She reached her fingers through the grate and touched the cat's ears. The animal began to purr: a deep, rumbling sound. The vibration sent a comforting shiver through Elizabeth's fingertips and down her spine.

She reached for the tag that hung on the carrier and turned it over. *Hi! I'm Mr. Darcy* it read. He had been turned in, it read, by his owner. She had said he was a wonderful cat but that she couldn't keep him any longer. *Will you provide me a loving home?* the tag read.

Elizabeth drew herself back. Mr. Darcy pressed himself against the grate of his crate and ran his head along her fingers. She most certainly would provide Mr. Darcy with a good home. Robert hated cats and was allergic to dogs. He'd forbidden her to get a pet, but she didn't have to accommodate Robert anymore. She picked up the carrier and took it into the shop to complete the paperwork.

She was back on the sidewalk twenty minutes later, laden with the cat carrier, a large sack of cat food, treats, and litter, and her now-cold lunch. Elizabeth and her new roommate headed for home.

Elizabeth struggled through the door, her arms aching from the weight of everything she had carried the few short blocks to her apartment. "This is your new home," she said to Mr. Darcy as she set the carrier on the floor.

He let out a plaintive "Meow."

"It's alright," Elizabeth cooed. "I'll let you out of there in just a minute." She moved quickly to the bathroom and set up the litter box underneath the pedestal sink. "I guess I'm sharing a bathroom again," she muttered as she retraced her steps to the cat carrier.

She sat on the floor, cross-legged, and looked into Mr. Darcy's eyes. He looked back, unblinking, and waited patiently for her next move.

"I hope you don't mind," Elizabeth said, "but Mr. Darcy just doesn't work for me. I don't think it suits you, either. You're way too modern." She pursed her lips and opened the carrier.

He stepped out and, ignoring his new surroundings, leapt into her lap.

She began to stroke his back.

He curled up and his throaty purr reverberated in the quiet apartment.

She leaned over him and ran a series of kisses between his ears. "I'm so glad I found you." He rolled his eyes up to hers. "We're both lucky, aren't we?" she asked him. A smile slowly spread from ear to ear. "That's it! That's what I'll call you: Kismet. From this day forward, you'll be known as Kismet."

Kismet stared into her eyes, then bent his head at an angle and rubbed the top of his head along her chest, purring mightily.

CHAPTER 26

Joe stood in the hallway, eyeing the door. The top half was frosted glass, bearing stenciled black letters outlined in gold. ACKERMAN FUNDING est. 1940. The font of the signage and the heavy wooden door in the dimly lit hallway all bespoke a serious business with a long heritage. Ackerman had been in business longer than Joe's parents had owned their butcher shop. Ackerman—presumably the current Ackerman's father—had started right before WWII and survived and thrived. As a small business owner himself, Joe had to admit that he admired Ira.

Joe checked his watch. The afternoon lull would soon be over. He needed to do what he'd come to do and get back to his own business.

He removed his cap and smoothed his hair into place before he turned the handle and stepped into Ackerman Funding.

The formidable door did not match the unimposing interior. Joe stepped into a small, square room. Smoke from Ira's cigar settled in the space like a low-hanging cloud. A desk positioned in front of a large window opposite the door commanded most of the space. Lateral filing cabinets lined the walls. Two coats hung from hooks on the wall and one straight-backed chair sat in front of the desk. A single door, partially open, afforded a glimpse of a smaller office beyond.

Elizabeth sat at the desk. She looked up at him as he entered. With the sun blazing in the window behind her, Elizabeth's features were in relief and he couldn't read her expression.

Joe approached her desk. "Hi," he said, turning his cap around in his hands.

"Hi, yourself." She motioned him toward the straight-backed chair. "Do you have an appointment with Ira?" She swiveled to her computer screen and clicked a button to display a calendar.

"No," Joe hurried to say. "I'm not here about funding or anything." She turned back to him.

He reached into his jacket pocket and pulled out a paper flyer. "These are our monthly specials." He handed the flyer to Elizabeth. "I wanted to make sure that Mrs. Ackerman knows about them." Even to his own ears, this excuse to drop by to see Elizabeth sounded lame.

Elizabeth took the proffered flyer and glanced at it. "Very nice," she said, laying it on top of a stack of papers on the corner of her desk. "I'll make sure Ira sees this." She smiled at Joe. "You didn't need to bring this by. I know how busy you are at your shop." She scribbled on a Post-it note. "Here's our email address. You can send it to him next time."

Joe took the note and placed it in his jacket pocket. He glanced at her, then looked away. "I also wanted to see you. I didn't know if you'd be back to work yet. I wanted to see how you're doing."

"I came back two days ago. Ira told me to take as much time as I need. He's been real kind that way." She leaned back into her chair. "It's funny. I thought I'd need to take some time off but, after a couple of days, I was just rattling around our apartment feeling miserable. It's actually helped to be back at work."

"Same for me—when Jill died," he replied quietly.

Elizabeth nodded. "I forgot. You know what I'm going through."

"Sort of." He cleared his throat. "I didn't have to deal with all of this craziness with the… package," he said, choosing his words carefully.

Elizabeth winced. "Packages."

"What do you mean?"

"Three different women received body parts."

Joe's heart missed a beat. He knew who those three women would be.

"It's certainly made all of this so much harder."

"Have the police identified the person or persons whose bodies they came from?"

Elizabeth shook her head. "Not that they've told me."

"I didn't hear about the other packages on the news."

"I don't think the press knows. They'll have a field day with it if they find out. I only learned about them when the police came by my apartment with a search warrant."

"What? Why would they search your apartment?"

"They wanted to get some of Robert's DNA. Said they need to find out if he had touched those packages."

Joe trapped a breath with his lips, then released it. "I suppose. Sounds like they're grasping at straws to me."

"I think you're right. They seem to be stymied."

Joe leaned toward her. "This shouldn't be your concern. They'll figure this out. You need to focus on yourself."

Elizabeth quickly turned her head aside and swiped at a tear that escaped and was making its way down her cheek.

"Are you sleeping? I remember how hard it was for me after Jill died. I was bone tired all the time—made it much harder to cope with things."

"I've got some pills from my doctor. I sleep but I don't wake up feeling refreshed."

"What about eating?" He looked pointedly at the sandwich that lay, open and uneaten, on a piece of wax paper on the far corner of her desk.

"I don't have much of an appetite these days."

"I understand how hard it is to do the everyday things that we need to do to take care of ourselves at a time like this." He tilted his head and held her gaze. "But you have to do it, Elizabeth. It doesn't help anyone if you let yourself get run down."

"You're right, I know." Elizabeth attempted a smile.

"Look at this beautiful afternoon out there." Joe pointed to the window. "We don't have many fine afternoons like this in winter. You should go out and take a walk. Enjoy yourself for fifteen minutes."

"I'm far too busy to just get up and go for a walk. I'm still behind from being out of the office."

"I'm sure Ackerman Funding can spare you for a few minutes." His eyes scanned her desk and stopped on the bank deposit bag peeking out from under a sheaf of papers. "I recognize that," he said, pointing at the bag. "Why don't you take the deposit to the bank right now? Is it ready to go?"

"It's ready," Elizabeth said. "But I always drop it on my way to the subway at night. I can't leave right now…"

"I'll bet you can," he replied, rising from the chair and walking to the coats hung on the wall. It was obvious which one was Elizabeth's. He returned and held it out for her in gentlemanly fashion. "Here. Let's go. I'll walk you to the bank and back again."

Elizabeth rolled her chair back and looked at Joe, her forehead furrowed. He continued to hold her coat.

She took a deep breath and then glanced out the window at the people on the sidewalk below. The afternoon sunshine was warm on her face. She turned back to Joe and a smile seeped across her lips. "I guess a few minutes wouldn't hurt."

She stood and slipped her arms into her sleeves. She picked up the bank deposit bag and stepped to the open door of the inner office. "I'm headed to the bank, Ira. I'll be back."

He replied with a muffled grunt.

Joe held the door for her and they stepped into the hallway.

"I have one request," Elizabeth said. "Can we not talk about Robert or Jill or anything sad? I want a break from it all."

"Absolutely." He searched his mind for topics. "Have you heard about anything new on Broadway?" He had no idea what was on Broadway these days—new or old. He remembered that she'd been a theater kid in high school, so he hoped this would be a good topic. Maybe he'd even find out if there was a show she wanted to see. He groaned inwardly. He'd better slow up. Her husband had just died. It would be a long time before it would be appropriate for him to invite her to see a Broadway play.

Elizabeth warmed to the topic and, by the time they stepped out of the building and onto the sidewalk, he knew he'd hit pay dirt. She chatted excitedly the entire way to and from the bank.

Joe made mental notes of the plays she mentioned. Happiness radiated through his extremities. Maybe—just maybe—this would be the start of something good for both of them.

CHAPTER 27

Derek arrived at his desk forty-five minutes before his shift was scheduled to start. The upholstered armrests of his desk chair were in shreds and the drawers on his old metal desk didn't seat properly when closed. He didn't care. Nothing was going to spoil his pride in his new position. He'd been promoted into the Detective Bureau and would now officially be working the Jensen case with Adam.

He took the black china mug with "#1 Dad" in white script that his kids had given him last Father's Day out of the plastic shopping bag that held his personal belongings. He placed it on his desk. *His desk*, he thought with pride. The only other personal items were two small, framed school pictures of his children. He moved them from one side of his desk to the other, then decided to place one on each side. Satisfied, he picked up his mug and headed for the coffeepot that stood on a low table along the back wall.

The pungent odor of the inky liquid told him what he needed to know. That coffee had been standing on the burner all night. He grasped the carafe, took it to the sink, and poured the offending liquid down the drain. He rinsed it, filled it with fresh water, and proceeded to make a fresh pot of coffee. He'd just finished filling his cup when Adam strode through the door.

"Derek," he called, extending his hand. "Congratulations and welcome to the Bureau."

"Thank you, sir."

"None of that, now. It's Adam." He picked a Styrofoam cup from the top of a tall stack and filled it with coffee. "We're thrilled to have you here." He took a swig of his coffee. "I'll be really thrilled if you continue to get in early and make fresh coffee every morning. That task usually falls to me."

"I woke up at four and couldn't get back to sleep. I finally decided to get out of bed and come in."

Adam nodded. "I'm not sleeping too well these days myself. This Jensen case has got me stumped."

"All we've got is a dead man—Robert Jensen—and three packages containing body parts that were supposedly sent by him. Except that they were mailed *after* he died. And they were all mailed to women he was either having an affair with or had recently had an affair with."

"Well put," Adam said. "None of it makes any sense." He drank his coffee. "We got the DNA report on Jensen yesterday. None of his DNA was found on any of the packages."

"That just confirms what we expected from the postmark date."

"I wanted to rule out Jensen's having been the person who packaged the body parts—regardless of who put them in the mail."

"So now we know that Robert wasn't the one who dismembered this person. Or persons."

"Correct. We can discard any theory about Robert trying to scare away or punish his mistresses."

"Unless he paid someone to do all of it for him," Derek suggested.

"True. I don't think that's likely, do you?"

Derek shook his head no.

We're supposed to have the ME report on the body parts this morning," Adam said. "Hopefully, that'll give us something to go on."

Derek nodded.

"In the meantime, contact the postal authorities at the post office branch in Las Vegas where the packages were mailed. Find out if they have surveillance cameras on the counters or if anyone reported an odd person or packages."

"Will do," Derek said, trying to squelch the excitement he felt over his new position.

"You wanted to see me?" Derek asked as he stuck his head inside Adam's tiny interior office that bespoke Adam's seniority and stature as a senior detective on the staff.

Adam remained bent over his computer screen. He cut his eyes to Derek. "Get a load of this." He relaxed into the back of his chair and motioned Derek into the folding chair on the other side of his desk. "The ME's report just came in."

Derek sat and leaned his elbows on the front of Adam's desk, peering at the computer screen.

"All three body parts are from the same person."

Derek nodded. "We suspected that would be the case."

"That's right. And that's good. At least we're only dealing with one dismembered body."

"Did they reach any conclusions about the victim? Can they make an educated guess as to the cause of death?"

"No cause of death. The victim was male and they think he was between six feet and six-three, 180–210 pounds. They think he was right-handed."

Derek blew out a breath. "That doesn't give us much to go on."

"They're not done yet. ME also remarked that the cuts were clean. No ragged edges. Says that they were made by a very sharp knife—by somebody who knew how to use it."

"A surgeon maybe?"

"Or a hunter." Adam shrugged. "They're running the DNA from the body parts through CODIS to find matches anywhere in the country. If there's a forensic or offender match, we'll find it. It just takes time."

"I know that working cases takes time but I didn't expect the waiting to be so frustrating."

"You'll learn patience in this job, that's a given," Adam replied. "What did you find out from the post office?"

"So far, no one reported anything suspicious on that date. The substation manager will ask everyone who worked that day if they remember these packages or anyone unusual."

"Any surveillance cameras?"

"Nope. And there's a self-service kiosk in the lobby, so if they mailed the packages from there, they wouldn't have interacted face-to-face with anyone."

"You can mail priority at a kiosk?"

"Yep."

"And pay with a credit card?"

Derek nodded. "I'm ordering the payment records to find out whose credit card was used."

"Perp would've used a stolen credit card."

"That would be my guess, so we may not get anything useful from that."

Adam blew out a breath. "And no cameras on the kiosk, either?"

"The substation manager asked if I was aware of the budget issues facing the post office." Derek shook his head. "No cameras."

"Well… now we know we have one victim. It's a start. Let's see what CODIS turns up."

CHAPTER 28

Elizabeth threaded her way through the throng on the sidewalk—people striding purposefully toward their midafternoon appointments or errands. A woman pushing a double stroller bearing two wailing toddlers careened toward her. She jumped out of its path and rested her back against the brick edifice of a shop. She breathed in deeply, the chill air singeing the insides of her nostrils.

She'd just left her first grief support group meeting during the lunch hour at Haven Funeral Home. Elizabeth had sat quietly in the circle of others sharing this unwelcome journey with her. She wasn't ready to open up about her feelings yet; she wasn't sure what they really were. Robert had been constantly two-timing her. Should she be heartbroken over a man that repeatedly broke his vows to her?

Elizabeth fixed her gaze on a rooftop across the street. Losing Robert was not the same as the loss suffered by the woman she sat next to in the group. The woman had been happily married to her high school sweetheart for more than forty years and they'd had six children. The woman had been kind to Elizabeth. She was grateful that—unlike Elizabeth—she hadn't been robbed of all those wonderful years with her husband.

Elizabeth squeezed her eyes shut. Even if they'd been married for forty years and had had six children of their own, Elizabeth knew that she and Robert would never have had the happy marriage that this older widow described.

Why had he always needed to have someone on the side? Elizabeth groaned inwardly. Evidently he had had more than one affair going at a time. How had she missed all the signs of his infidelity—the canceled dates and unexpected late nights "at work"? Why had she been blind to the flawed man that Robert really was?

Elizabeth's eyes flew open as she felt a tug on the strap of her purse. She reflexively clutched it to her chest as she swung on the would-be thief.

"Joe," she gasped, relaxing her grip on her purse and sinking back against the wall.

"Sorry, Elizabeth. I didn't mean to scare you."

Elizabeth stared at him, wide-eyed and quizzical.

"I saw you standing there with your eyes closed and I wondered if something was wrong. It's noisy out here and I didn't want to yell your name, so I touched your elbow."

"I thought you were trying to snatch my purse."

"I can see that. I'm sorry… I wasn't, you know."

Elizabeth smiled then. "Of course not. I know that."

Joe hesitated. "As I said, I was worried to see you leaning against my building with your eyes shut."

"Your building?"

Joe pointed to the shop window that bore the name "Porzek Meats".

"Frankly, I didn't know where I was," Elizabeth said sheepishly.

Joe held her with his eyes.

"I just attended my first grief support group—at the funeral home."

"I went to a group a couple times after Jill died. They can stir up a lot of feelings."

"That's for sure."

"Would you like to talk about it?"

Elizabeth paused. She should have returned to Ackerman Funding half an hour ago. They were busy and Ira would be looking for her. She also knew Ira wouldn't mind if she took another half hour. To her surprise, she heard herself agreeing.

Joe took her elbow. "There's a coffee shop in the middle of the next block."

Elizabeth fell in step with him and let him lead her into the shop and to a small round table at the back. A waiter approached their table. Elizabeth ordered a tall black coffee and Joe did the same.

Elizabeth leaned her elbows on the table and cradled her head in her hands. Joe remained silent, allowing Elizabeth to find her voice in her own time.

The waiter placed their coffees on the table. "Would you like—"

"We're fine," Joe said, cutting the man off and waving him away from the table.

"It's just that," came Elizabeth's small voice.

Joe leaned toward her.

"It's just that I don't know who I'm grieving." She raised pain-filled eyes to his. "I feel like a fraud. Robert wasn't a good guy. He was cheating on me right and left. The more I'm away from him, the more I realize how controlling he was. Those aren't good things."

"No," Joe replied.

"Then why do I feel so devastated—so lost and empty—now that he's gone? Am I that screwed up?"

"It's a big change for you. You've been with him for your entire adult life."

She shook her head slowly. "It's more than that. I feel like I'm never going to get over this until I find out who my husband really was."

Joe sank back into his chair. "How do you intend to do that?"

"I'm going to find out about the other women he had affairs with. Both the current women and any in the past that I can uncover."

A chill ran down Joe's spine. "What's the point of knowing?"

"I'll go talk to them. I need to find out about them; who they were, what their relationship was to Robert, what he promised them, and what he told them about me—about our marriage."

"How're you going to do that?"

"I don't know. If I had his phone, it would be easy, but it wasn't with his personal belongings that were returned to me."

Joe nodded mutely.

"I called the police officer who told me Robert was dead. He said someone probably stole his phone off the street. I'll never get it back."

Joe's jaw unclenched.

"I can always try to get his phone records. It's a company cell phone and I don't know if The Brandon Institution will share them with me or not."

"I understand your need to know, Elizabeth. I really do." He took a deep breath. "I snooped around in my sister's computer and learned some things that, in hindsight, I'd rather not have running around in my head."

"I'm sorry," Elizabeth murmured.

"Can I be honest with you?" Joe asked. He knew what he was about to say was true, but he also knew that he didn't want Elizabeth to discover that Jill was one of the women who had had an affair with Robert. If Joe had any chance of winning Elizabeth's affections, he didn't want Jill's betrayal to ruin it. "What good will learning these details do for you?"

Elizabeth stared into her coffee.

"Robert was having affairs—multiple affairs. Do you really need to find out with who and how often? If he were still alive and you were filing for divorce, you might need to know. But not now. The only thing this quest is going to do is to keep you focused on the past. A past you can't do anything about."

A tear ran off the end of her nose and splashed into her coffee. She nodded slowly.

Joe covered her free hand, resting on the table, with his.

"As hard as it is to move on, that's what you've got to do now."

She raised her chin and looked into his eyes.

"You're right. I know you're right. Maybe I've been fixed on the past because the future is unknown and so scary. I'm all alone now. My life revolved around Robert. Now I don't have him to anchor me."

Joe smiled and squeezed her hand. "I think you're going to find a happy future is waiting for you, Elizabeth. You're a lovely and kind person."

Elizabeth sniffed and withdrew her hand from under his. She plucked the paper napkin from under her cup of coffee and dabbed at her eyes.

"Do you believe what I've said?"

"I believe you believe it," Elizabeth said. "That'll have to be enough for now." She sighed heavily. "I think you're right about my trying to locate the other women. I'm not going to stir up the past. I'll let sleeping dogs lie."

Joe hoped she didn't notice the relief that washed over him. He reached into his pocket and took out one of his business cards. He turned it over and printed on the back. He pressed the card into her hand. "Here's my cell number. Call me if you need anything. Anytime."

Elizabeth nodded and placed the card into her purse without looking at it. "Thank you, Joe, but I'm fine."

"Just in case," he said. He held her gaze. "You never know when you'll need a friend."

CHAPTER 29

"We've been over this list a hundred times." Derek shifted his weight back until the chair balanced on two legs.

"So this will make it a hundred and one," Adam replied. "I can't tell you the number of times something has stuck out to me when I've taken another look at the evidence that we've already combed through. Maybe I review it in a different order or maybe my mind's fresh on a different day."

Derek brought the front of his chair back to the floor. "We need to do something. Waiting for the CODIS report is driving me crazy. Too bad the Las Vegas post office didn't give us anything."

"Not surprising, what with all the mail that runs through a postal substation. Without surveillance video, you have to rely on an employee's observation or memory of something or someone out of the ordinary."

"When you put it like that, it's a real long shot."

"What about the credit card records for the kiosk?"

"Nothing, yet. We should have those shortly."

"The thing that sticks out about the Las Vegas post office is that Las Vegas is where Robert traveled to—on business—and where he died."

"Accidentally."

The men looked at each other. "Lots of odd coincidences," Derek said.

"I'm not a fan of coincidences," Adam replied.

"If Robert caused these packages to be sent to his mistresses—or, in the case of Nicole Mills, a former mistress—why would he do it?" Derek asked.

"Some sick joke, maybe?"

"Those packages were designed to shock and terrify those women."

"Why would he want to do that to the women he was still having affairs with?"

"He wouldn't. Nicole—maybe. She didn't take their breakup too well. He might have wanted to punish her or scare her off—but not the others."

"Besides—how would he have gotten the body parts?"

"The most likely way would be to murder someone," Derek said. "Given the state of decomposition of the tissues, the ME estimated that the time of death was the day that Robert died."

"So Robert killed someone, cut up the body, packaged the parts, wiped his prints clean, and gave the boxes to someone to mail before he got hit by a bus?"

Derek snorted.

Adam began to methodically crack his knuckles. "If Robert had sent those packages, he wouldn't have used his own return address."

"Agreed," Derek said. "We have no reason to think he had the knife skills to make those cuts, either. I don't think Robert dismembered the body."

"Why would the real perpetrator put Robert's return address on the packages?" Adam asked.

"Someone hated him and wanted him to take the blame?"

"Maybe… but they must have realized that we'd figure out that Robert didn't send them."

"Not necessarily," Derek replied. "They were mailed shortly after Robert's death. The person who sent these might not have been aware of his death."

"I know it's far-fetched, but I've seen more implausible theories pan out. Remember—anyone who could dismember a body and mail body parts from a post office kiosk isn't exactly thinking straight," Adam said.

"We're right back to motive," Derek said. "Who would want Robert fingered for this?"

"That's a bit easier," Adam said. "Our guy Robert wasn't the proverbial nice guy. Plenty of people may have had it in for him."

"His wife is certainly at the top of the list. She was in Vegas when it all happened. He was cheating on her and she knew it. Maybe a no-fault divorce wasn't enough for her? Maybe she wanted to punish Robert and his women friends, especially after he walked in on her with another woman on his arm."

"That could be. 'Hell hath no fury' and all that. But pinning this on Robert would get him sent to jail, if convicted, or at the very least fired from his job. She'd be jeopardizing alimony she might get from him."

"Maybe she didn't think she'd be awarded any alimony. Seems like she's got a pretty good job. Or maybe she didn't care—she was blinded by the need to destroy him."

Adam pursed his lips while he considered this.

"Thing is, she doesn't seem like the type to dismember someone," Derek said. "I also think that if we're talking dismemberment, the perp would have murdered the victim that they dismembered. That's the simplest way to get a body."

"Maybe she hired someone to do the dirty work for her; kill him and dismember his body. She works for Ackerman Funding. He's well known for hiring mob enforcers to 'encourage' his customers to pay on time when they get delinquent."

Derek nodded his agreement. "That's the word on the street. But he never had anyone killed—and never went after anyone's family."

"Honor among thieves?"

"Something like that," Derek said. He stood and rocked from foot to foot. "Seems too far-fetched."

"Agree. Who else might have hated Robert enough to want to pin this on him?" Adam asked.

"Any of the girlfriends or former girlfriends."

"Start running down that list," Adam said.

"And his co-workers. I wouldn't be surprised if Robert hadn't made some enemies at work."

"Good thought. I'll go by The Brandon Institution to see how everyone's feeling about Robert now that he's gone." Adam rose from his chair. "I know this part of the investigation is frustrating. We're throwing stuff at the wall and nothing seems to stick."

Derek headed for the door.

"Don't worry. This is the way the 'middle' always goes. Something will turn up—it always does. Maybe even something we would never have considered in a thousand years. That's what makes this job the best in the world."

CHAPTER 30

"Two more body parts?" Ira shoved his reading glasses onto his forehead and leaned over his desk to stare at Elizabeth.

She nodded. "They arrived the same day as the foot."

"The packages were sent to different women?"

She nodded again.

"Were they…" he paused, searching for the right words.

"Sleeping with my husband?"

"I wasn't going to say that," he sputtered.

"Yes. Or one was having an affair with Robert and the other had recently had an affair with him." Elizabeth's eyes telegraphed her misery. "He'd broken it off with her."

"I'm sorry, Elizabeth. That husband of yours was an idiot. He hit the jackpot with you, but wasn't smart enough to realize how good he had it."

Elizabeth turned her head to stare out the window. "Thank you, Ira," she said in a small voice.

He cleared his throat. "Were they all feet, like the other package?"

She shrugged. "I don't know. They didn't say."

"Why were you talking to the police in the first place?"

"They were serving a search warrant," she began.

"What?!" Ira jumped out of his chair. "Why didn't you tell me this? Did you call Goldstein?" He came around the desk. "Tell me you had Jay with you while they were there."

She shook her head. "No. There was no time. They just show up and hand you the warrant. You have to comply."

"Did you call him later?"

"Yes." Elizabeth rolled her shoulders back and sat up straighter. "Jay said that I did the right thing."

"What were they looking for?"

"They wanted samples of Robert's DNA."

"His hairbrush would have been enough."

"They got that."

"Anything else?"

"His toothbrush and gym bag."

"That's it?"

"Yes. It was all very quick. And they were nice."

"They may have been nice to you, Elizabeth, but never forget that they are not there to be your friend."

Elizabeth's brow creased.

Ira regarded her closely. He decided that now was not the time to clue her in to the fact that the police would certainly have her on their short list of suspects. "Did they say why they needed his DNA?"

"They want to see if any of it is on those packages."

"Sounds logical." Ira returned to his desk chair and sat. "I know all of this makes..." he searched again for the right words, "your recovery harder. This isn't your typical death."

Elizabeth folded her hands in her lap and nodded.

"Are you still going to that grief support group?" He scooted forward in his chair. "That seemed to help you."

"We've been so busy. I haven't attended since the week before last."

"But it helped you, didn't it? You felt better after you went?"

Elizabeth drew a deep breath and held it, considering her answer. "Yes. I can't tell you exactly why, but I always feel more peaceful when I leave one of those sessions."

Ira tapped the desktop and she looked at him. He held her gaze. "I want you to go to those meetings whenever you want. Every day if they have them that often."

Elizabeth gave him a thin smile. "That won't be necessary—"

Ira cut her off. "Treat it like it's part of your job," he said. "In fact, starting now, it is part of your job." He sat up straight. "You are to go to your grief group or counseling—something that will help you cope with all of this—at least once a day."

Her eyes widened. She had always suspected Ira had a soft spot in his heart and now she knew it was true. "That's awfully kind of you, Ira."

He blushed. Ira quickly opened his desk drawer and began rummaging through the Pendaflex folders packed into the space. "I need to get ready for a call," he mumbled.

Elizabeth rose and started toward the door. She stopped after two steps, turned, and came to stand next to his chair.

He glanced up at her, over his shoulder.

She leaned toward him, put her arm around his shoulder, and brushed a kiss across his forehead. "You're a kind man, Ira Ackerman," she whispered.

Ira sat stock still. He didn't trust himself to speak.

Elizabeth headed out the door.

Joe couldn't suppress the smile that spread across his face when the door opened at twelve ten and Elizabeth entered the room. He'd arrived fifteen minutes early and selected a seat in the circle of chairs in the center of the room. He'd tried to save the seat next to him, in hopes that Elizabeth would show up to the meeting. She'd mentioned that she'd attended this grief support group when they'd talked in the coffee shop. Like most funeral homes, Haven's welcomed anyone into the group, whether the deceased had been in their care or not.

The clock had struck noon and all the seats had been filled with the last rush of mourners through the door. He'd settled into his chair and had tried to force his attention to the woman who facilitated the meeting. She was reading a short passage about the steps of grief when the door opened.

Elizabeth ducked her head as she slid into a chair along the outside of the room, behind the circle. The door was almost shut when an elderly woman pushed it open again.

Joe leapt to his feet and offered his chair to the elderly woman. She patted his arm as she took the proffered seat. Joe moved to the chair next to Elizabeth.

She swiveled her head and nodded to him, smiling.

Warmth surged through him. He was thankful when Elizabeth quickly returned her gaze to her hands, folded in her lap. He didn't want her to see him blush.

The meeting progressed as the strangers, united by the unwanted experience of losing a loved one, shared their experiences. When they'd completed going around the circle, the moderator turned to Elizabeth and Joe.

"Would you like to share with us?" she asked. "The hour is almost up, but we have a few minutes."

Joe held up a hand to indicate that he declined, and Elizabeth murmured, "I'll pass."

"Alright," the woman said. "Let's stand, join hands, and close with a prayer."

Joe and Elizabeth stood with the others. A woman in the portion of the circle in front of them stepped behind her chair and held out her hand to Joe. The man on the other side of her held out his hand to Elizabeth.

Joe took the woman's hand and reached for Elizabeth's. She took it and there was nothing tentative or submissive in Elizabeth's grasp.

Joe's pulse raced and he breathed in slowly through his nose. The warmth of her touch and softness of her flesh assaulted his senses. Desire washed over him. He closed his eyes and tried to concentrate on the closing prayer.

When the group uttered the final word, "Amen," Joe released the hand of the woman from the circle but he kept Elizabeth's hand in his own. She made no attempt to withdraw it from his. Joe's mind raced. How could he prolong this moment?

"Have you had lunch?" he asked.

Elizabeth shook her head no. "I was going to grab a slice of pizza from that little place on the next block and take it to my desk. I need to go back to work."

"Gino's?" Joe asked.

"That's the one."

Joe held the door open as they shuffled into the hallway.

"Have you tried it?" Elizabeth asked.

"No. I'm not usually in this neighborhood."

"It's the best on this side of town. You should try it." She glanced at him as they headed toward the stairs. "Are you hungry?"

"I am," he said truthfully.

"Walk over with me and I'll buy you a slice, too."

Joe almost missed the first step.

"In fact," she said, running her gaze over him, "I'd better make that two slices. I can barely get through one—they're huge—but I'm sure that won't be enough for you."

Joe didn't trust his voice.

"Veggie is my favorite," she said as they walked along the sidewalk. "But they have tons of choices all ready to go. You can buy as many slices as you like."

"I'm a sausage and pepperoni fan," Joe managed to say.

"You strike me as a traditional guy."

Joe cut his eyes to observe her profile as they strode along. He very much hoped that being a 'traditional guy' would be what she wanted right now.

CHAPTER 31

Derek leaned against the frame of Adam's door while the senior detective finished up a call. He replaced the receiver and slapped his desk with his palm.

"Not good news?" Derek asked.

Adam spun to face him. "No. Not good, but not unexpected." He pointed to the chair opposite his desk. Derek took a seat.

"We'll get the official report in the next day or two, but CODIS didn't find any matches for our body parts."

"So he wasn't a convicted felon or a victim whose DNA was in the index." Derek ran his hand over his chin. "We knew that this was a possibility."

Adam nodded. "Still disappointing. I can't help but feel that a murder is part of this."

"I agree. The whole thing is too macabre to be a prank."

"Did any of the three women who received the packages know about each other?"

"No. Brooks was the most realistic about her relationship with Jensen. Said it was all physical. She knew he was married—assumed he had other women on the side. Didn't care."

"You were the first cop on the scene, weren't you?"

"I was."

"Do you believe it didn't bother her that he continued with all of his other extracurricular activities?"

"I do. But I also think she cared about the guy more than she let on. She was shaken by the package…"

"Who wouldn't be?" interjected Adam.

"And I felt that she was grieving over Robert's death. Said she'd attended his memorial service the day before."

"Anything different in her story when you saw her again yesterday?"

"Nope. Everything's consistent. I don't get any sense of malice toward Robert. Or his wife."

"You say she didn't know the other women who received packages?"

"No. Robert never talked about the others." Derek smirked. "In fact, she said that Robert generally only talked about himself."

"He was a self-centered bastard," Adam said. "Did that seem to bother her?"

"She was pretty nonchalant about it. Reminded me that she wasn't in the relationship for conversation. The other two women didn't know about each other."

"It was worth a try," Adam said.

"I did get something interesting from Brooks and Mills," Derek said. "They knew about a woman named Jill. Neither of them knew her last name."

"Porzek." Adam supplied.

"What did they say about her?"

"She was having an affair with Robert. Brooks said that Jill believed he was going to leave his wife and marry her."

Adam nodded and remained silent.

"Jill made contact with Brooks. Tried to convince her to stay away from Robert."

"Brooks was not receptive to this request, I assume."

"No. She says she tried to convince Jill that Robert was not the marrying kind. That Robert had lots of women."

"That's all? Did she say how Jill reacted when she told her that?"

"She said that Jill was upset—crying—and asked Brooks not to mention Jill's visit to Robert. Brooks said that she started to feel sorry for her—that she may have gone too far in shocking Jill into reality."

"What about Mills? Robert had recently broken up with her."

"Mills said that she followed Robert and saw him with this other woman. She happened to see the woman in a coffee shop later—heard the barista call out the name "Jill" and saw her go to the counter to get her coffee."

"Anything else?"

"Mills apparently followed Jill outside the coffee shop, confronted her with some ugly accusations, and threw a cup of coffee in her face."

Adam winced. "What was it about this guy that drove women to act like he was the last man alive?"

"Who knows? He seems like a real piece of work to us. But I've seen plenty of women in fist fights over guys that should be locked up for the rest of their lives," Derek said. "Abusers, con men, derelicts."

"Now we know that Mills has a violent side to her."

"Throwing a cup of coffee into someone's face in a moment of pique is a far cry from dismembering a body and putting body parts in the mail," Derek said.

Adam sighed. "That's true, but Mills stays on the suspect list. How does Mills feel about this encounter now?"

"She acted genuinely ashamed of herself. It took a lot of talking to get her to tell me about it. She was mortified. Says she's never done anything like that before. Hopes she'll run into Jill again someday so she can apologize."

"That's never going to happen," Adam said. "I learned more about Jill. I went over to The Brandon Institution this morning and talked to Robert's coworkers. He wasn't well-liked over there, as it turns out."

"What a surprise."

"Seems he was an arrogant ass everywhere he went. Not a good team player. Always trying to take all the credit for every good idea. You know the type."

"There's a ton of them in Manhattan."

"The only person that had anything good to say about him was his assistant. I got the sense that she had a crush on him."

"Had he been having an affair with her, too?"

"She says 'no'. I got the impression that if he'd have suggested it, the answer would have been 'yes'."

"She didn't know what a bastard he was?"

"She suspected. She took all of his phone calls for him."

"His women called him at the office?"

"Only one that she knows of. When I asked her if she knew of any women—other than Mrs. Jensen—that Robert was involved with, she told me that there was a woman who called Robert repeatedly a few months before he died."

"She know the name?"

"She had one of those old spiral-bound phone message pads that make carbon copies. She pulled it out of her drawer and riffled through it. Found the name: Jill Porzek."

"Did you take the message pad with you?"

Adam pointed to it, sitting on the corner of his desk.

Derek looked at the date of the phone messages and flipped through the pages of his spiral bound notebook. He tapped a page with his finger. "Her suicide was shortly after these calls; after her encounters with Brooks and Mills." Derek shook his head. "Good God."

"We can't talk to Jill Porzek, but I think it's time we found out more about her. Maybe there's someone out there who cared for Jill and didn't take kindly to Robert's treatment of her."

Derek and Adam met in Adam's office late the following afternoon.

"Jill Porzek was a sixth-grade teacher at Most Holy Trinity. West side," Derek said. "Popular with her coworkers. Consensus is that she was quiet and shy. Very good teacher. Girl-next-door type."

"Did you find the co-worker that would have been her best friend at work? People her age always have one," Adam said.

Derek nodded. "Jill team-taught with the woman." He flipped a page on his notebook. "Sarah Tillman. Older than Jill. I'd say late forties. Married with children."

"They probably didn't hang out together, then," Adam said. "Do you think they were close?"

"I'd say they were. Sarah got so choked up a couple of times that we had to stop to let her compose herself."

"Did she know about Robert?"

"She knew that Jill was seeing someone and she finally got it out of Jill that it was a married man. Said that she'd warned Jill that he'd never leave his wife."

"How did she say Jill reacted to that?"

"Sarah said that Jill withdrew from her—didn't tell her anything. Until the breakup." Derek consulted his notes. "Sarah says that Jill called in sick three days running. Very unusual for Jill. Sarah said that she called Jill—repeatedly—and got no answer. She finally got so worried that she went by Jill's apartment."

"So she'd been there before?"

Derek shook his head. "Sarah said that the school nurse was also concerned about Jill and gave Sarah Jill's address. Against the school's privacy policy."

"We won't get anyone in trouble over that," Adam said. "What did Sarah find at Jill's apartment?"

"Sarah said that it took Jill quite a while to come to the door. Sarah kept pounding, getting more concerned all the time. This was about three weeks before Jill's suicide. She was ready to call the police for a wellness check when Jill finally came to the door."

"And?"

"Jill let her in and told Sarah everything."

"Sarah got to say 'I told you so.'"

"Sarah admits to thinking that but says that she was so concerned about Jill's mental state that she insisted Jill call her family."

"Did Jill do that?"

"Refused. Sarah finally convinced Jill to call a counselor. They have mental health benefits on their insurance plan from the school. Sarah told Jill that she wouldn't leave the apartment until Jill made an appointment with a counselor."

"Did she?"

"Yes."

"Did Sarah know if Jill kept her appointment?"

"Jill showed up for work the next day and told Sarah that she felt much better. Just needed to 'get it all out of her system' she'd said. Jill told her she'd canceled the counselor."

"So Jill seemed fine after that?" Adam asked.

"On the surface. She had the feeling that Jill was putting on an act. Said that she kept questioning Jill but Jill insisted she was fine."

"What happened then?"

"Jill committed suicide. Sarah says that she blames herself. She should have told the school nurse or gone to Jill's parents."

"That's a tough position to be in. I don't think I would have gone to anyone else. Did she know if Jill had other friends?"

"Sarah didn't think so. Jill kept to herself."

"Did Sarah know Jill's family?"

"Not personally. She knew that Jill's family owned an established butcher shop in Brooklyn: Brooklyn Family Meats."

Adam sat up straighter and turned to Derek. "Interesting. Who works there now?"

"Sarah didn't know much about it. She'd never been in the shop. Jill told her that her brother opened his own butcher shop on the Upper West Side. Sarah and her family are vegans, so she had no interest in butcher shops. Said that the brother's shop always donated turkeys for the teaching staff at Christmas."

"That's very generous. The butcher business must be good on the Upper West Side."

"I guess so."

"I think it's time you found out a little more about this Porzek family," Adam directed. "A butcher would know how to dismember a body."

Derek pushed his way through the front door of the Upper West Side establishment with "Porzek Meats" emblazoned in bold font in an arching semicircle on the plate glass window at the front of the store. It was late morning and people were stacked three deep at the counter. A chalkboard on the back wall displayed at least a dozen specialty sandwiches that could be ordered for takeout—complete with a homemade cookie and a bag of chips. The aroma of freshly baked chocolate chip cookies hung in the air.

Porzek Meats was doing a brisk lunchtime business.

Derek tucked himself into a corner along the side wall and observed the scene in front of him. An elderly woman efficiently worked the cash register while two women at the other end of the counter jotted down orders on slips of paper and posted them on a pegboard. In back of them was a sandwich assembly line manned by two men, working furiously. A third woman ferried the completed sack lunches to the register and called out the name of the customer.

Derek looked at his watch and began to count the number of bags handed out in the next ten minutes. Porzek Meats was selling an average of 2.4 sandwiches a minute. Not bad for something that wasn't their main business.

He didn't want to impose on Joe during a busy time of day. This would be voluntary questioning and Derek knew he wouldn't get Joe's full attention now.

His stomach growled and he realized he was hungry. He might as well eat while he waited. Derek was about to step to the counter to order himself a sandwich when the woman called the name "Ken" and a man ahead of him stepped to the register. Derek's view of the woman in front of Ken opened up. She looked familiar.

Derek shuffled to his left and leaned forward. The familiar woman turned her head over her shoulder, murmuring "excuse me". The woman was Elizabeth Jensen.

Derek stared at her and swallowed hard. Of all of the sandwich places in Manhattan, why was she here? Porzek Meats wasn't close to her office at Ackerman Funding. He shrunk back and kept his gaze fixed on Elizabeth.

She caught the eye of the woman whose job it was to ferry the white paper bags containing sandwiches to the register. He watched as Elizabeth leaned in and said something to the woman. The woman nodded and stepped quickly to the slats of plastic that separated the shop from the workroom. She parted the louvers slightly and leaned in. Derek couldn't make out what she'd called into the back room.

The woman resumed her activity with increased speed. The white bags were piling up even in the short time that she'd been conveying Elizabeth's message to the person behind the curtain.

Derek watched the opening to the back room. He didn't have long to wait. A tall, sturdy man parted the curtain and came around the counter. He looked to be in his late thirties or early forties. He wore a large white apron, tied in the back. "Porzek Meats" and "Joe" were embroidered in blue on the front. This had to be Joe Porzek.

Elizabeth nodded and approached Joe, taking a piece of paper from her pocket and thrusting it at him.

Derek released the breath. Apparently, she was just ordering meat. Maybe she was a customer. His eyes narrowed. Why would a recent widow be ordering meat from a pricey butcher shop that was nowhere near her apartment? This was more likely the kind of place that her boss—or her boss's wife—would frequent.

Derek made a mental note to find out where Ira Ackerman lived—and if he was married.

He watched as Joe scanned the paper Elizabeth handed him, removed a pencil from behind his ear, and made a note on the paper.

Derek decided he didn't need an overpriced sandwich. He'd brought a perfectly good lunch from home. He'd come back to question Joe in the middle of the afternoon. He'd return to his desk to eat and learn what Google could tell him about Ira Ackerman.

Derek was turning his attention away from Elizabeth and Joe when he stopped suddenly. Elizabeth had leaned into Joe and given him a quick hug.

Derek thought that was an unusual action for a butcher and a customer. The expression on the man's face when she did spoke volumes. He turned beet red and a look of sheer, unexpected joy spread across his face. This Joe Porzek had a serious crush on Elizabeth.

Elizabeth pulled away from Joe. "See you tomorrow," she said before she turned and proceeded out the door.

Derek forced his way through the crowd of customers and stepped onto the sidewalk. All thoughts of his own lunch were now gone. Jill

Porzek had been having an affair with Robert Jensen and now it appeared that Elizabeth Jensen and Joe Porzek were in a relationship. He had to find out more.

CHAPTER 32

"That was a good meeting," Elizabeth said. "The moderator made a good point about giving yourself permission to move on."

She and Joe stepped on the sidewalk outside Haven Funeral Home. The afternoon was clear and balmy. Spring had been damp and chilly so far, but today held the promise of a perfect day.

Joe barely trusted his voice to ask the question. "Are you ready to move on?"

"I think I am." Elizabeth glanced sidelong at Joe. "Are you shocked?" She hoped he didn't think less of her for her confession.

"Of course not," Joe quickly reassured her. "Remember what the group leader said—that everyone approaches the future in their own time and their own way. There aren't any rights or wrongs here."

"But it's been less than three months since he died," Elizabeth replied. "Even I'm shocked at myself."

They ambled along the sidewalk, neither of them in any hurry to get back to work. They passed a small French bistro. Its wrought iron tables, dressed in crisp white linens, spilled out of the French doors in the dining room and onto a street-level terrace separated from the pedestrian traffic by an ornate fence.

Joe took Elizabeth's arm and impulsively steered her to the hostess stand that was positioned on the sidewalk.

"Two for lunch, please," he told the host. Joe smiled at Elizabeth. "We've got to eat," he said. "I've heard about this place for years and have always wanted to try it."

"I guess it would be okay." She turned her head back into the gentle breeze. "I've got spring fever, for sure. This has been a horrible winter for me."

"Me too," Joe added.

Elizabeth glanced at him quickly. "I don't mean to forget about your loss. Jill's suicide is tough to cope with."

"Would you like to be seated inside or outside?" The host approached and interrupted.

"Outside," Joe and Elizabeth said in unison.

The host took them to a table tucked against the building. When they were seated, he handed them each an impressively large menu.

Elizabeth scanned the offerings and gasped.

Joe reached over and touched her hand. "My treat."

"Are you out of your mind? This lunch would cost almost a week's salary for me." She reached around to retrieve her purse from the back of her chair. "I think we should leave."

"No way," Joe said firmly. "The fact that we even got a table here is a miracle." He looked at Elizabeth and held her gaze. "Jill's death isn't gnawing at me every minute of every day anymore. If you're starting to heal, too, then I think we've got something to celebrate."

Elizabeth looked at Joe and a smile spread slowly across her lips. "Alright. What's the harm in enjoying myself?"

"Exactly," Joe said. "Like she told us today—don't feel guilty if you find yourself feeling better and taking pleasure in life again."

Elizabeth nodded. "Don't punish yourself for feeling happy again."

"Are you feeling happy again?" Joe asked.

Elizabeth breathed in slowly through her nose. "I don't know that I'm feeling happy again. But I'm starting to believe that I will feel happy again. Does that make sense?"

Joe nodded. "It does to me. What's holding you back?"

"Those packages with the body parts."

"Are the police still asking you about them?"

"No. But they haven't figured out who sent them or why they put Robert as the return addressee." Elizabeth took a sip of the expensive bottled water that the waiter poured into her glass when they sat down. "They don't even know who the body parts belong to."

"They still can't identify the victim?"

"Not that they've told me," Elizabeth said.

"The police are working on it," Joe said. "It's got nothing to do with you. It could take years to solve this case."

Elizabeth groaned. "That's the thing. I have a feeling that there's something really awful about those body parts... even worse than the fact that there are body parts at all." Her eyes widened. "Every time I start to feel happy, I think of all that and it pulls me back down."

Joe reached across the table and took Elizabeth's hand in both of his, bringing it toward him. She looked into his eyes.

"I hate that you're being drawn into all of this Elizabeth." He held her hand. "You know that Robert was involved in things…" He turned aside, searching for words. "Things that he shouldn't have been. You told me yourself that he'd been having affairs."

"And they weren't the first."

"You see," Joe said. "Robert had a lot going on that you didn't know about. Maybe it's best to put him out of our mind."

"Except I need to understand who he really was." Elizabeth dropped her chin to her chest. "So I won't make the same mistake again," she said in a small voice.

"Weren't you in college when you got married?"

Elizabeth nodded.

"You're older and wiser, as the saying goes. I don't think you're going to make the same mistake all over again."

The waiter stepped to their table. "I can come back, if you need more time," he said, looking between them.

"I've got to get back to work," Elizabeth said.

"We'll both have the luncheon special," Joe told the man. "Would that be alright?" he asked Elizabeth.

"Perfect."

"Give yourself permission to forget Robert—and whatever mess he got himself into—and be happy again," Joe said quietly, hunching over the table.

Elizabeth leaned toward him and looked into his eyes. "I'm trying," she said.

Neither of them noticed the man along the sidewalk snapping their photo with his cell phone.

CHAPTER 33

Aileen Garret, MD, sank back into the swivel chair behind her desk, taking care not to upend it. The chair was wobbly and decades past the time when it should have been hurled into a dumpster. The budget of the New York City Medical Examiner's Office, however, didn't run to new office furniture. Even for its sharpest ME.

She paused, enjoying the look of shock on Adam's face.

"You're certain?" he finally managed to croak.

"I am," she replied.

"The body parts—the foot, the hand, and the ear—are all from the same person."

Aileen nodded.

"And that person is—was—Robert Jensen?"

"Yes. Without question."

Adam cocked his head back and stared at the ceiling. "How in the hell did you find out?"

"I requested that they run a DNA match from the body parts and the sample we obtained from Jensen's gym bag."

"The sample was good enough?"

She nodded. "He had a hairbrush in his bag that contained hair follicles. The lab said it was an almost perfect sample."

"What caused you to request the match?"

Aileen pursed her lips. "I'm not sure, really. When the CODIS search came back negative, I almost closed my file."

"That would have been standard procedure."

"There's something about this case, Adam. I don't know why it stayed top-of-mind with me."

"Maybe it's the macabre aspects? Body parts in the mail. A dead man implicated."

"We see a lot of weird stuff in this job. Worse than this." She tapped her finger on a file on her desk. "But there was something about this case that stuck with me. All these women involved with this jerk of a guy."

"I'll agree with you on that."

"His name on the return address didn't make sense. I kept thinking that he'd be more likely to be the victim than the perpetrator." She leaned her elbows on the desk. "And the thought hit me: What if he was the victim? What if those body parts belonged to him and someone was trying to implicate him?"

Adam nodded. "So you put in the request for the DNA match?"

"What did we have to lose?"

"Why didn't you tell me you were having the test run?"

"It sounded like a crazy long shot, even to myself. I figured I'd say something if the result came back like it did."

Adam held her gaze. "Good work, doc."

Aileen blushed and looked at the desktop. "I just had a hunch. I'm glad it yielded something useful."

"Hunches are important," Adam said. "Instinct is crucial in a detective. Physical evidence doesn't usually present itself neatly to us. We have to use our intellect and our instincts to uncover the evidence we need to solve cases."

She raised an eyebrow.

"You'd have made one hell of a detective, doc."

A smile broke across her face. "Coming from you, that means a lot. Will you keep me posted on the case?"

"I will. This opens up a whole new can of worms." He rose from his chair. "If this Jensen guy died accidentally in Vegas, why was his body dismembered and parts mailed to people here?"

"I'm afraid I can't help you with that," Aileen replied.

"Will you send me the report on the DNA match?"

"I'll email it as soon as I get the final report."

Adam stopped in the doorway and extended his hand. "Thanks again, doc, for going the extra mile."

Derek stepped out of the cold morning into the super-heated interior of the diner around the corner from the ME's office. The warm air from the radiators caused his glasses to fog. He snatched them from his face and scanned the room.

Adam raised his hand in greeting from a booth near the window.

"A bit early for lunch," Derek said as he made his way to his partner. "It's only quarter after ten."

"I didn't get breakfast this morning," Adam said. "I got the call from Aileen Garrett and headed straight to the ME's office."

"Something urgent on the case of the body parts?" Derek pulled a thin paper napkin from the chrome dispenser on the table and wiped his glasses dry.

"That's what she said. Wouldn't tell me over the phone. Said I had to come in."

"And? Did CODIS come up with a match after all? Do we know who the parts belonged to?"

Adam gestured to a waitress and waited for her to approach their table.

"We're going to be here for a while," Adam said. "Could you bring us a pot of coffee? I'd like eggs, sunny side up, bacon, and pancakes."

Derek raised his eyebrows. "So much for watching your cholesterol." He smiled at the waitress. "I'm fine with coffee."

The woman took their menus and retreated.

"You're enjoying this, aren't you?" Derek asked.

Adam nodded. "Wait until you hear. We know who the body parts belonged to, alright."

"Who?"

"Robert Jensen."

"What?" Derek's head jerked back.

"Uh huh."

"How'd she find that out?"

"Said she had a hunch and sent a request for a match to the DNA we got off of his gym bag."

"Good hunch. I didn't see this one coming."

"That's what I said."

"She sure?"

"Positive."

Derek drummed his thumbs on the table. "So Jensen definitely wasn't involved with the sending of those packages."

"Nope."

"We know he died in Vegas."

Adam nodded. "But accidentally? And then dismembered after an accidental death?"

"Sounds far-fetched to me."

"Yep. Jensen was murdered."

"What about Jensen's body when it was brought to New York? The funeral home here would have reported missing body parts."

"Absolutely. They didn't."

"Was he cremated in Vegas before he was shipped home?"

"That's what we're going to find out," Adam replied. "What happened to Robert Jensen in Sin City?"

"And how did his hand, foot, and ear get separated from him without anyone noticing?"

The waitress came to the table with a pot of coffee. She turned over two mugs and poured. Fragrant steam rose from each mug. "Cream and sugar?"

"Black," both men said in unison.

"I'll be right back with your food," she said before she stepped away.

"I checked the ViCap database this morning," Derek said. "No reports of anyone else receiving body parts in the mail."

The waitress placed Adam's breakfast in front of him. He plucked a piece of crisp bacon from his plate and took a bite. "While I was waiting for you, I googled Jensen's obituary. It said that Haven Funeral Home handled his services. It's time I paid them a visit."

"They've been in business for years. They wouldn't be part of anything shady."

"Agreed," Adam said, "but it's the logical place to start. They'll be able to supply the chain of custody for his body or, more likely, his cremains."

"We're onto something heinous. I don't want the perp to get away with this because Jensen's death was ruled an accident."

"Neither do I," Adam said. "Neither do I."

CHAPTER 34

"You seemed awfully preoccupied in the meeting," Joe said as he and Elizabeth exited the Haven Funeral Home. They stood on the sidewalk at the bottom of the steps. The gentle breeze had lost the bite of winter. Joe let his jacket hang open.

Elizabeth brushed a strand of hair out of her eyes and tucked it behind her ear. "I've been struggling with something for a while. The discussion in the group today brought it all home to me."

"There was a lot of discussion about visiting a loved one's grave. A couple of the older widows go every day." He shook his head. "I don't see it, myself."

"Do you ever visit Jill?"

Joe shook his head no. "My mom does. I think she goes every Sunday after church."

Elizabeth caught her lower lip with her teeth.

"Do you visit Robert?" Joe held his breath, waiting for her response. He wanted—more than anything—for her answer to be no.

Elizabeth shook her head. "I didn't bury him. He was cremated and his ashes are in a cardboard box in my hall closet." She lowered her gaze to the sidewalk. "I didn't even buy an urn for him," she said softly.

Joe stood still, searching for something to say.

"After everything I learned about him—after his death—I didn't know what to do." She snuck a glance at him but kept her face lowered. "I've been hurt and heartbroken and furious. All at the same time. I hope," she gulped, "I hope you don't think I'm horrible."

Joe instinctively stepped toward her and stopped himself from taking her into his arms. "Of course I don't, Elizabeth. Anyone would feel the way you do."

"Hearing those other widows in there," she pointed to the funeral home, "made me realize I need to do something with Robert's ashes. I want to do something with them."

"Will you get an urn and keep them?"

She shook her head emphatically no. "That's the thing—that's what I realized in the meeting today. I don't want his ashes near me. I want them out of our apartment."

Joe nodded, encouraging her to continue.

"I won't go into the closet." She spread one hand across her chest. "I always used to hang this jacket up, but not anymore. I toss it over the back of a chair. It's like I'm afraid to open the door."

"That's not good."

"I'm never going to feel about Robert the way those other women feel about their husbands. And I want to quit thinking about him." She tilted her chin up to Joe. "I want that bastard Robert Jensen as far away from me as possible."

"What about his family? Can you give his ashes to them?"

"He was an only child and so were his parents. His parents and grandparents are all dead. I'm his only family."

"Did you ever talk with Robert about what he would want?"

"No. I really have no idea."

"Then I think it comes down to what you want, Elizabeth. He wasn't a good and faithful husband. Don't beat yourself up over the fact that you don't want to honor him in death in a way that he doesn't deserve."

Elizabeth sniffed loudly and dug into her purse for a tissue. "You really think so?"

"Of course I do. And as for his ashes, I think you should get rid of them. Scatter them somewhere. Have you thought of that?"

"I have," she said. "I was thinking of taking him to Central Park."

"Do you want me to come with you?"

"No. I'm not going to make a big deal out of it."

"Do you need a permit? I could google—"

Elizabeth held up a hand to silence him. "I'm not going to find out. I don't want to know if I'll be breaking the law. I'm just going to take the box and spread his ashes at the base of a tree. No prayers or scripture readings."

Joe nodded.

"Ashes aren't hazardous. I won't be putting anything dangerous into the environment."

"I'm sure people do it all the time," Joe said. "I wouldn't worry about it."

They turned and proceeded together toward Ackerman Funding.

"When do you plan to do it?"

Elizabeth checked her watch. "If I can get this week's receipts posted in the next hour, I'll leave early and do it this afternoon." She glanced over at him. "Now that I've decided, I want to get it done. I won't spend another night with him—his ashes—anywhere near me."

The receipts took most of the afternoon to post. The sun was making its descent to the horizon when Elizabeth poked her head into Ira's office.

Ira lifted his eyes from the profit and loss statement that he'd been parsing through, line by line, with a ruler. He raised an eyebrow at her.

"I'd like to leave a little early today, if you don't mind."

Ira's brows furrowed. "Can it wait? If you're done with the receipts, I could use some help with these statements." He jabbed his thumb toward the financial statements in an untidy stack on the corner of his desk.

Elizabeth's shoulders sagged. "It's just that..."

"If you have plans, go." Ira waved his hand dismissively. "I can stay and get through these."

"I want to scatter Robert's ashes," Elizabeth said quietly. "I can't," she turned her head aside, "I can't have them near me anymore. In the apartment. I need to get them away from me."

Ira dropped his ruler and pencil onto his desk and rose from his chair.

"Why didn't you say so? Of course, you can leave to do that. I didn't know you still had them. I guess I never thought about it." He crossed the room to where she was standing and glanced out the window. "It'll be dark in an hour. Where are you taking them?"

"Central Park."

"Where in the park? You don't want to be there after dark."

Elizabeth took her coat off the hook. "I don't have a spot in mind. Just under one of the big trees. I'm not going to make a big deal out of it. I don't want to draw attention to myself."

Ira regarded her closely. "If you've decided to do this, you'd better get going. Promise me you won't go too far off a busy path? And you'll get out of there by dark?"

Elizabeth patted his arm and smiled at her boss. His scaly exterior covered a soft heart. "I promise. Don't worry about me. See you in the morning."

Elizabeth raced up the stairs to her apartment and flung the door open. She grasped the knob to the hall closet door that she hadn't opened since she'd placed Robert's remains on the top shelf. She paused and leaned her forehead against the door. *Now is the time.* She took a deep breath, turned the knob, and yanked the door open.

She stood on tiptoe and stared at the eight-inch square box with the words Haven Funeral Home printed on the side. She extended a shaking hand and used her fingertips to pry it off the shelf. The box was heavier than she remembered and she brought her other hand up to catch it as it slipped out of her hand.

Elizabeth caught it before it tumbled to the floor. She took a ragged breath, shut the closet door firmly, and exited her apartment.

The sidewalk outside of her apartment was packed with people beginning the trek from job to home. She thought about flagging down a cab to take her to Central Park but knew that she'd be snarled in traffic. The quickest way to get there at this time of day would be on foot.

Elizabeth set off at a brisk pace, oblivious to the cries of people she brushed by or stepped in front of in her haste. She had to accomplish her mission before darkness made it foolish.

Elizabeth came to the corner of 59th Street and 5th Avenue, as the street lights flickered on and twilight descended upon the park. She waited impatiently for the light to turn and the walk sign to flash.

She positioned herself at the curb and ran across the street as soon as the light changed. The park—at least this portion at the southeast corner—was still full of people. She walked purposefully across the Grand Army Plaza and into the park, passing pedestrians as they hurried to make their exit.

She assessed the trees that lined the path. They were as familiar to her as old friends. She loved this park. Any of them would do nicely.

She kept going, deeper and deeper into the park. Her mind was whirling. She didn't want to be reminded of Robert every time she looked at one of these trees.

Elizabeth glanced around her. A mother pushed a stroller as a preschooler kicked stones on the path next to her. A jogger was making his way toward her. There were still a lot of people in the park. She would be fine. She'd go just a bit farther where smaller paths led away from the main trail. She'd find some out-of-the-way place to leave Robert. A place she wouldn't see when she came to the park.

Elizabeth strode on into the darkening park. A sign indicated that the Dairy was to the left. She was further into the park than she'd intended to be. She strained her eyes to see if anyone else was on the path. It appeared she was alone. She knew she should turn back but pressed on.

In another minute, she came to a small trail leading into a copse of trees. This would be ideal. She stood at the edge of the trail, silhouetted by a street light. No one was on the main path as far as she could see. She heard a taxi honk on 5th but the sound was muffled and distant. She hesitated, then turned onto the smaller trail. It was lit only by moonlight and she slowed her pace. A few minutes later, she found her spot. A large tree rose from level ground not more than five feet from the trail. She'd be able to make her way the short distance to the trunk without twisting an ankle.

Elizabeth crept cautiously toward the tree. A branch snapped under her foot and the sound echoed in the night. A chill ran down her spine. She needed to release Robert's ashes and get out of there.

She took the package from under her arm and placed it on the ground at the base of the tall tree. The trunk was shrouded in darkness. She fumbled with the lid of the box and cursed under her breath. The funeral home had taped it firmly shut with layer upon layer of packing tape.

The branches of the trees rustled in the wind. She glanced toward the path. Shadows rose and fell. A movement along the periphery caught her attention. Was someone out there? She froze, crouching over her package, and peered at the spot. It must have been a shadow created by the sweeping branches. She was alone.

Elizabeth turned her attention back to the package. She had to get it open. She felt along the side of the package for the ridge that would indicate the beginning of the tape. She found the edge and peeled a quarter inch section up with her fingernail. She tore off a one inch strip before it ripped.

She cursed again and slammed the box against the tree roots in frustration. She'd never get it open this way. Why hadn't she thought about this?

Elizabeth unzipped her purse and began churning the contents like a cement mixer. After what seemed like an eternity, her hand brushed against her keys. She'd be able to saw through the tape with her keys.

Elizabeth began stabbing at the tape. The sooner she got this done, the sooner she could get out of there.

"What you got there, girl?" came a husky voice from the edge of the path not five feet from where she knelt in front of the package.

Elizabeth dropped the package and her keys slipped from her grasp. A startled cry escaped her lips, to be borne off by the wind.

She leapt to her feet. A tall, stocky man was bearing down on her. His face was hidden in shadow and he swayed on his feet.

She was boxed in by trees. The only way out was past him. She hurtled herself forward and knocked him backward.

"What the…" he sputtered and staggered. He reached out his right hand and grabbed the sleeve of her coat.

She swung her purse, still slung over her shoulder, like a weapon and hit him on the side of the head. He grunted in pain and took a step back. She tore her sleeve out of his grasp and took off at a run.

She heard his footfalls behind her. She didn't dare look back to see how close he was. She put her head down and ran.

Her upper body got ahead of her feet and she stumbled, one knee crashing into the asphalt trail. She yelped in pain. The footsteps behind her kept coming.

She got to her feet and propelled herself forward. Traffic sounds grew louder and she saw the bright lights of the buildings along 5th Avenue, across from the park. Her lungs felt like they were going to burst. She increased her speed and exited the park onto 5th Avenue.

CHAPTER 35

Elizabeth emerged from the park and bent double, gasping for air. Saliva pooled in her mouth and she thought she would be sick. She closed her mouth and forced herself to breath evenly through her nose. The wave of nausea passed.

Elizabeth straightened and felt her purse on her side. Thank God she'd taken it with her. Robert's ashes and her keys remained in the park. She wasn't going back there tonight to find them.

She turned and began to walk slowly toward 59th Street. It would be a long walk home and the wind was cold now that it was dark. Her super would let her into her apartment and get her a new key tomorrow.

Elizabeth stopped suddenly. The package with Robert's ashes had her address on it. The man from the park could have both her apartment key and her address. She shuddered. She wouldn't be spending the night in her apartment. She'd have to get the locks changed tomorrow.

Elizabeth looked up and down 5th Avenue. She wasn't far from Ira's apartment. She'd call him. Surely the Ackermans would let her spend the night in one of their spare bedrooms.

She thrust her hand into her purse and found her phone. She punched Ira's cell phone number and listened to it ring. *Answer it, Ira.* On the twentieth ring, she gave up.

Elizabeth accessed the contacts on her phone and tapped on Ira's home phone. It rang once and went directly to voice mail. Elizabeth pressed her palm to her head. Now what? Should she take shelter in a coffee shop and keep trying to reach Ira? She didn't hold out much hope for the success of that plan.

She resumed her slow pace in the direction of her apartment. She'd just have to go to a hotel. Tears pricked the backs of her eyes. She'd hoped that she'd feel better at the end of this day but, instead, her spirits were at low tide. She wished she had a friend to talk to.

She was returning her phone to her purse when her hand brushed the business card that Joe had given her weeks ago when they'd had coffee. She pulled it out of her purse. His cell phone was printed in large numbers across the back of the card. Next to them, he'd scribbled: Call me anytime.

Elizabeth tapped the card against the back of her hand. Should she call Joe? What could he do about any of this? She didn't know the answers to these questions, but she knew she wanted to talk to him. He might not be able to help her, but hearing his voice would make her feel better. She reflected on this thought. Yes—hearing his voice always comforted her.

She punched his number into her phone and brought it to her ear. Warmth spread through her like butter on toast when he answered her call on the third ring.

"Elizabeth?"

She meant to say hello but burst into tears instead.

"What's wrong?"

Elizabeth gulped, trying to force out the words.

"Are you alright?"

"Yes," she managed to reply. "I… I almost got mugged in Central Park."

"What? Why were you in the park after dark?"

Elizabeth struggled to find her voice.

Joe said, "Where are you?"

"5th and 59th."

"By the Plaza?"

"Yes."

"Have you eaten dinner?"

"No."

"There's a trattoria a block and a half west along 59th. Do you know it?"

"I can find it."

"Let's meet there. Get a table and order yourself anything you want. I'm just locking up the shop. I'll be there soon."

"Thank you, Joe," Elizabeth said. She was right; hearing his voice made everything better.

Elizabeth spotted Joe, outlined in the open door of the cozy restaurant he had recommended. When she'd mentioned his name, the elderly host had smiled broadly and shown her to what he called his most romantic table.

She'd settled into her chair at a table placed in front of a working fireplace. She'd blinked, allowing her eyes to adjust to the dim interior. Every seat in the place could be described as romantic. Starched linen tablecloths created a sea of white. Heavy antique silver sparkled in the firelight and a single red rose surrounded by a halo of baby's breath sat in a crystal bud vase on every table.

Elizabeth rose from her seat and waved at Joe.

He nodded to her and made his way to their table. "What did you get yourself," he asked as he slid into the chair opposite her.

"Nothing," she replied. "I'm not hungry."

"Nonsense. They'll be insulted if we don't order." He gestured to the waiter. "Can you bring us an antipasto plate while we decide?"

"Of course. Wine with that?"

Joe raised an eyebrow at Elizabeth.

"Not for me. You go ahead."

"Cup of coffee for me," he said. "Elizabeth?"

"Yes. Coffee, please."

The waiter moved away.

Joe leaned over the table and had to stop himself from taking her hand into his own. "What happened?"

"I was in the park. It was dusk when I went in and there were tons of people around."

"You went to scatter Robert's ashes?"

"Yes." She took a deep breath. "After our talk earlier today, I decided that I needed to get his ashes away from me or I'd never have any peace."

"So what happened? There are lots of trees right inside any of the entry points."

"I know that," Elizabeth said. "But I didn't want him near one of the trees I usually see; didn't want to have to think of him every time I walked by that tree." She looked into his eyes. "Can you understand that?"

Joe nodded. "So what did you do then?"

"I kept walking and walking. Into the park. It was like I was possessed. I was walking fast and telling myself I'd know the spot when I saw it."

The waiter placed the antipasto platter and a crusty loaf of warm bread on the table. He poured a drizzle of deep green olive oil onto a plate and reached under his arm for an enormous pepper mill. He gave the mill a couple of twists, depositing a thin dusting of fresh cracked pepper over the oil on the plate.

"Go on," Joe said.

"I finally decided to take one of the smaller trails into a wooded area. I'd never seen it before so I thought it would be the perfect place for Robert."

Joe raised his eyebrows, encouraging her to continue.

"I was busy trying to slit the tape on the box with my keys when this guy steps out of nowhere and says, 'What you got there, girl?' "

"That must have been terrifying. What happened then?"

"He came toward me—he was staggering—I think he was drunk. All I know is that he scared the life out of me." Elizabeth leaned her elbows on the table and put her head in her hands. "I dropped the box of ashes and my keys and bolted. He grabbed my sleeve and I clocked him with my purse."

"Good going," Joe said.

"He stumbled back and I tore my sleeve from his hands. I took off and ran out of the park like my life depended on it."

"It might have, you know."

Elizabeth nodded. "I didn't turn around to see, but I think he followed me until I ran out onto 5th Avenue." She took a deep breath. "And now Robert's ashes and my keys are in the park."

"Did the box have your address on it?"

"Yes. I'll have my locks changed tomorrow, but tonight I'm going to stay at a hotel."

Joe nodded slowly. "That's a smart plan. Except you're welcome to come stay with me. I've got a very comfortable sofa."

"Of course not," Elizabeth said. "I wouldn't dream of inconveniencing you. I shouldn't have drug you out here tonight."

"It's no inconvenience," Joe said. "That sofa is fine. I fall asleep on it all the time. You can take my room and you can lock the door, if that will make you more comfortable."

"That's ridiculous. I'm not afraid of you." Elizabeth tore off a small piece of the warm bread. "In fact, I called you because you always make me feel better." She brought the bread to her lips, then set it back on her plate. "That whole incident in the park really shook me. And now I've lost Robert's ashes and my keys."

"They may be right where you left them. We'll go there at first light to look for them. Do you think you can find the place again? Central Park is awfully large."

"I think I can," Elizabeth said. "My memory of it is very vivid."

"It's settled, then. You'll spend the night at my place—where I will act as a perfect gentleman—and we'll go in search of your things tomorrow morning."

Elizabeth held his gaze. "You really are a kind man."

Joe flushed and pointed to the plate of meats and cheeses. "You'd better dig in. I've been known to eat one of these all by myself."

Elizabeth shook her head. "I don't think I could keep anything down. You go ahead."

"Sorry," Joe replied, signaling to the waiter. "Check, please. And can I have a box for this?" he said when the waiter approached their table.

"No, Joe," Elizabeth said in a rush. "You're hungry. Go ahead and eat. I'll be fine."

"Let's get you out of here," he said. "I can eat at home. Right now, you're my top priority."

She opened her mouth to protest further, then shut it. When had she ever been anyone's top priority? She had never been Robert's. She flashed Joe a shy smile as a warm feeling of calm washed over her.

CHAPTER 36

Joe swung his apartment door open and stepped to one side. "Mi casa es su casa."

Elizabeth stepped into the living room. The ceilings were higher than her apartment and the windows were larger. Wide baseboards and crown molding outlined the room. She surveyed the scene in front of her. A black leather sofa and a huge television, hung on the far wall, dominated the space. An end table held a sturdy brass lamp and a remote control. The only other piece of furniture was an unadorned rectangular coffee table. The space was neat and tidy, with no stacks of old newspapers, unopened mail, or dirty dishes anywhere.

Elizabeth turned to Joe. "Very nice."

Joe released the breath he had been holding. "You think?"

"For sure."

"It's pretty simple." He closed the door behind him. "Jill used to tease me about hanging something on the walls. Said I needed some color in here."

"That would be nice. Why haven't you?"

"I guess I don't know where to go or what would look good." Joe shrugged. "I see those makeover shows on TV and I don't understand what they're talking about. Jill was going to help me, but..." He turned his head aside.

"It can be pretty overwhelming. I agree with you there." She spun around. "I'd be happy to help you. We can go shopping together."

"That'd be nice."

"I'm not trying to take Jill's place," Elizabeth began.

"I know that. And I'd like to fix this place up but gridlock has set in, I'm afraid." He motioned for her to sit on the sofa. "Can I get you something to drink?"

"Just water for me, thanks," she replied.

Joe brought them each a bottle of water from his refrigerator and sat at the other end of the sofa.

Elizabeth took a long drink from the bottle and placed it on a coaster on the coffee table. She withdrew her cell phone from her purse and began typing into the screen. "Do you know what style you like?"

Joe's eyes grew big and he shook his head. "Style?"

"You know—modern, country, industrial, traditional?"

"Uh… no idea."

Elizabeth smiled at him and held out her phone to him. "Scroll through this website and show me what appeals to you. I'll be able to tell from what you choose."

Joe did as he was told and soon found something that appealed to him. "This," he said, leaning toward her and holding out the phone.

Elizabeth slid over on the sofa until their bodies almost touched. She leaned against him and looked at the screen of the phone.

"Ah…. Industrial." She smiled at him. "That makes sense for a guy like you—one who works with his hands."

"So we'll buy stuff that's industrial?" He sounded doubtful.

"Yes—in a decor sense. It's very popular right now. Very on trend."

"Wow. I never thought I'd be on trend."

"You see? You're hip and you didn't even know it."

Joe swallowed the lump in his throat. "Do you like this industrial stuff?"

"I do. It's interesting and practical. About the only style I really don't like is modern. I'm not a fan of chrome and glass and ultra clean lines."

Joe nodded. "I think I know what you're talking about. Too anti-septic looking for my taste."

"Exactly. So now that we know what you like, let's make a date to go shopping."

Joe's neck began to turn red. Had Elizabeth used the word *date*? "Would a Sunday work? The shop is closed on Sundays."

"Perfect. This'll be fun." She rested her shoulder against his. "Weekends have been hard since Robert's been gone. Too much time on my hands."

Joe sat quietly, luxuriating in the feel of her body next to his. "It can get lonely, living alone."

"I've got a cat. He's good company—acts almost like a dog. Greets me at the door when I come home and everything. Follows me everywhere."

"Jill had a cat like that; as sweet and friendly as they come."

Elizabeth cleared her throat. "What happened to him?"

"I don't know. When I went to Jill's place… when I found her… the cat wasn't there. I tried to find him but he was gone."

"Do you think he got out?"

"No. She must have given him away—she would have taken care of him." He sighed heavily. "That's what I tell myself."

"I'm sorry to hear that." She turned to face him. "You're worried about him, aren't you?"

Joe shrugged.

"I'm sure he's been adopted by someone really nice. Living a life of luxury. I'll bet he's had tuna for supper and is sleeping on someone's sofa right now."

Joe laughed. "I'd like to think so."

Elizabeth sat up straight and pulled away from him. "It'll be light by seven. Can we go to the park to look for my keys and the ashes then? Or do you have to be at the shop before that?"

"I normally start between four thirty and five, but I'll let my crew know I won't be there until after eight."

Elizabeth opened her mouth to protest.

"It's okay," Joe said. "We won't be that busy tomorrow. It'll be fine."

Elizabeth squeezed his hand. "Thank you, Joe. You've always been so kind to me." She ran her eyes along his profile. "Even when we were in school together. You were always the nice guy."

Joe felt himself flush.

"I was too stupid to go for the nice guy when I was young. I met Robert and he was full of polish and flash. One of the 'cool kids'. Part of the 'in' crowd. I felt like I was part of it, too, when I was with him."

She brought one hand to the side of her head. "I look back and can't believe I was so stupid. The only person that Robert ever really loved was Robert."

"Don't be so hard on yourself."

"I'm being truthful. It's only been since he's been gone that I've realized how messed up our relationship had gotten." She took a deep breath and faced Joe. "I was always trying to win his approval and affection. Even when he was on his way to the airport for the trip to Las Vegas—when I knew he was having an affair and was planning to leave me." She brushed the back of her hand across her eyes. "I practically threw myself at him. I'm not going to make the same mistake a second time."

"I'm sure you won't." He reconsidered his pledge to conduct himself as a perfect gentleman. He wanted to lean over and kiss Elizabeth. He paused, then straightened. "If we're going to be in the park at seven, we'd better get some sleep."

"You're right." She yawned. "I'm exhausted."

Joe stood and pulled her to her feet. "Let me show you to your room. You're in luck—I changed the sheets this morning."

"No, Joe. That's not necessary. I'll sleep here." She pointed to the sofa. "Just let me borrow a throw or a blanket."

"Nope. Not happening. Come with me." He took her hand and led her down a narrow hallway, past the kitchen, to a room on the left. He flipped on the overhead light. "I think you'll be comfortable, and the bathroom is across the hall."

Elizabeth smiled at him. "This'll be lovely. You really don't have to do this."

"Ah… but I do. It's in the Nice Guy handbook. I won't jeopardize my membership in the Nice Guy Society by breaking protocol."

She laughed. "We wouldn't want that, for sure." She faced him and held his gaze. "Thank you, Joe. You are a very nice guy."

His breath caught in his throat. "I'll… I'll see you in the morning. I wake up early so I'll have coffee ready in the kitchen."

Elizabeth's smile sent a wave of warmth to his toes. "Sweet dreams, Joe."

"I think it's just ahead, on the right," Elizabeth said. "Over the crest of this little ridge."

Joe walked along next to her. This was the sixth time she'd thought she'd found the spot where she'd exited the path to scatter Robert's ashes. He didn't care how long it took. He was enjoying walking in the park with her in the early dawn. "No worries. We'll find it."

Elizabeth hurried her pace. "Yep. This is it." She turned off the paved path and scurried along the dirt trail.

Joe followed her.

"It's here," came her excited cry from ahead.

He came to stand behind her.

"It's all here! The package with the ashes. And my keys."

"Good," he said. "Whoever that creep was probably couldn't find his way back here to take them."

She hugged both items to her chest. "I'm so relieved."

Joe nodded.

Elizabeth looked into his eyes. "Would you mind if we stayed another few minutes? To scatter these ashes."

"Of course we can," he said. He held out his hand to take the package. "I've got a pocket knife. Why don't I open it for you?"

"Yes. Much better than my keys."

Joe used his knife to deftly slit the tape. He opened the lid and carefully handed the box back to Elizabeth.

"Thank you," she said, a catch in her voice.

"I'll go back to the path to wait for you."

Elizabeth turned her head quickly aside and nodded. "That would be so nice, Joe. I know you have to get to the shop. I won't be long."

"Take whatever time you need, Elizabeth." Joe turned and stepped away.

Elizabeth watched his tall, solid form recede from view. She took a deep breath and knelt at the base of the large tree. Robert's ashes were contained in a sealed plastic bag. She carefully opened one corner of the bag and tipped it so that his remains emptied onto the ground at the base of the tree. His wedding ring made a pinging sound as it hit a shard of rock. She stared at it, glinting in a ray of morning sunshine.

She hadn't really known the man she had been married to. Perhaps she never would have understood him. The only certainty was that he wouldn't be part of her future. She stood and brushed a light dusting of ash from the front of her jacket. She inhaled slowly as she watched the breeze catch the earthly remains of her late husband and carry them away from her.

CHAPTER 37

Adam turned as the funeral director's door opened. The tall man closed the door behind him and crossed to where Adam was standing. "I'm sorry to keep you waiting." He gestured to a chair in front of his desk. "Please, sit down."

Adam perched on the edge of the chair as the man took his customary seat behind his desk. "The receptionist gave me your card and said you wanted to see me. How can I help you, Detective? I hope you're not here on official business?" He gave a nervous laugh.

"I'm here in connection with an ongoing investigation," Adam said.

The funeral director remained quiet.

"I understand that Haven Funeral Home provided services recently for a Robert Jensen."

The man nodded.

"Can I ask you a few questions about that?" Adam took the recorder from the inside breast pocket of his coat. "I'd like to record our conversation, if that's alright with you?"

"Of course. Our work for the Jensen family was all very routine."

"Have you seen any of the news reports about a body part that was mailed to a woman in the area? The package bore Robert Jensen's name and business office address for the return address."

"I read about it, yes. Nasty business. I thought that you determined that Jensen couldn't have been involved. He was already dead when the package was mailed."

"That's correct."

The man turned his palms up. "I'm not sure I understand why you're here."

Adam stared intently at the man. "We've recently uncovered information that we don't want revealed to the press or next of kin—yet. Can I rely on your discretion to keep what I'm about to tell you strictly between us?"

The man loosened his tie. "Of course you can. I'm used to keeping confidences."

Adam nodded. "Good. There were actually three packages with body parts."

"Good heavens. I didn't hear about the others."

"The press hasn't picked up on the other two." Adam locked eyes with the funeral director. "We've learned that the body parts in those packages belonged to Robert Jensen."

The man recoiled into the back of his chair. "What? That can't be."

"Why is that?"

"We cremated his body."

"So you took possession of his body? He wasn't cremated in Las Vegas?"

"No. We did it."

"He wasn't missing a foot, his right hand, or an ear?"

"Of course not," he cried indignantly. "Don't you think we would have notified the authorities if the body had been... desecrated?"

"Did you see his body?"

"I most certainly did. I'm the only person with the authority to sign cremation papers for the funeral home."

"And the body was intact?"

"Yes," he declared. "I told you that."

"Could someone else's parts have been sown onto Jensen's body?"

"No. Definitely not. We performed basic embalming. I'm absolutely certain that we had his entire body." He straightened his spine. "You must be mistaken."

"We're not wrong," Adam said. "DNA established that those body parts were from Robert Jensen."

The man stared at Adam in disbelief.

"How did you identify the body? How did it come to you from Las Vegas?"

"It was shipped to us from a funeral home there. We haven't had any dealings with the establishment before, but all of the paperwork was in order."

"What did that include?"

"We had a death certificate and the funeral home in Las Vegas is approved by the TSA as a Known Shipper."

"Can I see the death certificate?"

"Of course." The man turned to a filing cabinet behind him. "I keep a year's worth of records in my office." He flipped through the files in the drawer marked "G-M" and pulled out Robert's file. He placed it on his desk and opened it. "Here," he said, tapping the death certificate. "In addition to the date, time, place, and cause of death, it gives us the deceased's name, age, gender, place of birth, nationality, occupation, marital status, and residence."

Adam examined the certificate. "All of this is accurate for Robert Jensen," he said.

"And the physical description of the deceased matches the body that was sent with this certificate."

"You had no reason to think that the body wasn't that of Robert Jensen?"

"None whatsoever."

"Did you have any of his personal effects?"

"Just his wedding ring."

"What did you do with that?"

"We asked his wife if she wanted to keep it or if she would like us to place it with his cremains." He opened his laptop and typed into the keyboard. He brought up a screen and turned it so that Adam could see it. He pointed to a statement halfway down the page. "Mrs. Jensen had us add it to the cremains."

"That's it? You identified him based upon the certificate from this other funeral home and the wedding ring that you showed his wife?"

"We checked the physical description on the certificate with the body we received with it. It all matched."

"Did they enclose a photo?"

"No. Just height, weight, hair color, gender, and age."

"And the body you received matched all of that?"

"It did. But that wasn't all," he said.

Derek raised an eyebrow.

"Mrs. Jensen sent over a suit for us to clothe him in. She asked if she could see him before we cremated him."

"Is that customary?"

"Yes. Unless the deceased has suffered a trauma that would make the body… unpalatable for the family to view."

"He was hit by a bus. Was his body fit to view?"

"Yes. It was fine. Now that you mention his accidental death, I was surprised at the time that the body didn't bear any evidence of trauma."

"What do you mean?"

"No broken bones; no bruising."

Adam rested his elbows on the edge of the desk. "How can you be sure?"

"We notice these types of things when we get a body ready for viewing." The man leaned toward Adam. "If Jensen's body had endured any trauma—much less had body parts removed—I would have noticed it."

Adam inhaled slowly. "Mrs. Jensen observed the body?"

"She did."

"That couldn't have been Robert's body. What did she do when she saw him?"

The man shrugged. "That's just it—I don't know. I didn't go into the viewing room with her."

"Did she have anyone else with her?"

He shook his head. "She asked to see him by herself."

Adam raised an eyebrow. "Is that unusual?"

"People usually want someone with them but it's not unheard of. Elizabeth had her boss with her when she came in, if I remember correctly."

"Her boss didn't go in with her?"

"No. He waited for her in the area at the other end of the hall. I stayed in the hallway outside the viewing room."

"Could you hear anything from inside the room?"

He shook his head.

"How long was she in there?"

"I don't know—five minutes—maybe ten. Nothing unusual about it."

"And she didn't rush right out, saying that the body wasn't her husband's?"

The man continued shaking his head. "She did not."

"If it wasn't her husband's body, don't you think it's odd that she didn't say anything?"

"Extremely odd. I don't know what to think." He shrugged. "Grief can do strange things to people."

Adam ignored his observation. "How did she seem when she came out? Was she upset?"

"Nothing struck me as out of the ordinary."

"Was she crying?"

"She was emotional. I don't remember if she was crying or not."

"What did she do then?"

"I took her to my office," he gestured around the room, "here. I asked her about his wedding ring and she signed the paperwork authorizing cremation."

"I'll need copies of that authorization."

"Of course. It's all right here," he said, picking up the folder. He extracted two pieces of paper from the file and handed them to the detective.

Adam read the statement bearing Elizabeth's signature, then read it again. He looked up at the funeral director.

"Elizabeth Jensen certifies that the body she's just observed is her husband, Robert Jensen."

The man nodded.

"Based upon the papers from the other funeral home, the body you received was a similar age, height, weight, and hair color as Robert. Is it possible that she could have thought it was her husband?"

The man pursed his lips, considering. "I don't think so. Not in this case. As I said, the body was intact. We didn't have to do much to it." He sighed heavily. "She must have known that it wasn't Robert."

Adam got to his feet. "I'd like to take copies with me."

The man took the papers to a copier in the corner of the office.

"Thank you for your time," Adam said as the man handed him the copies. "I'd like to remind you that you cannot discuss our conversation or anything regarding your services for Jensen."

"I understand," the man said, looking Adam in the eye. "Believe me, I understand. Something isn't right here. I'm not going to do anything to jeopardize your investigation."

Adam nodded his thanks and stepped out the door. When he got to the street, he pulled out his phone and placed a call to Derek.

"You're not going to believe this," he said. "Wait until you hear what the funeral director had to say."

CHAPTER 38

Elizabeth was settling into her sofa with take-out almond chicken when the doorbell rang. She set the paper container and chopsticks on her coffee table and muted the television. She was making her way to the door when the buzzer sounded again.

"Coming," she called, realizing that the person on the other side of her door probably couldn't hear her. She pressed her eye to the peep hole and let out a cry of frustration. She recognized the detectives standing in the hallway.

"Yes," she called.

"It's Detectives Stanley and Harnet," the older man said. "We'd like to talk to you."

Elizabeth turned her back to the door and sank against it. What had Ira told her? Don't talk to the police without your lawyer? She checked her watch. It was almost eight. Surely her lawyer wouldn't want to be bothered at this time of night.

She sighed heavily and spun around, unlocking the deadbolt and turning the handle. She swung the door open and motioned them inside. Ira and his attorney would be furious with her, but she didn't see how talking to the police could hurt her. She hadn't done anything wrong.

"Come in," she said. "I was just about to eat." She led the way to the living room.

Elizabeth sat on the sofa. Adam drew up the other chair in the room and Derek took his position against the wall.

"Please," Adam said. "Continue. We can talk while you have dinner."

Elizabeth shook her head and secured the paper latch on the take-out box. "I'll eat later." She looked from one detective to the other. "What did you want to talk to me about?"

"We have something to tell you, actually." Adam switched on the recorder and placed it on the table. "It may be very upsetting."

Elizabeth took a deep breath and folded her arms around herself. "Go on."

"We've just received positive identification of the man whose hand, foot, and ear were mailed to the women."

Elizabeth furrowed her brow. "Okay…"

"We have a positive ID, based upon DNA analysis." He locked eyes with her.

Elizabeth didn't look away.

"They were all from the same person." He paused. "That person was your late husband: Robert Jensen."

Elizabeth's head snapped back. "What… what are you saying?"

"Those severed body parts were from your husband's body."

Elizabeth was shaking her head. "They can't be. I… I…" she stammered. "She swung her head wildly over to Derek. "I saw my husband. In the casket. Right before he was cremated."

"That's what we understand. We want to ask you about that," Adam said.

Elizabeth spun back to him. "Robert was there, in front of me. And he had all of his body parts."

"We've talked with the funeral director," Adam said. "He confirmed that you viewed a body that they presumed to be that of your late husband. You viewed it alone and then signed papers positively identifying him and authorizing cremation."

Elizabeth nodded, mutely.

"But it wasn't really Robert in that casket, was it, Mrs. Jensen?"

Elizabeth shrank back into the sofa cushions. "I… I'm not sure. I thought it was Robert."

"You signed papers that it was," Adam said. "Are you now saying you weren't sure?"

"I thought it was. He was the same size and had dark hair."

"Surely you would have recognized your own husband?"

"The truth is… I didn't really look at the man in the casket."

"Even though you signed a paper that said you positively identified him? A paper that allowed that person—whoever he was—to be cremated?" Adam cocked his head to one side. "And now you're saying you didn't look at him?"

"I didn't walk up to him. I got in there and it all seemed too much." Her words tumbled out of her. "The hair looked funny—not at all like Robert wore his hair—and his hands looked odd. I've heard people talk about how funeral homes sometimes make people look very unlike themselves. And how upsetting it is."

She clasped and unclasped her hands in her lap and looked from one to the other. "I was still in shock over his death. I didn't know if his body would look awful as a result of the accident. I figured maybe they had to make him look that way to cover up his injuries. I didn't want my last memory of him to be of his corpse looking grotesque."

"So you're now saying that even though you didn't get a good look at the body in the coffin, you signed the paperwork anyway?"

Elizabeth nodded vigorously. "That's exactly what I did. After I'd been in that room with him for a while, I'd had enough. I needed to get out of there."

"So you signed whatever they put in front of you so you could leave?"

Elizabeth lowered her gaze to her hands. "I guess so."

"You're a bookkeeper, aren't you, Mrs. Jensen."

She nodded but did not look up.

"Bookkeeping is a very detailed, precise occupation, isn't it?"

She nodded again.

"You're normally a very careful person, aren't you?"

"I am," she said in a small voice.

"I see," Adam said. "But this time—on the occasion of identifying your husband's body before cremation—you decided to sign papers certifying something you didn't know to be true?"

Elizabeth stared at her hands and remained silent.

"I've got a few more questions," Adam said. "You told us—before—that you suspected that your husband had been having an affair. We now know that he had been having multiple affairs."

Elizabeth hunched further over in her seat.

"Was your marriage in trouble, Mrs. Jensen? Were you and your husband contemplating divorce?"

"No…" she began, then stopped herself. "I wasn't."

"You were prepared to live with his infidelities?"

She shook her head no. "We'd been together since we met in college. And we'd been under a lot of stress the last few years, trying to get pregnant. We'd been undergoing infertility treatments. The strain of all that was taking a toll on our marriage."

"You weren't looking for a way out?"

Again, she shook her head no. "I wanted to stay with him; to work things out."

"What did he want?"

Elizabeth shrugged.

Adam fixed her with his stare. "Was your husband contemplating divorce?"

"Maybe." Elizabeth turned her face away. "He may have been."

"Why do you say that?"

"I overheard him talking to someone very late one night. He thought I was asleep. He was promising to 'tell me' when he got home from his trip."

"He was talking to a woman?"

"I think so."

"What did you believe he was going to tell you when he got home from Las Vegas?"

Her voice was no louder than a whisper. "That he'd found someone else. That he wanted a divorce."

Adam pressed on. "How did that make you feel?"

"I was devastated, of course."

"Were you mad at him? At her?"

"I was mad and hurt and sad all at the same time."

"What did you decide to do about it?"

Elizabeth drew a deep breath. "I figured that this woman was a passing fancy. I thought that if I could get pregnant, Robert would never leave me." She looked up and her eyes were drowning in pain.

"You thought a baby would fix everything."

"When you put it like that, it sounds like a ridiculous cliché. But that's exactly what I thought."

"Did you get pregnant?"

A tear rolled down her cheek. "No."

"You weren't mad at your husband?"

"I was furious with him, but I wanted to save our marriage, not destroy it."

Adam nodded. "One last thing."

"Yes?"

"Who inherited Robert's estate?"

"I did. I'm his wife." She furrowed her brows. "Why?"

"Was his estate significant?"

She took a deep breath and responded slowly. "He had a small amount in his retirement account and he didn't have any other property. He did, however, have two million dollars of life insurance."

Adam raised an eyebrow.

"I'm the beneficiary of those policies," Elizabeth said. "Robert's death left me a wealthy woman."

"What'd you think?" Adam turned to Derek as they took the stairs to the ground floor.

"She's got motive, in spades."

"That's a large part of it."

"But if everyone acted on a motive to kill someone, we'd have a lot more homicides than we do."

"You're right about that."

They paused on the landing and faced each other.

"I don't peg her as a hands-on killer."

"Neither do I. She would have hired someone to do the dirty work."

"You think she's the kind that knows a hit man?"

"Ackerman has the right kinds of contacts. Maybe she knows one of his guys well enough to ask."

"Possibly, but those types generally don't hang around the front office. I don't see it."

"She didn't hold back, either. She admitted she knew Robert had found someone else and was going to ask her for a divorce."

"My gut tells me that she's telling the truth."

"I'm not so sure." Adam resumed his descent. "But if not Elizabeth, then who?"

"How about someone sweet on the recent widow?" Derek stepped onto the sidewalk and held the door for his partner. "Like Joe Porzek? They've been keeping company—I've got that cozy photo of them at the restaurant."

"And Porzek's sister apparently committed suicide over that creep Jensen."

"I think it's time to pay a call on both Ira and Joe."

"We need to find out if Joe knew about Jill's affair."

"Agreed. Plus, he's a butcher. He'd know how to do the postmortem."

"This investigation is going somewhere."

"I told you. It's always like this. We're in the weeds and then, all of a sudden, we find the trail."

CHAPTER 39

"Mr. Goldstein," Adam said, shaking the attorney's hand. "I didn't expect to see you here." The detective took a seat in front of Ira's desk.

"I follow my attorney's advice," Ira said. "I never talk to the police without him being present. Never."

Jay smirked at the detective and sat in the chair next to him. "Mr. Ackerman is a busy man, Detective. How can we help you?"

Adam felt the hair on the back of his neck prickle. Jay Goldstein was a pompous ass. He leaned forward and placed a small recorder on the desk. "We record all of our interviews. You don't mind, do you?" He looked at Jay.

"I'll want a transcript," Jay said.

"I can arrange that," Adam said. He turned to Ira. "How do you know Elizabeth Jensen?"

Jay nodded imperceptibly at Ira. "She's my employee here at Ackerman Funding."

"What does she do for you?"

"She's a bookkeeper and office manager."

"How long has she been with you?"

"Just shy of twenty years."

"Do you have other employees?"

Ira shook his head.

"You'll have to answer audibly so the recorder will pick up your answer," Adam said.

"No. It's just the two of us."

"You run all of this with just the two of you?"

"I've got an outside accounting firm that does my taxes."

"Anyone else?"

"He's already told you 'no'," Jay said.

Adam ignored him. "Do you have a sales force? Someone that handles customer relations?"

"My business has grown by word of mouth. I don't need salesmen. I handle all of my customer issues myself."

"You make loans to businesses in the garment industry, correct?"

"That's right. I'm a factor."

"Your loans are at high interest rates, aren't they?"

"We loan to customers that can't otherwise qualify for bank loans and our interest rates reflect the higher risk of these loans."

"In other words, your borrowers don't have good enough credit for a bank loan?"

"That's right."

"These borrowers are more likely to default on their loans—be late on payments?"

"Right again," Ira said.

"Banks have departments that deal with borrowers in default. I believe they call them workout departments." He shifted his weight forward in his seat. "You make riskier loans than a bank but you don't have a workout department of your own? Why is that?"

"I talk to any borrower that's in arrears, myself. I want to understand the steps they're taking to bring themselves current."

"I see," Adam said. "You're very hands on."

"Exactly," Ira said. "I've got a lot of experience in this business and I can usually look at their books and point out problems that they might not have recognized. I can suggest solutions."

"So—due to your greater expertise, you can function almost as a business advisor?"

Ira leaned back in his chair and smiled smugly. "Exactly. My role is to help my customers when they have difficulties."

"And you do this all yourself? You never enlist the help of anyone else to 'talk to' your customers? Someone who might make it clear that they'll suffer unpleasant consequences if they don't pay up?"

Jay held up his palm to Ira and leaned toward Adam. "What are you implying?"

"Just that the factoring business is well known for its reliance on assistance from mob enforcers."

Ira raised his voice. "I don't employ mobsters. I'm a legitimate businessman and run a clean business."

Jay began to stand. "I think this interview is over."

"I've got a few more things to cover," Adam said, remaining seated. "They don't have anything to do with Ackerman Funding."

Jay sat back down.

"Did you accompany Elizabeth to the funeral home to identify Robert's body?"

"I did," Ira said.

"Why?"

"For Pete's sake—I thought it would be upsetting for her."

"You're concerned for her welfare?"

"I am."

"How do you feel about Elizabeth?"

"In addition to being one hell of a bookkeeper, she's a very fine person. I've come to care about her like she was one of my own daughters."

"So you know Elizabeth well?"

"I think I do. Her parents died years ago and she's an only child. Now that Robert is dead, I may know her better than anyone else."

"She's careful and precise, correct?"

"Yes. Essential qualities in a bookkeeper."

"She isn't prone to making careless decisions or taking rash actions?"

"I don't think so."

"When Elizabeth went to identify Robert's body, did you go in the room with her?"

Ira shook his head. "She said she wanted to be alone."

"Did that seem odd to you?"

"Not really. Elizabeth is a very private person."

"Did you try to convince her to allow you to go in with her?"

Ira turned his head aside. "Not really."

"Why is that? Didn't you think she'd need your support?"

"Frankly, I'm not too keen on seeing bodies in coffins." He swallowed hard. "I'd never go up to the casket. I was relieved that she wanted to do it on her own."

Adam nodded. "I see. Were you there when she came out of the viewing room?"

"I was down the hall. She went to the funeral director's office to sign the cremation papers before she came back to me."

"You were waiting for her?"

"Yes."

"How long was she gone?"

"I don't know. Fifteen or twenty minutes."

"How did she seem when you saw her?"

Ira furrowed his brows. "She was fine. Emotional and anxious to get out of there."

"Did her reaction strike you as unusual?"

"No. Why would it?"

Adam leaned toward Ira and held his gaze. "She identified the body in that casket before cremation."

"Yeah... so?"

"That body wasn't Robert Jensen's."

Ira jerked back in his chair. "What?"

"She identified it as Robert Jensen, but it wasn't."

"How in the hell do you know that?"

Adam breathed in slowly through his nose. "This isn't public knowledge and we'd like you to keep the information I'm about to give you confidential." He looked from Ira to Jay. "It's important to our investigation."

Jay inclined his head toward Ira. "You have our assurance."

"Two additional body parts were mailed to women here in New York. Las Vegas postmarks and bearing Robert's return address. Both of the recipients had had affairs with him." He cleared his throat. "The body parts that were mailed to all three women belonged to Robert Jensen."

Jay pushed his chair forward. "You must be mistaken. Elizabeth identified him at the funeral home."

"There's no mistake. We've got a positive ID of the parts through DNA."

"Maybe the body in the casket was missing those parts..."

Adam shook his head. "We've covered that with the funeral director. The body that they cremated—that Elizabeth identified as Robert Jensen—wasn't missing any parts."

Adam and Ira stared at each other.

"Any idea why Elizabeth would have identified the wrong body as her husband?"

Ira shook his head no.

"Audibly, please."

"No."

"Any reason that you know of why she would want her husband dead?"

Ira recoiled again. "Of course not. Besides, his death was accidental."

Adam shrugged. "This wouldn't be the first time that an accidental death was reclassified as a murder. Did you know about Robert's reputation as a womanizer?"

Ira's lips flattened into a straight line. "I did."

"And do you know if Elizabeth knew about her husband's infidelities?"

Ira remained quiet. He picked up a pen and tapped the end on his desk. "She knew. Or at least, she suspected."

"She came to you about it?"

"She was late to work a lot and making mistakes. Both very unlike her. I called her into my office and asked her what was wrong."

"She told you she suspected he was having an affair?"

"She did."

"What else?"

"That he was planning to leave her."

"What was her demeanor then?"

"She was heartbroken. Distraught."

"Was she angry?"

"No—not like she should have been. Ungrateful bastard. She quit college to put him through school. Truthfully—she was the brains of the operation between those two."

"What did you say to her?"

"I offered to talk to him—man to man. Remind him of his marital obligations."

"Was she okay with that?"

"Sure."

"And did you? Talk to Robert?"

"I did."

"How did that go?"

"How do you think? Arrogant prick told me to mind my own business."

"Did you relay this to Elizabeth?"

"No. Never got the chance."

"Why's that?"

"It was right before he went to Vegas." Ira tossed the pen onto the desk. "The whole issue quickly became moot."

"Do you think Elizabeth is glad that Robert is dead?"

"I don't know what she thinks. She's learned about the other affairs. She's having a hard time putting it all together. Elizabeth's at a grief support group at the funeral home right now."

"How often does she go to those?"

"Couple times a week. At lunch time. Depends on how busy we are."

"Are they helping?"

"They seem to. She's less stressed when she gets back."

"Getting back to the night of his death. Did Elizabeth work that day?"

"No. She was on vacation."

"She took an impromptu trip to Las Vegas to surprise Robert, isn't that right?" Adam asked.

Ira hesitated and exchanged a glance with Jay. "No. She went to Buffalo to care for her sick aunt."

"Would it surprise you to know that Elizabeth was actually in Vegas when Robert died?"

"That's not what she told me."

"She flew to Las Vegas to patch things up with him. But it didn't turn out that way. She was waiting for him in his hotel room when he returned—with another woman."

Ira winced. "How do you know that?"

"She told us. Says the woman left and she and Robert argued. He stormed out of the room and she chased after him but lost sight of him. She got scared—being out on the Strip late at night and alone— so she went back to the room, got her stuff, and flew right back home on a red-eye."

Ira swiveled in his chair to look out the window.

"She lied to you about going after Robert. Why do you think that is?"

"Probably embarrassed." He heaved a heavy sigh. "She knew what I thought of the prick—knew I wouldn't approve."

"Was she worried you wouldn't have given her time off?"

"Maybe," Ira replied. "I would've tried to talk her out of it, sure, but I wouldn't have denied her request for vacation."

"How did she sound when she called you to ask for vacation?"

"I believed she was upset about her aunt."

"She wasn't angry or agitated?"

"Not that I could tell."

"When was the next time you spoke to her?"

"She called me right after she got the call from the police that Robert had been killed."

"How did she take the news of his death?"

"She was shocked and barely coherent."

"What makes you say that?"

"She was crying so hard I could barely understand her."

"What did you do then? Did you go see her after she called?"

"No. I offered but she insisted she wanted to be alone. She asked me to make arrangements to have Robert's body brought home."

"Did you do that?"

"Yes. I took down the information she gave me and made some calls."

Adam rested both hands on the edge of Ira's desk. "Do you think Elizabeth could have gone to Vegas to kill her husband?"

Ira shot out of his chair and leaned toward Adam, both palms flat on the desktop. "Are you out of your mind? Of course not. Elizabeth didn't have anything to do with her husband's death."

Elizabeth strolled along the sidewalk as she headed back to work after the grief support group meeting. The mountain of paperwork she'd left required her immediate attention, but she didn't quicken her pace. She glanced in the familiar shop windows as she passed, enjoying the displays that she'd hurried past—unheeded—the past few months.

The camaraderie of the group was a new experience for her. She'd been isolated in her world of work and her devotion to Robert's needs for most of her adult life. What really lifted her spirits was spending time with Joe. His concern for her feelings—his interest in her world— was a balm to her battered soul. He'd been at the meeting today—as he usually was lately—and she'd hated to say goodbye to him. She sauntered along, savoring the happiness she was feeling.

Elizabeth rounded the corner of the block and approached the entrance to the building that housed Ackerman Funding. She was fifty feet from the entrance when the doors opened and a man stepped onto the pavement. A frisson of recognition ran through her. He glanced back at the building, then turned and melted into the pedestrians headed the opposite direction.

She stopped suddenly and her mouth went dry. She recognized the man. He was that detective that had come to her house to serve the search warrant and, later, to tell her that the body parts had been

Robert's. She shivered involuntarily. What in the world was he doing in her building?

She quickened her pace. All lighthearted feelings evaporated. Elizabeth pushed through the doors and waited impatiently as the elevator took her to her floor.

Ira looked up as she came in and hung her coat on its hook.

"Lizzie," he called. "Come in here."

Jay Goldstein was sitting in one of the chairs in front of the desk. Ira pointed to the other chair. The phone began to ring and she rose to answer it.

"Leave it," he said. "Let the machine get it."

Elizabeth turned wide eyes on her boss. He hated voice mail and never allowed the phones of Ackerman Funding to go unanswered during business hours.

She swallowed hard, looking from her boss to his attorney. "What's up?"

"I had a visit just now—from a detective working on the case of the body parts."

Elizabeth's mouth felt like cotton. She nodded.

"I understand…" he hesitated, looking at his hands, clasped on the desk in front of him. "I understand that those parts belonged to Robert." He looked up at Elizabeth.

"Yes," she said in a voice that was barely a whisper.

"I'm sorry, Lizzie. That must have been a horrible shock for you."

"It was."

"Why didn't you tell me?"

"I don't know. It's all so gruesome. I'm… I'm tired of thinking about it."

Jay gave Ira a sidelong glance and raised one eyebrow.

"You must know what the police were asking me about."

Elizabeth signed heavily. "They wanted to talk to you about when we went to the funeral home to identify Robert's body?"

"Exactly," Ira said. "I had to confirm that you went into that room alone. I couldn't lie to the police."

Elizabeth looked at Jay and then Ira. "No. Of course not. I wouldn't want you to." She began twisting her hands in her lap.

"Why did you sign the papers confirming that it was Robert's body in that casket? You must have known that it wasn't."

"I… I didn't go up to the casket to see him. I was in the back of the room." She brought one hand to her forehead. "His hair was dark like Robert's but it was all puffy and wrong. His arms were at a weird angle. I knew he'd been hit by a bus so I figured he must have been badly mangled and they'd done their best to make him presentable."

She leaned forward in her chair and turned to Jay. "I don't know what came over me, but all of a sudden, I just had to get out of there. It never occurred to me that it could have been someone else. The hair color and size were right." She looked at Ira. "I bolted. The funeral director was waiting for me in the hall."

"You signed the papers to authorize cremation. You identified the body as Robert's," Jay reiterated.

Elizabeth stifled a sob. "I know. I trusted the funeral home. The only thing I wanted to do was get out of there." She looked at Ira. "You believe me, don't you?"

Ira stared into her eyes, then nodded slowly. "I do."

Jay cleared his throat. "The problem, Elizabeth, is that the police may not believe you."

Elizabeth's brows furrowed. "What do you mean? Why wouldn't they?"

"Because those body parts are Robert's, that's why."

"What does that have to do with it?"

"The NYPD seems to be questioning the accidental nature of Robert's death."

Elizabeth gasped. "What do you mean? His death certificate lists the cause as accidental."

"I understand. And it'd be a lot of work to get that death cert changed," Jay said. "But the detective that just visited us seems to be very interested in Robert's death and your relationship with your late husband. Particularly your erroneous identification of his body."

Elizabeth groaned and bent over, wrapping her arms around herself. She rocked back and forth in the chair. "Does this mean they suspect me of… what? Pushing him in front of a bus?"

"We don't know," Jay said. "The point is, Elizabeth, don't talk to the police again without me."

Elizabeth's jaw dropped open.

"Jay's right," Ira said. "Don't worry about the expense—I'll take care of that."

"Don't… don't they have to read you your rights if they think you're guilty?" Elizabeth stammered. "They haven't done that with me."

"Your Miranda rights? Yes, they do. My guess is that will happen the next time they talk to you," Jay said.

"But I didn't do anything!" Tears rolled down the sides of Elizabeth's cheeks.

"I know that, Lizzie," Ira said. "Jay and I had to warn you. If the police try to question you again, call Jay right away."

"Okay," Elizabeth said. She turned wide eyes to Ira. "Maybe they won't want to talk to me again."

Ira shrugged. "Maybe. You know what to do if they do."

CHAPTER 40

"Should we bring Joe in to question him?" Derek asked. "Is it time to read him his rights?"

"Not yet," Adam said. "What would we charge him with? We've got an accidental death and dismemberment of a body—both out of our jurisdiction."

"And a violation of post office regulations."

Adam raised an eyebrow.

"Mailing of hazardous substances." Derek shrugged. "There's nothing that really fits this situation."

"The feds have jurisdiction with anything involving the post office. I don't want to get them involved," Adam said.

"Agree," Derek said.

"Why don't you go talk to Joe? See what you can turn up."

Derek checked his watch. "One fifteen. I should find him at his shop." He pushed his chair back from his desk. "The fact that he's an ideal candidate to have made those cuts is an odd coincidence. Let's see what the good butcher has to say for himself. I'll report back as soon as I'm done with him."

Derek grabbed his jacket from the back of the chair and headed outside. The sun was warm and the air held the hint of spring. He decided to walk the twenty-two blocks to Porzek Meats.

Derek entered the shop and waited until he was the last person in line at the counter. The woman working the counter handed a parcel and a credit card receipt to the person in front of him, then turned to Derek.

"I'd like to see Joe Porzek," he said, showing her his badge.

Her eyebrows shot up. "He's not here right now."

"Do you know when he'll be back?"

"Any minute now." She glanced over her shoulder at the clock on the wall. "Actually, he shoulda been back by now." She fidgeted with the tie on her apron. "He's gone to his grief recovery group."

"I'll wait," Derek said. "How often does he go to this group?"

The woman hesitated. "I'm not too sure… a couple times a week? You'd better ask Joe," she said, and turned away from Derek to busy herself straightening a stack of paper bags.

The door to the shop opened and Joe stepped inside. His jacket was unzipped, his cheeks were flushed, and he was whistling an upbeat tune.

"Joe," the woman said, the relief in her voice unmistakable. "This man is here to see you."

Derek stepped forward and produced his badge.

Joe looked from the badge to Derek's face, unable to hide his surprise. "What can I help you with?"

"Is there somewhere private that we can talk?"

"Ahhh… sure." He gestured to the area behind the curtain. "I've got a small office behind the workroom."

Derek nodded and followed Joe. The small office was cramped with a desk, a filing cabinet, and a desk chair. Joe pulled a folding chair from behind the door and set it up for Derek.

Derek flattened himself along the wall and managed to close the door before he squeezed himself into the chair. He turned back to Joe and, in spite of himself, smiled at him. "This is tight."

"It's not an office for two guys our size, that's for sure." Joe felt a bead of perspiration form on his upper lip. "What can I help you with, Detective?"

Derek took out his recorder and pushed the button. "I'm here to ask you questions about your sister, Jill."

Joe's face fell. "What do you want to know?"

"I understand that she took her own life several months ago. I'm sorry for your loss."

"Thank you," Joe mumbled.

"Do you know why she took her own life?"

"She didn't leave a suicide note. We really don't know."

"Had she suffered from depression?"

"Not that I know of."

"Had anything happened that might have upset her?"

Joe turned his head aside.

Derek remained silent.

"I'm… I'm not sure."

"What aren't you sure about?"

"I did some snooping in her computer—after she died."

"Why were you snooping?"

"I wanted to understand why she killed herself. She'd always been my sweet, fun-loving kid sister." His voice broke. "I just couldn't believe she'd done this to herself."

"That's understandable. Did you find anything?"

Joe nodded. "She'd been having an affair with a married man. Thought the bastard was actually going to leave his wife and marry her." He laughed mirthlessly. "She fell for that old line of bullshit. Even had a wedding dress."

"What happened?"

"He broke it off with her and she… she killed herself."

"Did she say who the married man was?"

"No, but I was able to find out."

"How'd you do that?"

Joe recounted how he'd photographed the man and used the Internet to find his name.

"Who was it?"

"Robert Jensen," Joe said. He cocked his head to one side. "That's why you're here, isn't it? Because Jensen's name was on the return address labels on those body parts that got mailed to the other women he was involved with."

"Did Jill know about the other women?"

"Three of them, yes. I've wondered if they're the ones that got the packages."

"We think so." Derek lowered his voice. "Did you contact any of them?"

"What? No!" Joe straightened in his chair. "Why would I do that?"

"I'm just asking." Derek paused.

Joe ran his hand over his eyes and leaned back into his chair.

"So you didn't know about this affair before Jill died?"

"No. I knew she had a boyfriend, but she didn't say much about him."

"You had no idea she was so serious about him."

"None whatsoever."

"What did you do when you found out it was Robert Jensen?"

Joe sighed heavily. "It got complicated. I know Robert's wife—I've known her for years. We went to school together, then lost touch until she started coming into the shop. I knew her by her maiden name—Newberry."

"How did you find out that she was married to him?"

"I saw her in a photo with him when I was trying to find the name of the guy Jill had killed herself over. The caption said she was Elizabeth Jensen. I recognized her as the woman I knew as Elizabeth Newberry."

"So now you've learned that the man your sister was involved with is the husband of your old friend and customer."

Joe nodded. The misery in his eyes was palpable.

"What did you do then?"

Joe drew in a deep breath and held it. His shoulders dropped as he slowly released it. "I went to see the guy."

"You met with Robert Jensen?"

Joe nodded.

"Where did this meeting take place?"

"I went to his office. At the Brandon Institution."

Derek nodded. "Go on."

"He didn't want to talk to me there so we went to a park across the street."

"What did you talk about?"

"He thought that Jill had sent me to convince him to take her back. He threatened to take out a restraining order against her." Joe's color rose. "He didn't even know she had killed herself."

"Did you tell him?"

"I did. The bastard had the nerve to tell me that he thought she was 'unbalanced'." Joe clenched and unclenched his fists.

"What else did you say?"

"I told him that he needed to quit with the girlfriends and be a good and faithful husband."

"What did he say to that?"

"Well… he didn't really say anything. Just nodded his agreement."

Derek furrowed his brow and stared at Joe.

"I had him shoved up against a lamp post," Joe said, turning aside. "I got physical with him."

"You fought with him?"

"No. He didn't resist. Wasn't really in a position to. I… I acted pretty Neanderthal with him."

"Any injuries? Did he file charges?"

"No. I just roughed him up and threatened I'd do worse if he didn't keep it in his pants from then on."

Derek's eyes narrowed. "What did you threaten to do to him if he didn't?"

"Nothing. I was all bluster. I think I scared him, though. I hoped that I got through to him."

"Did you ever 'talk' to Robert Jensen again?"

"No."

"Anything else you'd like to tell me?"

Joe stared at his hands.

Derek waited.

"I tried to talk to Robert again," he finally said.

"What do you mean, tried?"

"I decided he needed another reminder."

"Why?"

"Elizabeth's boss told me that she was upset because Robert was going to leave her when he got back from a business trip."

"You wanted to prevent that?"

"I didn't want that piece of shit Jensen ruining the life of another woman I... I care about." He looked at Derek. "I had a high school crush on Elizabeth and I've always liked her."

"And?"

"I wanted to get him alone—in a place where I would have his full attention. I found out about his trip to Las Vegas. I was overdue for some time off so I decided to follow him and talk to him there."

"You went to Las Vegas to talk to Robert?" Derek's thoughts raced. Joe nodded.

"You were there when Robert was?"

"Yes. I had his itinerary."

"How did you get that?"

"Elizabeth came into the shop with an order for her boss. She did that all the time. The order was to be delivered and she'd scribbled the address on the back of his itinerary and left it with me."

"So what did you do?"

"I booked a room at the same hotel and camped out in the lobby, looking for him. I figured I'd scare the crap out of him by being there."

"Did you... scare the crap out of him?"

"I didn't get the chance. I fell asleep in the lobby and woke up in time to see him leaving. I followed him and caught up to him just before he got... he got hit by the bus."

"Did you witness the accident?"

"No. I followed him but lost him in the crowd. I heard the brakes of the bus and people were screaming and pushing each other."

"What did you do then?"

"I stood on my tiptoes and saw the body on the pavement."

"Was it Robert?"

"It was."

"Dead?"

"Yes."

"Then what?"

"I wasn't in the mood for a vacation anymore. I went back to the hotel and tried to sleep. I packed up and flew home the next morning."

Derek nodded. "One more thing you should know: the three body parts—they were all from the same body."

"I'd heard that. From Elizabeth."

He regarded Joe carefully. "And that body was Robert Jensen."

Joe's recoiled. "What are you talking about? He was cremated here. I helped Elizabeth scatter his ashes."

"Those ashes you scattered weren't Robert's. We don't know whose they were, but we're going to find out. And we're going to find out who dismembered Robert's body after he died."

Joe brought his palm to his forehead. "Who could have done that?"

"Someone with motive, opportunity, and the requisite skill," Derek said, his gaze boring into Joe.

"Does Elizabeth know this?"

"She does."

"What did she say about it?"

"Not much. She's got a bigger problem."

Joe raised an eyebrow.

"She positively identified Robert's body at the funeral home. Signed the cremation authorization."

"What the—" Joe stopped himself.

"Seems you both have some explaining to do."

Joe stood suddenly. "I can't talk to you any longer. I need to get back out front."

Derek shut off the recorder. "We'll be in touch," he said as he managed to extract himself from the folding chair and pulled the door open.

"That's gotta be it," Adam slapped his desk.

"I just don't think so," Derek said. "My instincts tell me 'no'."

"Forget your instincts. Let's look at the facts. Elizabeth knows her husband is cheating on her and plans to leave her. She also knows that she'll cash in on a two-million-dollar policy when he dies."

"We don't know if she knew about the insurance policy before he died," Derek interjected.

"We can find out. Anyway, we also know that she and Joe are cozy. You said yourself that the guy admitted he had a crush on her in high school. You think he's still carrying the torch for her?"

Derek shrugged.

"They were both in Vegas when he died."

"And Joe had the ability to make those cuts." Derek stroked the stubble on his chin. "A hand, a foot, and an ear are each small. Easy to handle; easy to conceal. I wonder if they were chosen for their size or if the body part sent to each recipient is supposed to send a message?"

"I've thought of that," Adam replied. "A hand for the sculptor, a foot for the trainer, and an ear for the opera singer."

"They each got the part of him that corresponded to their common interest."

"Poetic justice?"

"Maybe the perp was trying to tell them something."

"Who knows. It's all sick and twisted."

Derek rubbed the back of his neck. "The dismemberment must have taken place at the funeral home in Vegas. That's where the bodies must have been switched, too."

"Makes sense. It'd be easy to find someone to bribe in Vegas."

"If that's what happened, we'll never be able to unravel all of it."

"Not without the cooperation of the Las Vegas police."

Adam and Derek stared at each other in silence.

"We won't get it," Derek said.

"No, we won't."

"So where do we go from here?"

"We keep the pressure on Elizabeth and Joe. See if one of them cracks."

Derek nodded. "Wouldn't be the first time one co-conspirator gave away the other."

"We can offer a deal to one of them. Since the murder—if there was one…"

"You can count on it."

"… and the dismemberment occurred outside of our jurisdiction, we don't have much of a case to begin with."

"What do we have for sure?"

"The packages were mailed from a self-service post office kiosk and Robert's credit card was used to pay the postage. We've got credit card theft of under a hundred dollars for all three packages and mailing of hazardous substances."

"The credit card is too minor to bother with and mailing hazardous substances is a federal offense."

"And a weak one, at best." Adam slumped back in his chair. "I talked to my contact at the US Attorney's Office. First-time offense— they'd probably get off with a fine. A small one, at that. She said that she'd draw up the papers if we want to cut a deal on those charges."

"Good to know we've got something as a last resort." Derek shook his head. "None of this seems right. Heinous acts were committed and nobody gets held to account."

"Happens all the time. You know that."

Derek threw his hands in the air. "The only thing that makes this palatable is that I'm not convinced that either Elizabeth or Joe were involved in this." He leaned toward Adam. "Why would Joe be so forthcoming with all of that stuff about his trip to Vegas and his talk with Robert if he was guilty?"

"He's got to know we can easily trace his whereabouts. Credit card receipts, boarding passes."

"That stuff isn't all that easy to get. We'd need subpoenas."

"He wouldn't know that. Maybe he's trying to throw us off by being cooperative."

Derek shook his head. "I just don't see it."

"He's a butcher, for heaven's sake. That's the clincher for me. He knew how to do what was done to Jensen's body."

"I'm not—"

"Convinced. I know. But there are too many coincidences to my liking."

"So Elizabeth and Joe conspired to do what? We still have an accidental death."

"Officially we do. I don't buy that anymore. Robert Jensen was murdered."

"Too bad that bus wasn't equipped with a dash cam. Video footage of the moment of impact could be crucial."

"Wouldn't that be nice? All of this new technology is great—when it's available."

Derek rose and began to pace. "Even if you're right, we don't have enough to charge either one of them. Or take it to a grand jury."

"Let's keep talking to them. Keep the pressure on."

"It's the best we've got. They may not be such a tight-knit unit after all. Elizabeth hadn't told Joe that the body parts belonged to Robert."

"You see? Maybe there's a crack in their wall already." Adam took a swig of his cold coffee and grimaced. "Why don't we both go to pay a visit to the grieving widow? I have a feeling we know things that she'll be surprised to learn."

CHAPTER 41

Elizabeth reached for the remote control and pushed the pause button. She reluctantly tore her eyes from the screen—she was coming up to the last scene of *Sleepless in Seattle*. Annie had just found the forgotten backpack. Elizabeth sniffled and dabbed at her nose with a tissue. She loved this scene.

She fished her cell phone out of the folds of the afghan billowing around her and noted the time. Who was knocking on her door at nine o'clock on a Friday night? She was preparing to restart the movie when the knock came again, more insistent this time.

She threw the afghan aside, stuck her feet into her shearling-lined slippers, and made her way to the door. She put her eye to the peephole. It was the two detectives.

"Yes," she called through the door.

"Mrs. Jensen? We'd like to have a word with you."

Elizabeth leaned her forehead against the door. Ira and Jay had made her promise not to talk to the police without Jay being present.

"We have some information that you need to know."

Surely she could open the door to receive information. If they waited for Jay to arrive, she'd be up until midnight. Elizabeth stifled a yawn and opened the door. She stood in the doorway.

"May we come in?" Derek asked.

She eyed them warily, then turned and led the way to the living room. Elizabeth sat on one corner of the sofa and gathered the afghan around her.

"Sorry to interrupt," Derek said, taking his spot along the wall while Adam claimed the chair.

"It's okay," she said. "I was just watching a movie that I've seen a zillion times."

"Which one?" Adam asked.

"*Sleepless in Seattle*."

Adam nodded. "That's one of my wife's favorites. We've watched it more times than I care to remember." He removed the recorder and placed it on the coffee table between them. "I'd like to record this, like we did last time."

Elizabeth nodded. "You have information for me?"

"I believe you know Joe Porzek?"

She nodded again. "We were friends in high school."

"And now?"

"We're still friends. Why?"

"We believe that you've been seeing each other."

"We meet up at a grief support group at the funeral home, if that's what you mean."

Adam nodded. "Is that all?"

"I go to his shop to place orders occasionally. Mostly for my boss's wife—when they're having a dinner party."

"Have you done anything else with Joe Porzek?"

"No."

"Would it surprise you if I told you that Joe says he helped you with Robert's ashes?"

"Oh... that." Elizabeth gulped. "What did he tell you?"

"That's what we'd like to hear from you."

"I... I only spent the night at Joe's because I was terrified after almost being mugged in Central Park."

Adam and Derek exchanged glances. "Tell us about that," Adam said.

Elizabeth recounted her experience with the drunken stranger in the park and how Joe had come to her rescue. "He was a perfect gentleman—nothing happened. He only let me stay there because I'd left my keys in the park and that guy could have taken them."

"And obtained your address from the box containing the ashes."

"Yes. Exactly."

"You couldn't have gone to a hotel?"

"That's what I had planned to do," Elizabeth sputtered. "Joe talked me out of it. Said that he'd help me look for my keys and the ashes as soon as it got light."

"I see."

"Seemed like it would be easier to spend the night at Joe's so we could make a start as early in the morning as possible."

"What did you do when you got there?"

"We talked and then I went to bed—in his bedroom and he slept on the sofa. As I said, nothing happened."

"Alright. And did you go out first thing the next morning?"

"We did."

"Did you find your keys and your husband's ashes?"

"Yes. I said I wanted to scatter them by myself. Joe opened the box for me—it was taped shut. He stepped away and I scattered them at the base of the tree where I'd dropped them the night before."

"How long did that take?"

"No more than five minutes. I knew that Joe needed to get to his shop."

"So you and Joe are just friends?"

"I've told you that already."

"Would it surprise you to know that he may be romantically interested in you?"

Elizabeth felt her color rise. She focused on a loose stitch in the afghan, running her fingers up and down the errant thread. "I don't know. I guess I thought he might be interested." She lifted her face to Adam's. "He's always been kind to me."

"Did you know that he talked to Robert before he went to Vegas?"

"Wait… what?"

"Joe visited with Robert in a park across from Robert's office. Told him to stop having affairs and behave like a good husband."

Elizabeth jerked back in her seat. "No. Joe never told me and Robert never said anything."

Adam nodded.

Derek pushed himself away from the wall. "Did you know that Joe traveled to Las Vegas the same time that Robert was there? Stayed in the same hotel."

"I didn't know that. I knew he'd gone on vacation but I never knew where. I didn't ask."

"Did you know that the purpose of his trip was to talk to Robert again? About his marital duties?"

"No. Of course not."

"But you'd talked to him about the problems with your marriage?"

"Yes… but in no great detail. I never would have expected him to talk to Robert on my behalf."

"Did you know that Joe flew to Las Vegas?"

"I've already told you that I didn't."

"Did you supply your husband's itinerary to Joe?"

"No."

"So you didn't enlist his help in taking care of your problem with Robert?"

"No," she replied. "I'm stunned that he would have done all of this for me."

"About that," Adam said. "Helping you may not have been Joe's only motivation."

"What do you mean?"

"Joe had another wrong he was trying to avenge."

"What are you talking about?"

"Did you know that Joe's sister—"

"The one who committed suicide?" Elizabeth interrupted.

"That's the one. Did you know that Jill and Robert had been having an affair?"

Both men watched Elizabeth's reaction carefully. She gasped and the color drained from her face. "What are you talking about?" she sputtered.

"Jill Porzek and your late husband had been having an affair for months. Evidently he had promised to leave you and marry Jill. She had even bought a wedding dress."

Elizabeth covered her mouth with her hand and shook her head. "I had no idea," she whispered.

"Robert apparently broke it off with Jill. Joe feels that she was so despondent, she took her own life."

Elizabeth's eyes were rimmed in red. "I didn't know any of this." She choked on the words.

"Joe didn't tell you?"

She shook her head.

"Seems like there's a lot Joe isn't telling you."

Elizabeth pulled at the loose thread until it broke free and created a run in the stitching.

"Did you and Joe discuss Robert?"

"I told him that we'd had problems in our marriage. I wouldn't call that a discussion."

"You said that you knew Joe had feelings for you?"

She turned her face aside, then nodded.

"And now you know that he had reasons to talk to Robert—reasons that had nothing to do with you. Reasons to hate Robert."

"I guess so."

"And that Joe was with Robert when he died."

Elizabeth sat stock still.

"Do you think Robert died accidentally, Mrs. Jensen?"

"Yes... that's what they told me."

"Does that make sense to you, knowing that his body parts were mailed home?"

She stared at them.

"Both you and Joe had plenty of reasons to want Robert dead."

"No!" She cried. "I didn't want my husband dead. I followed him to Las Vegas to patch things up."

"Well, then, your friend Joe may have wanted him dead. Plus, he was there when it happened and he had the skill necessary to remove those body parts."

"How would he have done that?"

"We were wondering if you could tell us that, Mrs. Jensen. Maybe you and Joe worked on this together?"

"No!" Elizabeth clutched the afghan to her chest. "I'm not going to say another word without my lawyer being present."

Adam reached for the recorder and shut it off. He nodded to Derek. "We'll be in touch."

Elizabeth trailed after them in a daze. She needed to call Jay Goldstein, but first she wanted to talk to Joe.

CHAPTER 42

Joe shoved his hands into the pockets of his jeans and paced along the narrow aisle at the back of the bookstore. Elizabeth suggested that they meet here, saying it would be private in the rarely used reference section at the back of the shop. They shouldn't be seen together. He ran his finger absently along a shelf, making a path in the thick coating of dust. He put his nose into the elbow of his sleeve and sneezed.

He turned when he heard the click of heels approaching along the worn wooden floors. Elizabeth rounded the corner, unwinding the scarf from her neck to allow her blonde hair to tumble around her shoulders. Her cheeks were red from the brisk early morning air.

His pulse raced and, in spite of the serious questions he had for her, an undeniable longing stirred in him. A smile forced its way to his lips. "Elizabeth," he began, reaching for her hands.

She ignored him and looked over her shoulder. No one else was in sight. She stepped to him and lowered her head. "We've got to be quiet. No one can hear us. And we've got to be fast."

Joe bent toward her. "The police talked to you." It wasn't a question.

She nodded. "Did they talk to you?"

He nodded. "Why didn't you tell me that those body parts were Robert's?" he asked. "I think I deserved to know. Not find it out from the police."

She jerked her head up to face him. "I never thought the police would talk to you. Why would I? I didn't know that Robert had been having an affair with your sister," she hissed.

Joe turned his head aside.

"Why didn't you tell me? Did you think I wouldn't find out?"

"I… I'm sorry, Elizabeth. I should have." He shrugged. "I guess I thought you wouldn't want anything to do with me if you knew."

"You're right about that." Her voice quivered. "When were you going to tell me?"

"Soon. I swear it."

"You're just like Robert. Only telling me what you want me to know."

Joe grasped her by the shoulders. "I'm nothing like Robert," he forced himself to lower his voice. "I've never cheated on anyone in my life. And I was going to tell you. I wasn't even aware that you were his wife until after she died." He dropped his hands to his sides.

"What did you know about the two of them?"

"I only learned that she was having an affair with a married man after she died." He raked his fingers through his hair. "She didn't leave a note so I went snooping on her computer."

"You found out about Robert there?"

He raised his eyes to hers, wondering how much to tell her. "I had to dig to find out he was Robert Jensen. Even then, I didn't know he was your husband."

"How's that possible? I came to the shop all the time. You knew I was married."

"You placed all your orders in Ackerman's name. I knew you by your maiden name. You were Elizabeth Newberry to me."

"When did you find out Robert was my husband?"

"Before he went to Las Vegas. I saw you in a Facebook photo with him."

"They said that you went to Vegas. To talk to Robert. That you were there when he died."

Joe nodded.

"Why didn't you tell me that?" Elizabeth leaned close. "Why did you go there?"

Joe put his hand under her chin and lifted her face. "Because I cared for you. That bastard ruined my sister's life. I wasn't going to let him ruin yours."

"What did you plan to do?"

"Talk to him. Remind him of a few things."

"The police think that you went there to kill him."

"His death was accidental. You have the death certificate to prove it."

"They're not buying it, Joe. They think that you killed him and dismembered his body. That you'd know how to do that." Her voice broke and she turned wide eyes to his, leaving the question hanging in the air.

"I didn't kill Robert. And I didn't cut off his body parts and mail them to those women." He stared at Elizabeth. "Do you believe me?"

She averted her eyes. "I don't know what to think. You lied to me about Jill and Robert. What else are you keeping from me?"

"Nothing, damn it. I'm not a killer and I didn't do anything to that bastard of a husband of yours." He drew a deep breath and leaned back. "Talking about keeping things from people: when were you going to tell me that you positively identified a body as Robert that most definitely was not Robert?"

Elizabeth winced.

"The police told me about that." He waited for her response.

"I... I know it sounds stupid, but I was so rattled that I couldn't force myself to go up to the casket."

"Oh... come on."

She put up her hand, palm facing him. "I swear it. The body in that casket was the same size as Robert. Same hair color. I never in a million years thought that the funeral home could have made a mistake. All I wanted to do was sign the papers and get out of there."

He released the breath he'd been holding. "Seems like we've both been hiding things."

Elizabeth nodded. "Can you understand?" Her voice wobbled.

"I don't know what to think, either, Elizabeth. You were in Vegas when he died. You lied about the body in the casket." His eyes bored into hers. "The police now think Robert was murdered. They think one—or both—of us are somehow involved in it."

Her eyes grew large and telegraphed her fear.

"We're in trouble, Elizabeth."

"But I didn't do anything," she said.

"Neither did I."

She brought her hands to the side of her head. "I haven't had time to think. It's all so sudden."

"What're you going to do now?"

"I think I'd better call my lawyer." She pulled her phone from her purse and lost her grip on it.

The phone clattered to the floor and the screen saver came into view.

Joe bent to pick up the phone and froze. He looked up at Elizabeth. He held the screen out to her. "Who is this?"

"It's my cat. Kismet. I told you about him."

"This is Jill's cat." He choked on the words. "How in the hell," his voice rose, "did you get Jill's cat?"

Elizabeth took a step back. "I adopted him. From a shelter." She put her hand to her forehead. "I can't believe this. I have Jill's cat."

"I can't believe it either," Joe said in icy tones.

"What do you mean?" Elizabeth took a step back. "How do you think I got him?"

"Maybe you were there when Jill died. Maybe it wasn't a suicide? You found out about Jill and Robert. Killed her. Took her cat when you were done."

Elizabeth recoiled. "You can't think that! I couldn't kill anybody. I didn't kill Jill."

Joe grasped the bookcase to steady himself.

Elizabeth reached for his arm.

He snatched it away from her.

"Listen to me. I can show you a receipt from the place where I got him."

Joe's eyes were wary. "You can falsify a receipt."

"You can check with the shelter. It's called Home Fur Good. They won't know him as Kismet. I renamed him. The tag on his cage said that his name was Mr. Darcy."

Joe breathed in slowly through his nose. "That's what Jill named him."

"You see? I wouldn't know that if it hadn't been on the records of the shelter. Call them and check it out." She reached back out for his arm and this time he didn't pull away. "I didn't kill her."

"I know; I'm sorry. The police suspicion and scrutiny is making me crazy."

"It's making us both crazy. We'd better call our attorneys."

"They'll tell us we shouldn't meet again."

"That's probably best," she said, and her eyes were rimmed in red.

"I didn't kill Robert, Elizabeth. You've got to believe me."

"Neither did I. But one of us is going to get accused of it." She turned away from him. "Goodbye, Joe."

Elizabeth perched on the edge of the client chair in front of Jay's desk. He looked up from the yellow legal pad where he'd been furiously taking notes.

"That's it? That's all the police asked? All you told them?"

She nodded. "As far as I can remember."

"Which is why you shouldn't have been talking to them without me," he replied curtly. "You know that. You even promised Ira and me. Why didn't you call?"

Elizabeth shrugged. "It was late. I didn't want to disturb you. And I didn't do anything."

"That's not what the police think."

Elizabeth gulped. "How much trouble am I in?"

"I don't think they're going to go after you for perjury for signing that certificate." He tossed his pen on his desk. "That's small potatoes."

"Then what?"

"My guess is that they think you hired a hit on your late husband."

Elizabeth gasped.

"Unless I'm wrong, they think that you hired your boyfriend—"

"He's not my boyfriend," she interrupted.

"—Joe Porzek to do the dirty deed."

"But the authorities ruled it an accidental death."

"A fact very much in your favor. It'll be extremely hard to get that ruling overturned—unless somebody has a video showing otherwise."

"And why would I have his body parts cut off and mailed to these women? I didn't even know about them."

"If that's true—if they can't prove you knew about those three women—that's very helpful to you."

"Of course it's true. But what about Joe?"

"He had his own reason to want to punish them."

"I don't think—"

Jay interrupted. "The prosecutor will make the case that he was seeking revenge for his sister."

"Sounds far-fetched to me."

"Maybe, but this is a very odd case."

She rocked back and forth in her seat, clutching her purse on her lap. "This can't be happening."

"But it is."

"It's not fair. I want this to be over."

"If this Joe of yours—"

"I've told you—he's not 'my Joe'."

"—would confess to cutting off and mailing the body parts, this whole thing would probably go away."

She jerked her head up. "Why would he do that? He shouldn't go to jail for something he didn't do."

"Are you so sure he didn't?"

She turned her head aside.

"He might not even get jail time if he's got a clean record. This is a high-profile case. Got a lot of media attention when the first package arrived. The press will go nuts if they find out about the other two. The NYPD won't allow this to go unresolved." He raised his eyebrows at her. "It's better than one of you getting prosecuted for murder. Maybe somebody should suggest this to him."

Elizabeth's chin trembled. "I don't know…. I just don't know."

"I'll talk to him," Ira said, and hung up the phone. Jay Goldstein could always be counted on to put Ira's interests first. Getting Joe to confess to dismembering and mailing those body parts—on his own volition—would take the heat off of Elizabeth. And if Artie Savio had pushed Robert—a fact that wouldn't surprise Ira in spite of Artie's protestations to the contrary—the confession could protect Ira, as well. He didn't want to find himself explaining his relationship to Artie to the police. Jay's proposal was the ideal solution.

He stepped into the living room. His wife was sound asleep in front of the television. He padded down the hall to his office and retrieved one of the burner phones he kept secreted in the concealed compartment in his desk. He rummaged through the stacks of papers on his desk and found the card that Joe had given him weeks ago. He tapped the numbers on the screen and waited. Joe picked up on the third ring.

"Hello," Joe said.

"It's Ira… Ira Ackerman."

Joe waited for Ira to continue. His call at this time of night wouldn't be about an order of meat from the shop.

Ira cleared his throat. "I understand that the police have," he paused, then continued, "circumstantial evidence against both you and Elizabeth."

"They think they do. I didn't do anything and I don't think Elizabeth did, either."

"I agree with you. One hundred percent. That's why I'm calling." He waited for a response but Joe remained quiet. "You know that innocent people get convicted all the time. This is a sexy case for the cops. They're under a lot of pressure to solve it."

"What's that got to do with anything?"

"They won't drop it unless they can tag someone for something," Ira said. "Elizabeth is a very likely target. I think we both know she could never have done anything like they're insinuating."

Joe remained silent.

Ira waited.

"Agreed," Joe finally replied.

"And that she's not going to fare very well if she has to go to jail. I can't even think of that," Ira said, his voice cracking with emotion. "Unless I'm wrong, I think you've got feelings for her. You don't want to see her behind bars, either."

"That's true."

"You don't want to lose your sister and Elizabeth over that worthless piece of shit Robert Jensen."

He could hear Joe's deep intake of breath.

"So what do you want me to do about it?"

"Have you hired an attorney?"

"I was going to call a guy tomorrow."

"Why don't you let me set you up with one? He'll take good care of you and I'll pay his fees."

"Why would you do that?"

"Because he's going to go to the police on your behalf and offer up a confession to mailing the packages."

"No. No way. I didn't do that."

"Hear me out. He'll negotiate out any charges of dismemberment. You'll be fined for mailing hazardous materials. No jail time. I'll pay the fine."

"I can't do that. My business will go to hell if I do."

"We'll insist on a confidentiality clause. I'll make sure you're okay."

Joe was silent.

"Where will you be if Elizabeth goes to jail? Will your clean reputation be worth it?"

"This is crazy."

"Think about it," Ira said. "And one more thing—think about how grateful Elizabeth will be that you took this on to save her. She's never had anyone put her first—ever. If you want to win her over, this will do it."

"I can't see myself confessing."

"Think about it, Joe. You're a smart kid. Think about how your life will look with Elizabeth. Or without her."

CHAPTER 43

Elizabeth draped her coat over a chair in the kitchen and pulled the bottle of aspirin from the shelf next to the sink. She put two tablets on the back of her tongue and swallowed. Her head had been throbbing ever since she'd left her attorney's office.

Why were the police after her? She hadn't done anything.

She rummaged in her refrigerator and brought out a bag of mixed greens. She carried it to the counter and tore it open. A rancid smell filled her nostrils and she peered into the bag. The contents had turned to a green slime. She turned the end of the bag onto itself and rolled it shut, stowing it securely in the trash. She wasn't hungry anyway.

She retreated to the living room. What about Joe? Surely he couldn't have done the things the police had implied. She couldn't believe that of him; didn't want to believe it.

She sunk into the sofa and turned on the television. The funny home video show flashed onto the screen. She normally enjoyed the show and marveled at the silly things people captured with their video cameras and cell phones. She wasn't in the mood tonight, however, and muted the volume.

She was reaching for a magazine from the stack on her coffee table when something Jay had said caused her to stop short.

What if someone had made a video of the bus colliding with Robert? It would prove that he'd stumbled into the street and hadn't been pushed, as the police seemed to think. People recorded everything these days and posted their videos to social media. It was a long shot, for sure, but a video could provide the answers she needed. The answers the police—and Joe—needed. She had to try.

Elizabeth pulled her laptop onto her lap and typed "bus pedestrian accidents" into her search engine. Google produced over twenty-five million entries.

She scrolled through the first ten pages of entries, then clicked on YouTube and entered the same search. She was astounded to find over one hundred million results. She forced herself to click on one of the entries and watched the horrific recording of the final moment of life for a middle-aged man. She lifted her eyes from the screen. What kind of person films such a thing—and then posts it on YouTube?

She shuddered and closed her laptop. She didn't want to see Robert's death, even if she were able to find it in the hundred million entries.

She turned off the television and went to her bedroom. She brushed her teeth and deposited her clothes in the hamper in the corner. She turned back the blanket and reached for the bottle of sleep aids that lived on her nightstand. She shook the two customary tablets into her hand and brought it to her lips but stopped. Finding out what really happened to Robert wasn't just about her. Joe was under suspicion as well. She needed to help him, if she could. If she were truthful with herself, she wanted to know if Joe had pushed Robert into the path of the bus.

Elizabeth got out of bed and returned to her laptop. She brought it to her kitchen table and settled in. She opened the screen and refined her search term: bus pedestrian accidents Las Vegas. There were only twenty-seven thousand hits. She hunkered down and began culling through the results.

By the time she turned out the light and went to bed shortly before four the next morning, she had found what she needed.

Joe and his attorney walked up the steps to the Detective Bureau where Adam and Derek waited for them. "Remember, let me do all the talking," Terry Norton admonished his client.

"I know. That's why I'm here with my attorney—you're going to handle this for me."

"We've cut a deal. I'll want to review the paperwork before you sign anything."

"What if they decide to arrest me?"

"They're not going to do that. They don't have the evidence."

"And you don't think I'll go to jail?"

"No jail. Just the fine that Ira will pay."

"That's it? All done?"

"Yes. The US Attorney put this together."

"You're sure about this? I'm not ruining my life by signing?"

"I think it's a good deal, but it's your decision. It'll let the police close the case on those body parts."

"And they'll stop trying to make Robert's death a murder?"

"That's right." He turned to his client. "But you don't have to do this, you know."

Joe inhaled deeply through his nose. He looked over his attorney's shoulder, into the distance. "I know. But I've thought about this and it'll spare both Elizabeth and me months of uncertainty and worry."

"What did she say about it?"

"I don't know."

"You didn't tell her?"

"I tried calling this morning and sent a text, right before I met up with you."

"She didn't reply?"

Joe shook his head. "What's there for her to say?"

"And you're sure you want to do this?"

Joe squared his shoulders. "I'm sure."

Elizabeth rolled over in bed. The sun streaming through the crack in her curtain told her that it was much later than her usual wake-up time of six thirty.

She grabbed her phone from her nightstand; it was almost ten. She groaned. She'd slept through her alarm and would be really late for work. It was month end and Ira would be furious. She checked her phone for messages. There was only one text.

She punched the message icon and saw that it was from Joe. She frowned. They'd decided not to contact each other for the foreseeable future. She'd been anxious to tell him what she'd found the night before, but had decided it would be wisest to send the message through her attorney.

She tapped the message icon and read the terse line of text:

Confessing this morning to save us both from months of suspicion and anxiety. I need you to know I didn't do it but I won't watch you suffer. Don't worry.

Elizabeth choked on her saliva as she flung herself out of bed. What the hell was he doing? He didn't do anything wrong. She believed him. And she couldn't let him make some ill-conceived confession.

She dove toward her clothes hamper and pulled on the clothes she had deposited there the night before. She stuffed her feet into her shoes, grabbed her coat and purse, and headed out the door.

Elizabeth punched the button for the elevator while she stuck her arms through her sleeves. The light over the door showed that the car was still on the first floor. She turned to the stairwell and raced down the stairs.

She came out on the pavement and rummaged in her purse until she found the card that Adam had given her. She tapped in his number. The call went immediately to voice mail.

Elizabeth noted the address of the detective bureau. It was a long walk—at least thirty minutes. Her news couldn't wait thirty minutes. She scanned the street in front of her. A cab turned the corner and headed toward her. A woman along the curb raised her hand. Elizabeth muscled past the woman and began frantically waving her arms.

"Hey," the woman yelled.

"Sorry. It's an emergency," Elizabeth called over her shoulder as she opened the door and threw herself into the back seat. She leaned forward and gave the driver the address. "As fast as humanly possible." She took a couple of twenties from her wallet and waved them in his direction.

The cab took off and began weaving through traffic.

Elizabeth placed another call to the detective. Once more, it went directly to voice mail.

"Detective Harnet," she said. "This is Elizabeth Jensen. It's ten o'clock and I'm on my way to your office. I have a video that shows

Robert wasn't killed accidentally. He was pushed in front of that bus. I'll be there in a few minutes."

She scrolled to her text messages and replied to Joe.

Got proof that you didn't kill Robert. Don't confess. On my way. Don't do anything!

"It's all in order," Terry said, turning to Joe. "You can sign."

Joe nodded and picked up the pen. He brought it to the signature block when the phone in his pocket vibrated. He looked at his attorney. "I'd like to read these papers for myself."

"Go ahead," Adam said. He got up from his chair. "Take your time. You need to be sure."

He looked at Derek and jerked his head to the door. "We're going to step outside for a moment."

Joe nodded and picked up the papers and began to read. His phone vibrated a second time in his pocket. He'd look at his message as soon as he finished signing the papers.

Derek closed the door behind him. "You're not happy about this, are you?"

"I'm not," Adam said. "Something's wrong. That kid didn't do anything."

"Then why would he confess?"

"He may be trying to save her. Guy's got a serious crush on the lovely widow."

"Maybe. Wouldn't be the first time we got a false confession."

"Exactly," Adam replied. He took his phone out of his pocket and looked at his messages. "Speak of the devil. I've got two missed calls and a voice mail from Elizabeth Jensen."

Derek raised his eyebrows.

Adam put the phone on speaker and replayed the message. They listened to it a second time.

"What do you think we should do now?" Derek asked.

Adam stepped to the room where Joe and his attorney waited and flung the door open.

"I'm almost done," Joe said.

"We're going to hold off on those papers," Adam said, extending his hand for them.

"We've got a deal," Terry said.

"We have new information," Derek said. "This deal is off the table."

"What?" Joe gave the papers to Adam and turned to Terry.

"We're not going to hang around here while you reshuffle your deck," Terry said. He rose and took Joe's elbow. "Call me when you get your act together."

He and Joe moved out of the meeting room and into the reception area. Adam and Derek followed on their heels. The outside door flew open and Elizabeth bounded into the space. She stopped short when she saw Joe.

"You didn't sign, did you?"

He shook his head.

"Thank God! She brought her hand to her chest. "You got my text?"

Joe's brow furrowed. "What text? When?"

"Twenty minutes ago."

"I haven't looked at my phone yet."

"Then why…?"

Adam stepped between them. "I got your voice mail. I decided we needed to see what you had before we went any further."

"What's this all about?" Terry asked.

"She says she has a video that shows that Robert was pushed in front of the bus."

Elizabeth waved her phone in the air. "I've got the link right here. It's on YouTube."

"What?" Terry asked.

"There's a video that shows Robert being pushed in front of that bus." Her voice broke. "It's unmistakable. And he was pushed by a short, stocky man."

"Do you recognize the guy?"

"I've never seen him before in my life. You can't see his face—it's hidden by Robert's body. But I can tell you—*it's not Joe.*"

A shocked silence descended on them as they considered her statement.

Elizabeth took a step toward Joe. His hand shook as he retrieved his phone from his pocket. His eyes grew moist when he read her message.

"Let's go inside and watch this video." Adam said.

"If it shows that Robert was pushed by someone other than my client," Terry looked at Joe, "he won't sign those papers."

"Maybe he'll need to explain to us why he was willing to perjure himself," Derek shot back.

Joe opened his mouth to reply and Terry raised his hand to stop him. "My client isn't going to say another word."

Adam stepped between Derek and Terry. "If the video shows what she says it does—and our IT team verifies that the video hasn't been tampered with—we won't need these," he said, raising the papers he'd retrieved from Joe. He gestured toward the room that they'd just exited. "We can watch it in there." He stepped to one side and Derek led the way. Joe and Elizabeth fell in line behind him. Their hands touched and he squeezed hers quickly before letting it go.

CHAPTER 44

"That's one for the books," Derek said to Adam as they hunched over the screen of Adam's laptop.

"For sure. He was definitely pushed. And not by Joe Porzek."

They both stared at the image on the screen. They'd paused the video at the moment that Robert had been pushed into the path of the bus.

"We've watched this over and over. You just can't get a good look at his face."

"Maybe IT can zoom in and get us something to work with," Derek said.

Adam shook his head. "I don't think so. We're never going to find out who did this—at least not from this video."

"It could still be somebody that Elizabeth hired to kill her husband."

"Maybe, but I'm not sure how we'd connect those dots."

"So we let it drop?"

"It's not in our jurisdiction." Adam swiveled his chair away from the laptop. "We've got no evidence and I don't think Elizabeth's guilty of anything. Do you?"

Derek inhaled slowly through his nose, then shook his head. "I don't. Someone else wanted Robert Jensen dead."

"Who do you think's responsible?"

"Who knows? Guy was an asshole. Probably rubbed a lot of people the wrong way." He tapped the laptop screen.

"We'll never know." Adam swung his chair back and forth. "Why didn't any of the witnesses see the guy push him? Why did everyone say it was an accident?"

"You saw how packed the sidewalk was. Maybe no one was aware of what really happened."

"What about the person that took and posted this video?"

258

"You know how people are—they don't want to get involved." Derek rose and began to pace. "Would we be able to find the person who took this video?"

"IT says it's a long shot."

"So we're at a dead end?"

"It appears so. We'll need to forward this to the Las Vegas police so they can open their own investigation."

"Still bothers me that Joe was willing to confess to mailing those body parts. Maybe he still did that?"

"Do you really think that he got his hands on a body that someone else murdered and cut off and mailed body parts? Even if he mailed them, he didn't kill Robert."

"The guy in the video has to be the one who mailed those packages. Means he had a lot of detailed knowledge about Robert's private life."

"More than his wife had," Adam said.

"Joe knew about the girlfriends."

Adam shrugged. "Doesn't mean he mailed those packages."

"You believe what his attorney told us? That Joe confessed because we were tightening the noose on Elizabeth and scaring her to death? He didn't want her to commit suicide like his sister did? Sounds iffy to me."

"I know it sounds improbable," Adam faced Derek, "but it makes sense. I don't think he did it. He's been holding a torch for Elizabeth since high school and now he's almost got her. He wasn't going to let anything get in the way of that. Paying a fine is nothing."

Derek rubbed his hand over his eyes. "My gut tells me you're right." He sighed heavily. "So where do we go from here?"

"We close our file and move on to the next case. There's nothing else we can do."

Derek's lips settled into a hard line.

"We can't solve everything that comes our way." Adam clapped Derek on the back. "Let's get back to the cases we can solve. There are plenty of bad actors in this city. The NYPD is depending on us."

"You're right," Derek said. "I hate that this guy got away with murder."

"Me too," Adam said. "You never know. Fate has a way of catching up with people."

CHAPTER 45

Artie Savio waited on the crowded subway platform. He much preferred to drive everywhere—even in the city—but his car was in the shop.

He glanced at a newspaper discarded at his feet. The headline of an article in the middle of the page caught his attention. No Leads in Mailed Body Part Case: Police at Standstill.

He bent and picked up the paper. A smile spread across his lips. Those stupid bastards were never going to pin it on him. That arrogant prick Robert Jensen had it coming. You didn't disrespect Artie Savio. Artie chuckled. He'd gotten away with murder.

Artie put the paper under his arm as the subway train approached. The crowd on the platform began to jostle for position. He felt two hands grasp his shoulders in a vice-like grip. He swung his head over his shoulder and his eyes bulged.

The last thing he saw in this life was the face of an enforcer from a rival mob. He felt the rush of air from the incoming train as his body was propelled into its path.

CHAPTER 46

Elizabeth startled as the woman in the circle next to her touched her elbow and thrust a stack of papers at her.

"Oh… sorry," Elizabeth murmured as she took a sheet off the top of the stack and passed the remainder to the person seated next to her.

Elizabeth looked at the clock on the wall. The grief support group meeting was almost over. For the third day in a row, Joe had not been in attendance. She hadn't seen or talked to him since their meeting at the detective bureau.

Jay had confirmed that the police had closed their case. Neither she nor Joe need fear being charged with anything. There was no longer any reason for the two of them to avoid each other—unless Joe didn't want to talk to her. That had to be the reason. Joe wanted nothing more to do with her.

The moderator announced that it was time to rise, join hands, and recite the closing prayer. Elizabeth followed along and spoke the prayer from memory, her thoughts still fixed on Joe.

She dropped hands and headed for the door as soon as the group said "Amen." She hurried down the steps and turned immediately in the direction of Ackerman Funding. She'd lost her appetite for lunch the moment she'd entered the room and saw that Joe wasn't there. She had bank statements to reconcile when she got back to work. Maybe it would take her mind off of his absence in her life.

Elizabeth set out at a brisk pace. She didn't hear her name being called from behind her. She approached an intersection, stepped around a vendor handing out flyers promoting a comedy show, and hurried across as the signal on the other side of the intersection counted down the seconds for pedestrians to safely cross.

She didn't see the man that cursed when he stopped short and couldn't make it across the street before the light changed.

Elizabeth wove in and out of the pedestrian traffic, making good time. She was about to cross another street when someone grabbed her arm from behind.

"Hey," she cried, spinning around while attempting to wrench her arm free. "What the—" The words froze on her lips.

Joe stood in front of her, breathing heavily. A smile flooded his face. "You can really move when you want to. Didn't you hear me calling you?"

Elizabeth shook her head, unable to believe that he was right there, in front of her.

"I wanted... needed... to talk to you. I've picked up the phone to call a dozen times but this conversation had to be in person."

The passersby on the sidewalk split to go around them. A student's backpack clipped Elizabeth's shoulder, almost knocking her off her feet.

Joe reached out his other hand to steady her. "Let's get out of the way," he said, tucking her hand into the crook of his arm and covering it with his hand.

Elizabeth leaned into him and they made their way to the curb in the middle of the block on 59th Street.

"Come on," she said, stepping between parked cars. "We can talk in the park."

They checked for traffic, then dashed across the street and made their way into Central Park. He released her hand but she kept it wrapped around his arm. They began to stroll down the path in the gentle spring sunshine.

"I've wanted to talk to you, too." She glanced up at him. "My lawyer tells me it's all over. The police have closed the case."

"That's what mine said, too. No one's going to ask any more questions."

"I'm relieved," Elizabeth said. "Not because I had anything to worry about," she added hastily.

"I know that. Neither did I."

Elizabeth stopped and turned to face him. "Then why in the world were you confessing? What were you confessing to?"

"Mailing hazardous materials," he replied. "I was doing it so that the police would stop digging around. They were convinced that Robert was murdered—"

"They were right about that," Elizabeth interrupted.

"And they wanted to get somebody on the line for something before they closed the case."

Elizabeth nodded. "That's what Jay said. That it was such a hideous, unusual case, they weren't going to let it go."

"My attorney said that they'd have been way more aggressive if the crimes had taken place in New York."

"If their case was so sketchy, why did you offer to confess?"

Joe lifted her chin with his hand. "Because I could see that their questions and suspicions were tearing you apart. I was afraid that you'd spiral into depression, and I know—firsthand—what that can do to people." He looked away from her.

"Jill's suicide."

Joe nodded. "I wasn't going to let this get to you."

"So your confession was to protect me?"

"It was."

"That's very selfless of you, Joe. Crazy," she said, running her hand along his arm, "but kind. Robert wouldn't have done this for me."

"I'm not Robert."

"He wouldn't hold a candle to you, Joe." She looked long into his eyes.

"I loved you more than twenty years ago, Elizabeth. I've loved you every moment since then. And I love you now."

Elizabeth took a step into his arms.

"Do you think—in time—when you're over Robert—we can start seeing each other?"

"I think we can start right now." She stood on her tiptoes and pressed her lips to his. "You're the most wonderful man I've ever met, Joe Porzek."

They kissed again, this time allowing their lips to give expression to the depth of their feelings.

Joe was the first to step back, breathless. "You'd better be careful, kissing me like that. You'll never make it back to work this afternoon."

Elizabeth tilted her head to one side. "You know what? I think Ackerman Funding can survive one afternoon without me."

"Really?"

She nodded and smiled. "What about you and Porzek Meats?"

"They're about to find out." He tucked her hand back into his elbow and they continued walking into the sunshine.

THANK YOU FOR READING!

If you enjoyed DEADLY PARCEL, I'd be grateful if you wrote a review.

Just a few lines would be great. Reviews are the best gift an author can receive. They encourage us when they're good, help us improve our next book when they're not, and help other readers make informed choices when purchasing books. Reviews keep the Amazon algorithms humming and are the most helpful aid in selling books! Thank you.

To post a review on Amazon or for Kindle:

1. Go to the product detail page for DEADLY PARCEL on Amazon.com.
2. Click "Write a customer review" in the Customer Reviews section.
3. Write your review and click Submit.

In gratitude,
Barbara Hinske

ACKNOWLEDGEMENTS

I'm blessed with the wisdom and support of many kind and generous people. I want to thank the most supportive and delightful group of champions an author could hope for:

My insightful and supportive assistant Lisa Coleman who keeps all the plates spinning;

My life coach Mat Boggs for your wisdom and guidance;

My kind and generous legal team, Kenneth Kleinberg, Esq., and Michael McCarthy—thank you for believing in my vision;

The professional "dream team" of my editors Linden Gross, Kelly Byrd, and proofreader Dana Lee;

My friends Teddy Gingrich and Bruno Park for your insights and advice; and

Elizabeth Mackey for a beautiful cover.

ABOUT THE AUTHOR

BARBARA HINSKE recently left the practice of law to pursue her writing career full time. Her novella *The Christmas Club* has been made into a Hallmark Channel Christmas movie of the same name (2019), and she feels like she's living the dream. She is extremely grateful to her readers! She inherited the writing gene from her father who wrote mysteries when he retired and told her a story every night of her childhood. She and her husband are slaves to their two adorable and spoiled dogs. They live in a historic home that keeps her husband busy with repair projects and her happily decorating, entertaining, and gardening. She also spends a lot of time baking and—as a result—dieting. Together they have four grown children.

Please enjoy this excerpt from **FINAL CIRCUIT,**
the second installment in the "Who's There?!" Series:

CHAPTER 1

Olivia Osgoode turned up the collar of her heavy woolen coat against the icy wind that skimmed the concrete block wall of the parking garage. She glanced around her. She was truly isolated. She should have paid to park in the underground garage down the block instead of this shabby municipal parking structure that rose six stories, like a blemish on the face of downtown. Her grandmother had raised her to be thrifty and Olivia's penny-pinching ways were firmly set, now that she was in her late twenties. If she'd thought about the fact that she'd be returning to the garage after the end of normal business hours—alone—she'd have spent the money on the other garage.

She pushed the button to summon the elevator. The last rays of afternoon sunshine failed to penetrate the elevator lobby of the garage. The sole fluorescent bulb flickered, scattering shadows into the corners. The elevator arrived and she hurried in, pushing the button for the top floor.

The heavy metal doors crept together. Olivia steadied herself for the chug of the car as the motor engaged, but the elevator sat motionless. She stabbed at the button for her floor. The elevator didn't move. A frisson of fear ran up her spine. How long will I be trapped before help arrives? She rubbed her hands together. It wasn't much warmer in the elevator than it had been in the garage.

She located a red button on the control panel and bent over to read the words that had been worn off by frequent use: Call Help. She pushed the button but no alarm sounded and the dented speaker grill next to the button remained silent. Will I be here until people arrive for work in the morning? She racked her brain—how cold was it predicted to be that night? Will I freeze to death while I wait?

Olivia shook her head to clear her thoughts. Stop letting your imagination run away with you. She leaned into the button for her floor, then jabbed it three times in succession. The motor shuddered and the elevator began its sluggish ascent. Olivia moaned softly and fished a crumpled tissue out of her coat pocket to dab at the tears that came so easily since her grandmother's death.

The elevator lurched to a stop at her floor. She stepped out and the doors closed behind her. She shielded her eyes from the glare of the setting sun with one hand and hoisted her purse onto her shoulder with the other. A movement at the far end of the garage caught her attention. She froze and stared in disbelief.

Silhouetted against the crimson sky along the outside row of parking spaces, a tall figure in a black jacket leaned over the open trunk of a dark sedan, his face obscured by a ski mask. He struggled under the weight of the large object he carried.

Olivia blinked hard against the blinding light and focused. He was carrying a woman wearing a black skirt and low heels. A scarf draped across the woman's body provided a slash of crimson against her inky clothing and white hair. Her head dangled at a precarious angle. The woman was dead.

Olivia heard herself scream. The sound reverberated in the concrete structure. Bile rose in her throat.

The figure lifted his masked face to hers. He stood no more than two hundred feet from her.

Olivia stumbled backwards until the closed elevator doors stopped her escape. No! She pressed against the unyielding metal surface. I've got to get out of here! She jerked herself around and fumbled for the button to summon the elevator. She punched at it frantically and watched the readout over the door as the elevator worked its way back to her, floor by floor. Come on! For God's sake, come on!

She whipped her head over her shoulder and forced herself to look at the man as he threw the body into the trunk and slammed the lid. The victim's head and one foot caught on the opening of the trunk and the lid sprang back up after hitting them with a sickening thud. He abandoned the body and began to run toward Olivia.

She tried to scream for help but this time no sound emerged. The elevator was still two floors away. It's not going to make it in time! She swung to her right and saw the door next to the elevator marked "Stairs." She lunged at the handle and tugged, but the door wouldn't open. Shit, shit, shit!

The man was coming fast.

Olivia thrust herself back to the elevator as the doors began to part. She flung herself into the elevator and searched for the Close Door button. Focus! she screamed internally as she looked at the symbols for Open Door and Close Door. Which is the right one? The arrows pointing toward each other? That had to be it.

Her hand shook as she reached out to push the button. She couldn't make a mistake. If she hit the wrong one he would capture her. And kill her. I have to do this.

Olivia took a deep breath to steady herself. She pushed the button and the elevator doors started to close. She looked up to stare in horror at the man running toward her. He'd covered half of the distance between them and was picking up speed as the elevator doors made their steady progress toward each other. Her heart hammered in her chest and she flattened herself against the back of the elevator.

The man dove toward her as the doors shut. He grunted as his torso hit the ground outside the elevator. He thrust one gloved hand into the opening and curled his fingers around the edge of the door. The doors stopped moving toward each other.

Oh, my God, he's going to open the doors! Olivia's breath caught in her throat. If she didn't do something—now—she would be his. She bounded toward the door, her eyes fastened on his hand as he tried to force the doors open. She brought the heel of her right foot up and lashed out at him, kicking viciously at his fingertips. Her heel connected firmly with his gloved hand but he held on. She brought her foot back and struck again. She hit her mark and lost her balance, sprawling on the floor of the elevator. She tilted her head back and stared into the dark eyes behind the killer's mask. Olivia recoiled at the malice that glittered there.

He lost his grip and his wrist hit the metal threshold of the elevator. She tore her eyes from his and crawled to the control panel, leaning into the Close Door button. His hand slid out of sight and the doors closed.

The elevator shook as the masked man pounded on the closed door. Olivia propelled herself, crablike, into the far corner of the elevator and drew into a ball, hugging herself. She held her breath, expecting the doors to reopen, but the motor engaged. The elevator began its descent. Olivia bent forward as another wave of nausea washed over her. For one frightening moment, she thought she might pass out. She swallowed hard. Don't give in. Keep your wits about you. She wasn't safe yet. He could be waiting when she got out of the elevator. She needed to call the police.

Olivia tried to pull herself into a standing position but her legs were too shaky to support her. She crawled to her purse and retrieved her cell phone. She sat cross-legged on the filthy floor and brought the phone's screen into view. A guttural moan escaped her lips. She had no cell service in the elevator. She flung the phone back into her purse. Now what?

The elevator bounced to a stop on the first floor and the doors began to part. Olivia forced herself to her feet, placing one hand on the opening to steady herself. She reached for the Close Door button with her other hand. What if he's out there, waiting for me?

She leaned out of the elevator and quickly looked right and left, sweeping her eyes over the shadowy scene in front of her. Everything was still. She could see most of the first floor of the garage from her vantage point. The only vehicles remaining were an SUV and a minivan. There were no dark sedans in sight. The first floor of the garage was deserted and the masked man was nowhere to be seen.

Olivia gulped in a deep breath. She couldn't stay where she was. She had to get out of there and call for help. She propelled herself from the elevator, swiveling her head wildly, searching for the killer as she ran. She stumbled, almost sprawling on the ground, but managed to keep her feet under her. She rounded the corner and ran out of the garage, darting across the street mid-block. A van screeched to a halt, narrowly avoiding her, and the driver laid on his horn. Olivia ignored him and raced to the double glass doors of the office building where she had been meeting with the lawyer for her grandmother's estate less than fifteen minutes earlier. She'd be safe with him. Howard Asher would call the police; he'd know what to do.

Olivia tugged at the heavy doors of the building. They didn't yield. She checked her watch; it was almost six thirty. The doors were locked. People had been streaming out of the building when she'd arrived at five thirty for her appointment with Mr. Asher. She thought he'd been kind to agree to wait for her when she'd telephoned to say that she'd be an hour late—now she was sorry that he hadn't insisted she reschedule.

She had been ready to leave work for her appointment when she'd taken the call from the father of the teen that had died in a tragic car accident over the weekend. She'd spent over an hour with him, discussing the details of the funeral that would be held at Hilton Mortuary the next morning. What the grieving man had really needed was the sympathetic ear of a compassionate listener. Olivia hadn't had the heart to hurry him off the phone so she could attend to her own business.

Now, here she was, standing on a deserted sidewalk with a killer on the loose, looking for her. She wouldn't find a safe haven at Asher Law, PLC. *I've got to call the police.*

She turned to the street, searching for any sign of the masked man. A streetlight further down the block was out, leaving the entrance to the next building in deep shadow. She narrowed her eyes, straining to detect any movement in the darkness. Her hands shook as she tried to punch 9-1-1 into her phone.

Available at Amazon in Print, Audio, and for Kindle

DEADLY PARCEL ("WHO'S THERE?!" BOOK 1)

Novels in the Rosemont Series

Coming to Rosemont

Weaving the Strands

Uncovering Secrets

Drawing Close

Bringing Them Home

Shelving Doubts

Novellas

The Night Train

The Christmas Club (adapted for The Hallmark Channel, 2019)

UPCOMING IN 2020

Guiding Emily, the first novel in a new series

FINAL CIRCUIT ("WHO'S THERE?!" BOOK 2)

The seventh novel in the Rosemont Series

I'd love to hear from you!
Connect with me online:

Sign up for my newsletter at
BarbaraHinske.com to receive your Free Gift,
plus Inside Scoops and Bedtime Stories.

Search for **Barbara Hinske on YouTube**
for tours inside my own historic home plus tips
and tricks for busy women!

Find photos of fictional Rosemont and Westbury,
adorable dogs, and things related to her books at
Pinterest.com/BarbaraHinske.

Email me at **bhinske@gmail.com** or find me at
Instagram/barbarahinskeauthor
Facebook.com/BHinske
Twitter.com/BarbaraHinske

Made in the USA
Las Vegas, NV
11 March 2025

19336953R10163